Beijing
*Peking*

CHINA

Jiujiang
*Chiu-chiang*

Nanchang
*/Nan-ch'ang*

Yangtze River

Guangzhou
*Canton*

Hong Kong
*(est. 1841 by British Empire)*

SHANE
JOHNSON

offspring

of a

deathless

soul

# offspring

## of a

## deathless

## soul

*A Timeless Story of Spritual Triumph*

beth nonte russell

**BIG MIND**
PUBLISHING INC.
McLean, VA

*In grateful acknowledgement* of those who have been instrumental in bringing this book to life. Thank you especially to Antoinette Carr, Paige Ohliger and Paula Bansch for your friendship, encouragement and guidance, without which this book would never have been. Thank you Pat Keiffner and Brad Dixon and all those at IBJ Corp. Contract Publishing who have worked so hard on this project and made it your own. Thank you, Randy, for believing in this book and in me when no one else did; but mostly, thank you for saying "yes" and allowing this to be. And Lily...for being the inspiration.

Published & distributed by

**Big Mind Publishing, Inc.**

McLean, VA.

*www.bigmindpublishing.com*

in association with

**IBJ Corp. Contract Publishing**

Indianapolis, IN

Library of Congress Catalog Number
ISBN 0-9745673-4-5
First Edition
Printed in the United States of America

For those left behind

You will be what you will to be
Let failure find its false content
In that poor word, "environment,"
But spirit scorns it, and is free.

It masters time, it conquers space;
It cows that boastful trickster, Chance,
And bids the tyrant Circumstance
Uncrown, and fill a servants place.

The human Will, that force unseen,
The offspring of a deathless Soul,
Can hew a way to any goal,
Though walls of granite intervene.

Be not impatient with delay,
But wait as one who understands;
When spirit rises and commands,
The gods are ready to obey.

The river seeking for the sea
Confronts the dam and precipice
Yet knows it cannot fail or miss;
*You will be what you will to be!*

*-Ella Wheeler Wilcox*
*1896*

prologue

*How is it possible to be reborn if you do not die? It is my most urgent wish to be reborn. It is the only wish I have now, the only desire left to me. Everything else, all passion, all hope, slowly fades to the point that I cannot see it anymore. It is difficult for me to even imagine a time when passion moved me, or hope lifted me. I want nothing that I used to want, which makes me not the person that I used to be. We create ourselves through what we desire, and I don't know who I am anymore.*

*Dying is nothing like what we suppose. It is an unshackling, a freedom I never knew in life. Strangely, I am not less myself, but more. And those things I am losing as life ebbs from my body are the very things which kept me enslaved. The fears and desires, all the time mistaken for my real self, now recede into unreality. They are dying, not I, not I...*

*In this state between life and death I can see both where I am going and where I have been. It is the realization of continuity that allows me to release myself from this earth, from the loves I have known here. For when fear and desire die, only the unspeakable reality of love remains. My daughter, my Little Bird.....my love will follow you through time until you too break free from this existence, triumphant. I see you laughing into the wind as you run, knowing that the sun which warms you is me, and the song of the birds is me, and the deep longing you have is me also. We are one, and in this oneness we will be together forever.*

*You will live, and as I spiral upward into the next phase of my existence I use all my strength to hold the thought of you, to pull the essence of this love into the center of my heart where it will remain a dormant seed of joy until we meet again. My wish now is to be reborn, a most urgent wish, and the only true longing I have ever known.*

"Dying is nothing like what we suppose..." This, I know to be true. I put down my pen and stare at the words that have just been written. A part of me had just stepped aside, a space had been made, and something else...someone else...had come pouring through the opening, and out onto the page. A voice, familiar and yet unknown to me, had emerged full-blown into my consciousness, expressing a love and longing beyond my known experience. What does that mean about who I am?

"My daughter, my Little Bird...." The poignant words could not have come from me; I am childless, there is no daughter of my own to speak to or long for. The intensity of the longing expressed makes me ask myself for what, for whom, would I die in order to be reborn? Something has been winding down in me for a long time and that is why I came here, to this rented house near the sea, to decide about my life. Whirling inside myself here for a month with no resolutions. And now this....what was this?

I put the paper away; perhaps I'll never look at it again. Where could this beauty, this terror fit into my life? It is time to go back, though I have no enthusiasm for the way I have been living. If I had the courage I would stay in this house alone forever, letting whatever voices needed to speak through me to come. But I cannot; I have to return for reasons I may never know.

I pack up my things and pull the door to the tiny white house closed behind me. The sea air whispers in the pines, it speaks of who I will become and not who I have been. In a few hours I will arrive home and my husband will greet me, happy I have returned. I will hear myself speaking, saying things in the ways I have before, but now a part of me will be listening for the voice I have heard and cannot forget. I will be waiting for that golden moment it whispered of when fear and desire die in me, and only the unspeakable reality of love remains.

That night I had a dream that was so disturbing that I woke from it choking on my tears. I dreamed that I suddenly, inexplicably, remembered that I had a baby. Somewhere, there was a baby that I had given birth to and then placed aside, forgotten, neglected. It was not a deliberate neglect; my mind had suffered a complete erasure of memory. Until the moment in the dream when the knowing came with a shock, I had been living in complete ignorance of her existence. Now that I remembered, the utter horror and shame of forgetting made me question whether or not I deserved to live.

I thought, where is she? Where did I last put her down? All I knew was that it had been too long...too long for a baby to go without care, to be without love. I moved in the agonizing slow-motion way of dreams down a long hallway toward where I thought she might be, and in the weird perfect logic of the dream world, it happened to be the room in which my mother had died, in the house where I grew up.

I entered the room, which was darkened and had a closed-up feeling. There in the corner next to the window was a crib, and I knew that my baby was inside it. The cold dread of what I would find was almost too much to bear. If she were dead, if I had not found her in time, my life was over; I could not live with the knowledge that I had been responsible for my own baby's death. The crib loomed up before me; it was all I could see. I looked down and there she was, my child, and I knew instantly and with a wave of disbelief that she was still alive, that I had found her just in time.

She was barely breathing as I lifted her from the crib and looked into her face. Her eyes were huge and dark and luminous, and they held no recrimination for me. The eyes reflected that the soul behind them was at peace, and in that peace I saw my own salvation. I put my finger to her lips and she began sucking, hard, and with each pull she grew stronger and stronger until she was a robust glowing baby, alive in my arms.

I could not shake the dream for days. The feeling that I had been expiated from some guilt which I could not name permeated my waking life. It was as if a secret truth had been revealed to me, and that truth is that in remembering what we have denied, we save ourselves.

時間

time

When I wake I don't know where I am. It takes several minutes before I remember I am on my way to China, I am traveling with Alex, we are going to bring home a baby. The sun is still shining though according to my watch it is ten o'clock in the evening. We have been following the light since this morning as we have flown over the top of the world, and it has been eerie, a day with no night. We could be anywhere, it could be any time, in this moment, suspended between heaven and earth; I am flying into tomorrow, or is it yesterday?

There are still several hours before we are scheduled to land in Tokyo, and from there, we will take another three-hour flight to Beijing. I have an entire row to myself; this airplane is almost empty. Several books, all of which I am having trouble concentrating on, surround me on the seat and the remains of a half-eaten lunch still waiting to be taken away by the flight attendant. I look across the aisle and Alex is stretched out, sleeping. After more than a year of planning for this adoption, it must finally be starting to seem real for her; she seems distracted, withdrawn, and not in the mood to chat about the new baby or anything else.

I have spent the time trying to read, looking out at the clouds, thinking—the things I prefer to do anyway. At some point I had begun to meditate but I must have fallen asleep; there was a dream, something intense...what was it? I try hard to bring it back; I recall a structure, bathed in dream-light, and as I concentrate on this image more details begin to emerge from the shadows of sleep. I take out my notebook and pen to record what I remember:

*I am standing in a pagoda, surrounded by water. I am looking at my reflection when suddenly, another reflection merges with mine. I look up to see a young Chinese man, in some type of military or royal dress, and he is coming toward me. My heart rises up in joy and yet I am also afraid. I can see that I am dressed in some type of elegant robe, with elaborate embroidery and color.*

The dream is a shimmering little jewel, so vivid in color and feeling. I have had so many dreams about China since I agreed to come on this trip with Alex: dreams about babies, dreams that I am Chinese and that Alex is Chinese, and a dream in which Alex's husband is a Chinese soldier trying to warn me of some danger.

As I think back over this dream-trail, I make a note to myself that I must remember to tell Antoinette about this one. Though I have known her for only a short period of time, Antoinette has become the first person I think of when anything of interest occurs. I had spoken to her for the first time just two months ago, after my friend Paige had insisted that I call her, pressing her phone number into my hand.

Paige and I had been sitting in her garden on a warm sunlit morning in late summer. We had met in a yoga class a year before. When she walked into the room the first evening of class, I knew we would be friends. Within weeks we were as comfortable with each other as sisters, and part of each other's lives.

Many of my other friendships that were of much longer duration had never evolved to that state; like my friendship with Alex, for instance. I had known Alex for over ten years, but there was something in me that remained wary of her, though I was not able to say why.

On the morning when she spoke to me of Antoinette, Paige and I had been talking about the practice of psychology. I was telling her that there seemed to be something missing in all the techniques and theories, and I didn't know how much it was really helping people. I had been working as a counselor for a couple of years and had become disillusioned with the promise of psychotherapy. Understand the mind and problems would be solved, went the theory; but somehow in practice it never seemed to work out that way.

Perhaps it was a dead end, I said to Paige, and there needed to be something more for people to truly heal. After sitting for hundreds of hours with clients suffering from every imaginable permutation of misery, I began to sense that the dysfunctional behaviors, the longings, the pain had some sort of underlying logic or meaning which was impossible to discover with the conventional tools of therapy.

"I think you should talk to Antoinette," she said, though when I pressed her she could not tell me why. Paige had known Antoinette for years, and had mentioned her many times to me. But she had never really offered details about her, and she didn't seem to want to now, either. It all seemed somewhat mysterious, and I was skeptical.

Paige said that Antoinette had an interesting way of looking at these issues, and had made them her life's work.

She seemed to feel so strongly that Antoinette and I should talk, so I did call, the next afternoon. When Antoinette answered, her charming English accent was the first surprise, the first of many. One of the first things she said to me was, "Things are not as they appear."

Things are not as they appear. All of my searching over the years had led to dead ends. My study of psychology, science, religious thought, yoga and Buddhism had led me to a place where I had to accept that there was something more, something beyond my understanding, something not explained fully in any of the books I had read. What the 'something more' was, I had no idea. I thought of the experience I had had several months before, when I had written, spontaneously, words that belonged to someone else. I still had no explanation for it, and it haunted me.

"What do you want, what are you looking for?" Antoinette asked, questions no one had ever asked before, at least not so directly. She asked the only questions that matter. She told me that she worked as a spiritual guide and teacher. I told her that she was exactly what I was looking for, though until the moment those words came out of my mouth, I had not known it was true.

"Antoinette, I'm looking for the real thing," I said, hesitating, not knowing if she would understand what I meant, not knowing for sure if I knew what I meant.

Antoinette laughed. And when she laughed, it sounded like the tinkling of bells I had heard in a dream—long, long ago.

A month later, Paige and I were standing in the airport in Charleston, South Carolina, waiting for Antoinette to appear. We had agreed to meet and spend a long weekend at the beach, and now I was nervous, not sure if I was ready for this. Antoinette and I had talked several times on the phone since our first conversation, and each time she had led me in prayers, or meditations, which opened up a new world that was intriguing but which made me uncomfortable.

I had resisted prayer for most of my life; I didn't understand how it was supposed to work. It seemed like wishful thinking, magical thinking; everyone prays, yet how many prayers are answered?

A weekend with Paige and Antoinette, talking about God, joining in prayers…I had always been suspicious of the overtly religious, those who talked about their faith. I had kept my spiritual longings to myself. I found it difficult to utter the word "God." If I had not been so desperately in need of answers, I would never have opened this Pandora's Box which Antoinette presented me. But on that bright weekend I did open it, and found within the promise of a power which I had denied myself: the power to live life itself as a prayer, to purposely join myself to what is beautiful and true.

The captain announces we are preparing to descend. Alex joins me in my row, and we begin to gather our belongings. She is still quiet and withdrawn, her face white and tired-looking. A tiny twinge of homesickness rises in me, and there are butterflies in my stomach. It already feels as if we've been gone a lifetime.

This morning when we met at the airport, it was cold and dark, a crystal clear December morning; our husbands and Alex's son were there to see us off. Alex lingered with them while I stood off to the side with my luggage. This was a big moment for their family, a turning point, an ending and a beginning. No longer would it be just the three of them; a new baby would join them and change their lives. I could tell they were unsure about this, hesitant, not smiling, clinging to each other. I thought of the little face in the picture Alex had shown me a few days ago, a black-eyed girl with sparse hair and a determined look. The orphanage had sent the picture of the baby assigned to her, and when Alex showed it to me I asked for a copy of the photo, and then pasted it onto the front cover of the journal I would be keeping for this trip.

I liked to look at the picture. Last night, when I showed it to my husband, he said, "That's the cutest thing I've ever seen! Why don't you bring one back for us, too?" He was obviously joking, but for some reason, I got angry.

"You can't just DO that," I said; "you can't just bring back a baby." I wondered now if my anger was a tell-tale sign of a desire to do just that. I wondered if seeing these orphaned babies would make me want to have one, too; maybe it would awaken that maternal instinct that has seemed to be lacking in me all this time. Just yesterday, when

16

I was having breakfast with Paige, we were talking about the trip and I said, "I'm really glad it's not me bringing home a baby!" And I was glad, for now, that it was not me.

But I am excited for Alex, even though right now she doesn't seem very happy herself. The day before we left, she called and told me that she had "freaked out" the night before; she had been preparing the nursery and suddenly was overcome with the need to run from the room, from the house, from her life.

"I've never felt that way before," she said, "Never felt that desperate." She told me it had taken several hours to calm herself down, and that she was sure it was just exhaustion, concern over the details of the trip and the adoption, and last-minute jitters. But the effects seem to be lingering, she is definitely not herself. When I ask her if she is okay, she barely answers.

We exit the plane silently and move into the terminal. Almost at once I am hit with a strong wave of nausea; I feel as if I'm going to pass out. Somehow I make it through the corridor to our gate, and then I have to sit down against a pillar and put my head between my legs. My mouth is watering profusely, if I move I know I will vomit.

It happened as soon as we entered the terminal and were met with a sea of Asian faces. A virtual wave of humanity, all with Asian features, moved toward us in the corridor, and for some reason, that was a shock to my system. I had felt a surge of energy hit me in the gut, in the solar plexus, and I became disoriented and weak. I am feeling this strange sense of fear, not just discomfort, but anxiety, an anxiousness; it's as if I were in danger. It is irrational, and I don't mention it to Alex. She has enough on her mind right now so I suffer in silence.

The dream I had on the plane…the Asian faces surging down the corridor toward me. They swirl together and I can feel the earth spinning wildly beneath me and for all I know it is wobbling off its axis. I hold my knees tightly and keep my eyes closed, praying for this to pass. I am in a dream, this is all a dream now and the way back home is closed to me until I wake up. But into what reality will I awake? In this moment nothing seems certain. I breathe, and breathe; it is all I can do. For more than an hour I sit like this, trying to hold it together, wondering if I'll be able to go on with the trip.

Finally, our flight is called. Alex has to help me onto the plane, which is packed with Japanese and Chinese businessmen. Except for the flight attendants, we are the only women on this flight, and that makes me very uncomfortable. The men don't acknowledge us at all; it is as if we are ghosts, we don't exist. I still feel so sick and I settle into my seat and fall asleep right away, a deep, dense sleep, my mind opaque, trying to escape. When I wake up we are landing in Beijing, and I wonder, what have I done?

How can we know where our journeys may ultimately take us? We think we know, and try to prepare. We make plans and itineraries, pack clothing for certain types of weather. We take our bodies to specific geographical locations, but how often do we think of the effect it may have upon our souls? How often do we wonder, why this destination, and not some other? Why have I chosen it, or has it chosen me? What part of myself awaits me there, where I am going?

Traveling to China from the United States is a long journey, but I did not know how far inside myself I would travel by going there. A day's journey which took me to a forgotten lifetime; in the end, I did not know exactly where I was or how to return to the life I had left. The confusion of being on the other side of the world forced me to see things differently. China sleeps while we are awake, our biological clocks set at exactly opposite poles. Their night of remembering is our day of forgetting; we speak a different language of time. The American and Chinese collective minds swirl in opposite directions, ours toward the future, and theirs toward the past.

During this journey I lost a day, and gained it back upon my return. How does this happen, time getting lost? Think too deeply about the absurdities of this and it becomes apparent that the human invention of time, of days following days in a tidy linear progression, is an illusion, a trick we forget we have played upon ourselves. We are conditioned to accept time as an absolute, and yet, in one sense there is no time at all. It is always now, and everywhere that exists, exists now, though in one place the sun is shining and it is called "Tuesday morning," at the very same moment in some other geographical location it is dark and we say "Wednesday." A day ahead? No; the same moment, exactly. Tuesday and Wednesday, happening at the same time. Past and future, dark and light, today and tomorrow, always inseparable.

For the past year and a half Alex has been going through the arduous process of international adoption, a marathon of paperwork, red tape and delays. She called six months ago to tell me that she had been matched with a child. The trip was set but she needed a companion as her husband could not make the trip; they had decided he would stay home to care for their 8 year old son. When she asked would I come with her, to China, I heard myself saying "yes" before even thinking. It would be an exciting adventure, another country to add to my list of places in the world that I had seen with my own eyes, and a chance to see how this business of international adoption actually works.

I was surprised when Alex asked me to come. We had known each other for years, and yet, I would not consider us close. We had met as neighbors, and ours was a social friendship; we saw each other a few times a year, at dinner with our husbands or in groups with other friends. Our families had celebrated birthdays and holidays together on occasion; but there was something about Alex, a reserve or detachment, which I never felt I could breach. In some sense she remained aloof and unknowable, an enigma, a mystery.

And then to ask me this, to come to China….after my initial positive reaction, I began to have reservations. This trip was so important; I asked Alex if there was a family member or a very close friend who could provide the kind of support necessary. What I meant, but didn't say, was "why me?" Would our friendship withstand the intimacies of travel, not to mention an adoption?

Alex explained that she had asked me to come because she needed an experienced traveler to go with her, someone who would not easily be thrown off stride. She had heard tales of my travels over the years, the places I had visited sometimes on a whim—the long trip by myself to Europe. She explained, but I had the sense that deep down, even she did not know why she had chosen me, as if she knew by doing so she had pushed outside the bounds set for the relationship.

She had settled on my travel history as her reason, but what she did not know was that it was not travel for the sake of travel alone, but always a looking, a searching for something, some piece of myself. My life had been made up of attempts to bury an old self, a person who no longer existed, a person who perhaps never existed, a self patched together from borrowed ideas. My trips were a way to tunnel into the dark country inside myself, a place I could only visit when I was outside the geographic bounds of my day to day existence.

It had dawned on me the day Alex called, a day after I had returned from a trip that had exhausted me and left me depressed, that perhaps looking for a piece of myself in some far-off location might not make much sense. Was travel just an escape, a way of fooling myself into believing that my life was moving forward when in fact it was standing still?

A vague sense of emptiness, of something missing, of not being where I should be had haunted me for a lifetime. I was ready to admit that travel had not cured me, that nothing had cured me. The day before Alex called I had decided to stay put for a while—to try living inside the life I had created in my suburban house, with my husband, my dogs—and my chronic discontent, the source of which I had yet to identify.

"It" eluded me, the "it" that would pull the world together and show it to make imminent sense. I was looking for an answer, searching for a system, grasping at this and experimenting with that, but nothing coalesced, nothing calmed my spirit for long. As my discontent became more entrenched, as it became like a sort of grief, I began to panic...what was it, what was it, what was it? I did not know, and I began to think there might not be an answer, that maybe there were no answers at all. I had a growing sense that life was moving on and my dreams were dying. My life stretched out before me, a wasteland of time.

It is dark when we land in Beijing, and flurries of snow swirl outside the window and across the tarmac. A set of stairs is wheeled up to the plane, and standing just outside the doorway as I am about to descend, I experience a wave of déjà vu. This scene looks so familiar, and it takes a moment to realize that I am remembering something I had seen long ago. It is the image in my mind of former President Richard Nixon's visit to China, and his arrival, nearly 30 years before. I had seen it on television and in news photos, the fat flurries of snow, men in drab green military uniforms scurrying about with dour expressions on their faces, hurrying to complete some unknown, probably sinister purpose. Where have these memories been stored for all this time? In some dusty drawer of my mind, waiting for just the right moment to spring open and display its contents.

Perhaps if that visit had never occurred, I would not be arriving in Beijing today, and somehow my subconscious mind has tied the two events together. I muse on the fact that every seemingly isolated event has repercussions through time. President Nixon's choices, decisions and policies affecting me some 30 years later, in a way he could never have conceived of at the time.

The terminal inside is nearly empty, yawning and eerily vacant. Though modern, clean and brightly lit, it has the feel of a mausoleum. I have the feeling we are being watched. Going through customs and having my passport scrutinized by someone holding a gun unnerves me. I watch a skinny old man as he moves a dirty mop in slow circles around the floor. At 8pm on a Friday night the airport of our nation's capital would be chaotic with travelers, but there is hardly anyone here.

Alex and I stand alone as the empty baggage terminal goes around and around. When we finally see our bags it is a relief and we tug them off the belt and move uncertainly toward the exit. Now what? We scan the crowd, and spot a young woman holding a sign with Alex's name on it. She is from the China Women's Travel Service and will be our guide for this trip. She wears round glasses and has a shy demeanor as she tells us to call her "Anna," though that is obviously not her real name. She speaks excellent English. She helps us load our bags into a small white van parked at the curb; we drive off into the night, into a huge and strangely quiet city.

During the drive Anna tells us that there are two other couples in our group who are also adopting and that they have already arrived at the hotel. Tomorrow we will visit the Great Wall, she informs us, and the next day, the Forbidden City. After that, we fly on to Nanchang, where we will meet the babies. A giddy excitement starts to return; this will be a grand adventure. I'm feeling much better now, since I slept on the plane. I stare out the window at the dark streets, looking for any type of life, and though I see none, I know it exists. Right now China is hiding, and tomorrow I will begin to find her.

Anna is singing. It is a song about a Chinese girl who lost her beloved, a man who dies while being forced to help in the building of the Great Wall. The girl, distraught, travels across the countryside, looking for her love, whom she never finds. She ends up dying at the Wall herself, and is buried inside. Anna tells us that the Wall was built to keep out invading armies. It never did. Instead, it served as an invitation to invasion, rather than a deterrent, because building a wall indicates weakness, a perceived vulnerability to attack. And once built, the separation and isolation that the wall enforces weakens the society further. To an enemy, the Wall was like blood in water is to a shark, it whetted the appetite.

We are driving there, to the Wall, through the traffic-choked streets of Beijing. The van inches through the clogged intersections, trying to break clear to the outskirts of town to the tourist point two hours beyond. Anna starts singing another song, this one about a butterfly. The way that she so unselfconsciously sings to us is endearing. It is something that a little girl would do. It indicates a naiveté, innocence and a lack of cynicism that is refreshing. An American, of the great entertainment society, might do this in a similar situation, but it would be a joke-y thing, staged and false. Anna was offering herself wide open, unprotected. Perhaps we were witnessing just that part of the Chinese character that so needed a wall.

Anna's singing turns an ordinary drive into a festive occasion. We are a little family, riding in a non-descript mini-van, and yet most of us have known each other less than a day. Alex and I, Judy and Curtis, Louise and Jimmy with their daughter Maggie, and Anna, plus the driver…we have been brought together under unusual circumstances. A most intimate act, the adoption of a child, the creation of new families, being carried out amongst virtual strangers. But now Maggie, six years old, comes to the front of the bus and wants to sing into the microphone. Maggie herself was adopted from China five years ago, and her parents are here for their second child. Maggie is gorgeous, funny and smart, a poster child for Chinese adoptions. She has been teasing Curtis throughout the trip and she has enraptured him with her natural charm. He keeps filming her with his camcorder, and though she is Chinese by blood, her actions are completely American. She is a performer, and wants us all to respond with approval, with praise.

Anna and Maggie alternate their musical offerings, and the contrast could not be more stark. Anna with her songs of lost loves and ancient China, sung in her high clear voice; Maggie with her selections of tunes from Sunday school and T.V., belted out with gusto in a husky alto. I almost regret when we finally reach the entrance to the Great Wall tourist point, so entertaining is the show.

We pile out of the van and it is so cold, the wind whips our faces and I pull my hat down over my ears and suddenly I am alone in my own silent world. Small trinket shops line the walkway—you can buy tee-shirts and stuffed pandas, jade and chopsticks, any kind of thing which will collect dust once you get it home, but which seems like a good idea at the time. Red flags fly from a high archway over the road, their frantic flapping not festive but alarming. They make me think of danger; they are red daggers in the cold. We move quickly, but separately, like deep sea divers who can see each other but cannot communicate except with hand signals. The cold takes our breath away and drives between us, but we re-group at the entrance and Anna shouts over the wind that we should meet back at this spot in one hour, pointing with exaggerated gestures at her wrist watch.

Alex and I climb the stairs leading to the wall, together, silent. The stairs are steep and when we reach the top of the first section, a vast barren landscape spreads out before us, and in all directions, rolling brown hills and leafless trees. The bright sunshine has no warmth, but infuses everything with a brittle sharp luminescence, throwing harsh shadows in its path. We continue along the Wall, and it is surprising how steep it is; you don't so much walk the Wall as climb it, like a mountain. At intervals there are stone staircases crowned by parapets where you can stop and take in the view, which is stunning at every point. To see a structure of this length and height snaking along the spine of this stark countryside, rising impossibly out of nowhere, leaves me speechless. The sheer manpower needed to construct it is incalculable, and then to think that all that effort was futile in its purpose. The Wall reminds me of a grand loneliness and painful separation, a cleaving of the land and a cleaving of China from the world.

A sadness rises up in me with each step. I take photographs, fully knowing they will never capture the essence of this place. Alex and I walk the Wall for that hour, not speaking much, under-dressed for the cold, and yet when we reach the steps to the plaza where we are to meet the others, I tell Alex to go on without me. I want to linger a moment, take some final shots with my camera, and try to discover what exactly it is that I am feeling. Alex moves on to the trinket shops, and I turn and place my hands upon the stone and look out over the rolling countryside. I close my eyes, breathing in the cold air, and focus on that breathing until my mind is as clear as the crystalline sky. There is a question inside me that will not quite form into words, and so I wait; after a moment, an image begins to form within my mind. It is a red dragon, a mighty beast breathing smoke and fire. The dragon is holding something, and he holds it out toward me. I look for what feels like a long time, the sight is so beautiful, jewels of many colors twinkling and shining. I want to reach out to touch it, for this object seems so familiar: it is a crown, and I feel sure I have seen it before, but where or when I could not say.

The van crawls through the evening rush hour of Beijing. I have been lost in my thoughts the entire drive back, exhausted from the hike and trying to absorb the experience. I watch people outside the window, people on bicycles, people walking with huge bundles lashed to their backs and people pushing carts laden with a jumble of cargo. Not one Caucasian face do I see, no blond hair, no blue eyes. I think of other foreign capital cities where I have seen a raucous mix of ethnicity, but not here.

There are modern buildings alongside dilapidated shacks. I see a man selling something from a steaming pot in front of a Western-style bank. I catch a glimpse of a woman inside a brightly lit storefront; it seems to be a beauty shop. The woman is young, dressed in sophisticated black, her hair beautifully coiffed. She is stunning; her face arrests my attention as we roll slowly past. She would not look out of place in Paris, or New York, especially with the bored and jaded expression she expertly wears. Just past this shop, I see a woman walking in her drab grey Mao jacket and dusty shoes; she smiles and she has no teeth. Then and Now, sharing the same sidewalk.

I am so tired, hungry and cold. Jet lag has begun to take its toll. When we reach the hotel I go straight to my room and to bed, and once I lay down I cannot move. It is as if something has pinned me there. I drift in and out of sleep, beyond exhaustion, yet overstimulated. The Wall....fragments of Chinese songs....people's faces that I saw from my window....all move through my mind, a whirling ballet of images. At some point I hear Alex moving around the room, and I hear her say it's time to leave. We are scheduled to attend a Chinese opera performance. I hear her but I can't respond, and after she goes I fall into a deep cavernous sleep, into a land of palaces and pagodas, dreaming of some time in China's past which seems like my own.

*The world rushes by outside my window. I don't know where I am in relation to where I am going. The emptiness of the countryside has given way to scores of people, animals, and all manner of conveyance hauling fruits and vegetables, building materials, or household goods along the dirt streets and wooden sidewalks. I am in the middle of a city but I don't know which one as I have never been anywhere outside my home.*

*My village is small and squats in a valley, like the women squat while tending the rice fields. The people are poor but are proud of the lives they eke out of the stingy land. My father farmed the land like his father before him, but I am a girl child and must marry and bear children. Everyone I know wanted to bear sons, and only sons, to carry on the family name, to care for them when they grew old and were no longer able to perform the back-breaking work of feeding themselves. A son could do that, could work until well after they passed on, while a daughter would be preoccupied with her own husband, her own children and not be able to consistently provide food and shelter. A woman must be provided for, she cannot be the provider.*

*But my own father never wanted a son, he said, only a daughter who could look after him with devotion and love, not obligation. In this as in many other things he was far different than anyone else in the village. Father said that because of the burden they are yet to be, a son will always resent his parents. My father told me this and many other things by the light of the fire each evening; he believed that leaving girls in ignorance will cost society half its potential power and is not wise. Father taught me mathematics and read literature and poetry to me, taught me to write and encouraged me to do so. I would show him my writings, little essays about the birds or trees, about words I heard on the wind. He took delight in these and read them over and over again.*

*My mother had died when I was very small of a terrible fever that raced across the land. Many died, as there were no doctors to care for villages such as ours, so far away from the large cities. We were responsible for our lives here, for our health and for our food and for our shelter. No one from the Empire ever gave to us; they merely took, each year at tax time, a portion of that which we had grown by our own sweat and toil. But it did not concern us, for we lived in a world of peace, however poor or sometimes hungry we might be.*

*My mother died long before I could memorize her face. My father says a mirror will tell me all I need to know about what she looked like and I plan to ask for one the minute I am in my new home. I wish my father could be with me; I will miss him terribly, as we have never been parted. And I will miss the long hours I spend running, running in the fields with one of the many kites he would make for me. My favorite, the one he gave me for my last birthday, was a delicate butterfly, made of gossamer silk. Father had painted tiny tigers onto the wings of the butterfly, one for each year of my life. I was born in the year of the tiger and this was my symbol for luck. "Combine the best aspects of both creatures, my child, and you shall roar as you fly to the Heavens," he had said with a laugh. I smiled, but his remark troubled me, for this was my conundrum. I was always either a butterfly or a tiger, but never both. Either too delicate and flighty or roaring too loudly, using my claws as weapons. Was it possible to be beautiful and fly free, while at the same time, being fierce and courageous? Perhaps my new life would help me to answer this question and many more.*

*I am to be a virgin bride for the Emperor, a bride he had chosen for himself while riding through the fields that surround my village on the way to a military engagement. He had come upon me there, had spoken to me from the back of his giant black steed. I had said not a word; I was too shy to respond to his queries. He had asked my age and my father's name, to which I responded in silence. But my eyes must have flashed for he looked into them for a long moment before he rode off across the countryside with his guards and soldiers trailing behind. I ran home breathless to my father, legs bare as I had tied the hem of my garment into a knot at my hip. I had been flying my kite, hair loose and free; I knew I must run with the wind, though the village women shook their heads and clucked their tongues at my behavior.*

*Chen was with me in the fields and now he followed behind, lurking outside my father's door as I recounted the story of my meeting with the Emperor. Father had looked at me for a long while with a sad expression and then said "Run along now, and start our dinner, it will soon be the end of the day." And he walked past me out of the house without looking at Chen standing just outside the doorway.*

*I told Chen to go, too, as I had work to do. Chen had a sad expression just like my father's and I did not want to see it* anymore. "We'll meet tomorrow as usual," I told him, and gave him a smile and a pat on the cheek. We will be together always, I thought, in this little village. It made me happy to think of life in that way.

But one day a few weeks after my encounter with the Emperor, everything changed. His Majesty had sent a summons to my father asking that I be released to him to serve as a concubine in the royal palace. Father's hand shook as he read the parchment and then slowly rolled it back into his hand, gripping it to stop the trembling. I had cried bitterly when he told me of its contents. "No, no, no, I will not go away from here!," I shouted. My father had educated me too well, I knew exactly what a concubine was, the life that was required. "No, father!," I cried. "I want to marry and have a child, to live in the village and have a home. I cannot be a concubine, Father; I would die!"

My poor father, the dilemma this placed him in, between his beloved daughter and the sovereign ruler of China. In law and in tradition his daughter had no worth, no right to say no. A father could sell or give a girl child away to anyone he chose. Should the Emperor himself make an appeal, it was little more than a formality. The understood reply was always 'yes' to whatever he requested of his subjects. And I was asking my Father to say no, to put himself at risk for the daughter he had taught to speak for herself.

My father sat that night in front of the waning hearth light until the rooster crowed to signal the arrival of a new day. He got up slowly from his chair and came to my bedside where he knelt to whisper "No my daughter, I will not send you away." I wrapped my arms around his neck and then bounded out of bed to gather eggs for his breakfast, which I would cook with all the love of a grateful heart. As I left the house that day, my father was gathering his writing tools, his brush and ink and parchment, to make a formal reply to the Emperor—to refuse his request for the life of his daughter.

In my naiveté I had thought this was the end of the matter. There were millions of girls in the kingdom for the Emperor to choose; if one were to refuse, he would surely find another. Why would it matter if a village girl such as me said no? During the week it took for my father's reply to reach the palace via horseback I had gone about my usual life, playing with Chen, cooking for Father, studying my books at night. A week in the village was an eternity, time moved so slowly there; by the time the royal courier returned in a blaze of speed on a horse flecked with foam I had almost forgotten all about the matter. It was a shock, then, to see a man in uniform standing at our door as I returned from filling the water pails at the well; I almost spilled them out onto the ground in surprise.

Father had come out of the house and bade me to come in. I set my pails down and wiped my hands upon my apron as I walked slowly past the courier, who did not even glance at me. He stood with eyes straight ahead in a posture of waiting, for what I did not know. Inside, my father took my hands and we sat down together. On the table was a parchment scroll with fancy calligraphy and an official seal in red wax. "Daughter," my father said, "the Emperor has requested once again that you be brought to him at the palace. The man outside is charged with the task of bringing you to town, where there will be a carriage waiting. We must hurry to ready your departure."

"But Father," I could hardly choke out the words, my eyes stung with tears, my heart pounding in sudden fear. "Father, you promised I would not be sent away! I cannot become a concubine; it is not the life I choose. I could run away, I am very fast. I could be across the field before the guard knows that I've gone, I could...."

"No, daughter," my father interrupted, "you must listen to me, as circumstances are not what you have assumed. When I wrote to the Emperor in refusal of his request I stated that it was based upon my desire that my daughter not live the life of a second wife, as a concubine, as you are my only and most beloved child, and the status of First Wife is the only appropriate marital arrangement and the only one to which I would agree. And now it seems the Emperor has agreed and wishes to confer upon you status of First Wife, should you satisfactorily complete the training necessary to Imperial life."

"But Father," I wondered, "how can that be? The Emperor has seen me only once; surely he has many girls and concubines from which to choose a wife, I cannot believe..."

"Daughter," father interrupted, "the Emperor has found you pleasing and has indicated in his reply that it is not possible for any man to place a value upon a daughter which is lower than that conferred upon her by her own father. In my refusal to acquiesce to his request the Emperor saw that I have placed you upon a pedestal in my heart and he wishes that sort of woman as a wife, a woman of value. In the letter, he has likened you to a sparkling jewel and he has promised to place you swiftly into a setting which befits your rare beauty and quality. The life you may now have far surpasses that which I could have dreamed for you. You must go, and with a happy heart spread your love and beauty to the highest and furthest reaches of this land."

"Oh father," I cried, "but how can I leave you? I only go because you ask me to, because it brings you honor. But father, I will not go without Chen! He must accompany me as my companion, and live and serve in the palace, too. I love him as a brother; surely there would be no objection?"

*My father had risen then and gone to the door and in a low voice had spoken to the guard posted there. The man listened with no expression and then slowly nodded his head in assent, speaking a few words back to my father, who then turned to me. "You must hurry daughter and tell Chen to ready his belongings. You are to leave tonight and there is much to do."*

*As I ran across the field which separates my house from Chen's I dreamed of us riding happily along in the royal carriage, laughing and anticipating this great adventure. He will be so surprised, I thought, and I was happy that because of me he would now have a chance to live a life of privilege. And yet I worried that Chen would not want to go, as there was a girl in the village who loved him; they had already planned to marry. I was his friend, his sister in spirit; but she....Lo Ming would bear his children, she was the lotus of his heart.*

*I saw Chen from across the field, he was waiting in the doorway as if he knew I would come. Smoke curled from the chimney of the little house and made a white pathway to heaven above his head. His face held an expression of acceptance and anticipation; now that destiny had arrived for him, he was ready to take its hand. It was this I loved in Chen more than any other thing: his willingness to embrace life in all its uncertainty.*

*"Chen!" I gasped as I reached the dirt courtyard that had been swept clean and was smooth as stone. "Chen, I must ask you..."*

*"Shall I gather my belongings? When do we leave?" he asked softly, a slight smile tugging at the corners of his mouth. And seeing my confusion he continued by explaining, "I knew he would be back for you, my dear friend; for I saw the light that burned in his eyes that day in the field, and knew that he meant to have you."*

*I fell silent, and looked up to see a flock of birds splitting the* sky with the arrow of their configuration, and it seemed to me that though they flew together they were lonely in their journey. Should one bird fall behind, would its fellows slow to protect it? Or was the safety of the group an illusion hiding the reality that each is alone in striving to reach its destination?

"And you are willing to go?" I asked, "To leave all you have known, to leave all you have loved..." and the face of Lo Ming came to my mind, and her eyes glowed softly with love for Chen, with happiness for their future.

"There is much that I may do," Chen answered. And I thought of the ambitious plans of my friend, how so many hours in the fields we talked of changes that could be made to help the village. Chen had talked of trade with other villages, of increasing our farmers' yield of food and grain, of law and justice to create an orderly system of commerce. Chen's skill with numbers and the ways of business were well known to the village elders and there had already been talk of his being certain to rise to a position of great authority in time. In what ways might he use these talents within the palace, how many more might he help?

"I will send for Lo Ming when all is settled," he said, and raised my hand to his lips, kissing it softly and sealing our pact. I had never felt so close to another human being before and love flooded my heart. Such a good and true person was my friend; with humility I thanked him and told him that I would always want him near me.

I wake with the sensation that I have just been falling. What time is it, isn't there something I should be doing, or should have done? The clock says 8 a.m.; I have been asleep for 15 hours. I sit up, look over and Alex has rolled with her back to me on her bed, still asleep. The last thing I remember is that she was getting ready to go out with the group, to the opera performance.

I get out of bed and move to the window, pull back the dingy curtain and sit on the cold metal ledge with my notebook and pen. There was a dream last night, and for the time being I can remember it from beginning to end. Another dream about China…I need to scribble it down before it fades away, like the morning mist above the rooftops of Beijing. The sun is trying to find a reason to shine today, through the gloom of pollution haze. A sea of continuous rooftops spreads out before me, punctuated here and there by an interior courtyard where I can glimpse the mundane activities of daily life. A man is walking, holding a cage, inside is a live chicken. I watch as he turns into one of the narrow alleys, and then a few moments later he emerges into the courtyard of a house and sets the cage down, and then disappears. Dinner for this evening, still alive this morning; but not for long.

This is not a beautiful city. Even in the pristine stillness of dawn it seems dirty and sad. I notice five birds circling in the air above the rooftops. They circle the same patch of air, moving higher and higher in a slow, elegant maneuver. Up in a spiral, and then lazily down again to alight on one particular rooftop, all in a row. Moments pass, and the cycle repeats, the birds taking off into flight, performing this silent air ballet. Someone has trained them, has spent many hours shaping their natural grace into something of even greater beauty, and I find comfort in this. At least one patch of this chaotic cityscape was made beautiful by the hand of man, by intention.

The strange night of dreams has left me disoriented. Catching hold of fragments here and there…there were birds in my dream as well, doing something at my bidding. What was it? I was in a place I did not recognize, from another time, ancient Imperial China. I write,

> I am in a carriage, an opulent carriage, as it moves from the country to the city. I am looking out the window; the scene outside is first rural fields and hills and then becomes a city where there are many people moving about. I am leaving my home and going somewhere else to live and I am sad about it, yet hopeful that this may be a better life. I will miss my father, who is my father now, but he is Chinese. It's funny how I know it's him even though he has Chinese features. There is someone in the carriage with me, my brother, and he is Chinese too. He is not my brother but my friend in the dream, and we have been friends for a long time. We are going to live together in a palace. I know that I will be married to the Emperor. I am wearing an elaborate embroidered robe, but it feels like dress-up. I am very young and so is my brother (I wonder, am I Chinese too?).

This dream seems beyond any type of Freudian analysis, a favorite pastime of mine. It is a story, like watching a movie, but the feelings are so real that it's as if I actually lived it. My dreams are becoming more and more like this; they are whole and resist reduction. I am living another lifetime in the night. Sometimes it takes the entire next day to recover my bearings, and the "real" world of my daily life seems pale in comparison to my dream experiences.

I close my notebook and start to dress, looking for my running shoes amidst the clutter of our suitcases. There is a gym downstairs in the hotel, and I run for three miles on the treadmill, listening to Chinese rock music blaring over the stereo, staring at a blank wall and trying to figure out what the lyrics might mean. A young male attendant stares at me the entire time with a blank expression, which at first makes me uncomfortable and self conscious; after a while, I don't even notice.

An hour later we meet the others in the lobby and begin loading the bags into the van before climbing in ourselves. During the ride to the center of town, I am again amazed by the people coming and going, on bicycles piled with pots and pans, crates, chickens, children, or whatever needs transporting. The riders weave in and out of the vehicular traffic with the boldness of experienced daredevils. Riding to work or the market, purposeful and without a moment to waste, oblivious to the danger or accepting it as part of the price of daily life. These people appear to meet the mundane challenges of daily living with flair.

The van stops along a busy thoroughfare, and we pile out and assemble on the sidewalk directly across from a huge two-story McDonald's restaurant on the edge of Tiananmen Square. The Golden Arches bracket one side, while a huge portrait of Chairman Mao smiles from the other. East and West, each holding its ground while keeping a sharp eye on the other, staring each other down.

As we get closer to the Square my excitement builds as it starts to sink in where we are, this historic place. I keep saying to anyone who will listen, "Do you believe we're here? Do you believe we're here??" because I can't, it is surreal. I think of the tanks rolling through this square, mowing down the students who had staged a protest calling for democracy. I think of the staged military parades and the communist leaders waving to the rows and rows of soldiers from their viewing stand, high above the fray.

Tiananmen Square is the symbol of modern China, as the Forbidden City is the symbol of ancient China, and it is a surprise to me how they nestle up against each other, somehow I had not imagined they would be so close in proximity. Tiananmen is a vast space, much larger than I expected, and though the expanse is so large and open, the high brick walls surrounding the perimeter give the unmistakable feeling of entrapment. Once again I have the feeling we are being watched. Every soldier in the square, and there were many, carries a large gun over his shoulder or strapped to his waist, a reminder that we are really just fish in a barrel, easy targets.

Judging by the hard expressions on the faces of the soldiers, wearing the drab green uniform confers upon its wearer a terrible burden. They attempt to hide this with arrogance as they patrol around the Square, pushing people around with their don't-mess-with-me attitude. Most of the Chinese people here in the Square ignore it, used to a lifetime of authoritarian rule. But for me, an American, it comes as a shock. It is an affront to my sensibilities; I feel a wave of disgust every time I look at one of their faces. Where in the United States would we see military personnel patrolling a public square like this, armed to the hilt? The disturbing aspect is that they are not here to protect the people; they are here to squelch any type of dissent aimed at the Communist party. There is no one to protect the people here; their own government suspects them, spies on them, restrains them and inhibits them, and they must toe the line. They must acquiesce because of the guns on the backs of their own young countrymen, who will do the bidding of the state against them. Their faces say they will, and I believe them.

Anna moves us along as we snap pictures in front of the giant smiling portrait of Chairman Mao, architect of this system. I have read a bit about him, and his image gives me a feeling of unease. The cruelty he perpetrated, the repression of his people, is well known, and yet here he is, his influence still hanging over everything. He is fully present though he died so many years ago, the people yet unwilling to let him go.

The past is so oppressive here in this ancient land, and perhaps the Cultural Revolution was an attempt to smash and destroy the burdens of time. But as is so often the case, one way of oppressing people is substituted for another and the cycle continues, until oppression itself is seen as the real enemy, and all forms of it are rejected by a people.

A throng waits at the entrance to the Forbidden City just underneath, and we join the line of people waiting to get in. Suddenly, a commotion directly in front of us catches our attention. A group of people is sitting in a circle, holding hands, eyes closed in peaceful silence, surrounded by a crowd of onlookers. Sirens begin blaring in the distance, coming closer, the shrill sound piercing the air. The men in drab green finally have something to do, and they come rushing forward from all sides of the square, as if racing to put out a fire. They move in, violently parting the crowd, pushing aside anyone in their way, women, children, old people. They begin grabbing the arms of the meditators, screaming at them, ordering them to do something, to move, to acquiesce. The circle of sitters does not move and the soldiers begin dragging them by whatever body part they can grab, hair, arms, legs; they are punching them and kicking them, though they are not resisting. A police van comes screeching to a halt in front of the melee, and the soldiers start dragging, pushing and stuffing the offending individuals into the van. One man shields his face from the blows of a night stick, a woman holds her arm in pain as a soldier twists it behind her back. The crowd looking on makes no move of protest, the guns, after all.....but I see no signs of revulsion or even surprise evident on their faces.

Anna hisses at us to keep moving, don't even look in that direction; and no matter what, do NOT take any pictures! We are shaken; we do as we are told. Our little group moves slowly past the scene, trying hard to stay together and not to be separated in the crowd. Anna pulls us along, shepherding her flock to safety.

Something is oddly out of balance here. I know now why these young men's faces are so hardened and immobile. If it were not so deadly serious, it would be almost comical, a farce. Skinny men barely out of their teens dressed in ugly uniforms, rushing around and hitting people on the head with nightsticks for sitting down and thinking. The insanity, the complete insanity of fear is obvious here. I look up at the smiling Mao. And you! You are dead now, but somewhere beyond, are you witnessing this? Are you proud of what you have wrought? And I think how all the players in this sordid little drama I have just witnessed will also be dead in the not so distant future and I am sad for them, sad that they have used so much of their life energy to perpetuate such a system.

When we are at a safe distance and the shrill call of the sirens has died down, I turn to Anna. "What do you think of this? Does it bother you?" I ask. Her face goes slack, and she moves away a little, she doesn't want to talk. "Really, what do you think? Do you talk about this with friends, with family?" I press her, move toward her. She looks around, side to side, and then steps closer to me, with a gesture of her hand that shows her practiced restraint.

"What can we do?" she says, and it is obvious to me that she feels she is taking a risk in answering me. "We just want to live our lives. If we protest, they'll arrest us too; and we want to live!" she says, in a low, strained voice. I start to speak, I am set to argue, to say "But then nothing will change!" The look on her face deflates my intention as I see, as she had said, that it was no use. The Chinese had lived with this type of authoritarian system for thousands of years, both under the old Empire and now under the Communists. For me, an American child of the 60's and 70's, this acceptance of powerlessness was unthinkable; and yet I saw that here, perhaps acceptance was the intelligent thing, and protesting tantamount to suicide. It was the way things were. And in that moment, I saw that even my questioning Anna along these lines was a dangerous thing. For her to have this kind of job, guiding Americans who were here to adopt babies, she must have been in some way a trusted member of the establishment. Perhaps she had had to profess loyalty to the Communist party many, many times in her life; and I was asking her to criticize it, and put herself and her job at risk. My first reaction upon seeing the arrests in the square was to assume that anyone would find it and the state which sanctioned it abhorrent. But I had forgotten that it is possible that not everyone would long for freedom. Some who have been imprisoned for long periods start to fear the outside world, preferring the comfort and security of the known.

My vehemence dies down and I think of the entire tableau that has just played out before me. Tiananmen Square....soldiers....Chairman Mao...people meditating...meditation? As a threat to the state? What exactly are they so afraid of, to unleash so much force for so little reason? The Chinese government seems to be acknowledging that meditation, which is a going within, a strengthening of the mind, is dangerous, and they are right. True power for change starts within the individual, within the mind and heart. A free mind and heart is beyond the control of any government, and this freedom cannot be taken away, no matter what you do to the body. Throw it in jail, starve it, even kill it; it makes no difference. Meditation is a danger to any system which seeks to control others through fear, which seeks to maintain external power over others at any cost. And many minds, millions of minds, focused together on change, on freedom, on self-realization would bring down this totalitarian government if sustained for any length of time.

These people, the ones just arrested, may be beyond being hooked by fear; but the ones watching, the ones who have not yet tasted the freedom that lies within, perhaps they can be frightened into believing that even beginning is dangerous or even evil. I look at Anna's face and absorb her words, and it dawns on me, that she knows this, she knows. I nod to her slightly and we move away from each other, and though we don't speak of it again for the rest of the trip an invisible bond is now between us, a meeting of the minds.

Stepping through the doorway into the Forbidden City is like entering a place where time has stopped. After the melee of the arrest and the hubbub of Tiananmen Square, the empty silence of the Imperial fortress is death-like. Nothing lives here. I feel a chill as we begin walking across the first of the many open courtyards, and pull my thin coat more tightly around my body. The air is crisp and sharp, the cold is reaching into every part of me, covered and uncovered, until even my toes inside my heavy boots are numb.

We walk slowly through the courtyard, looking around, no one speaking, as if we have entered the hushed interior of a library. There is nothing to say, and I am having difficulty formulating complete thoughts. I think of a scene from a favorite movie of mine, "The Last Emperor," when the orange-robed monks fill the courtyard with chants as they bow before the new Emperor, only three years old. The little Emperor only wants to run through the ranks of the monks, to play hide and seek. That scene always stayed with me, though I had seen the movie only once many years before. It was the chanting of the monks that most affected me, and I could imagine the faint echoes of the tones as I stood here, in the now abandoned city.

Emperors lived here once, Emperors and Empresses. This is a vast, orderly and spacious sanctuary that protected its occupants from the rest of the unruly city, and yet they must have been unhappy here, isolated as they were from the outside world. The buildings are beautiful, but I feel nothing here. It is as if all traces of human energy were somehow removed, and all that remains is a void.

As the group moves through the site, I keep thinking of the people just arrested outside the Forbidden City. They were arrested for meditating. Actually, they were arrested for being members of a group deemed a "cult" by the Chinese government, as most religions have been. This particular group practiced an unsanctioned form of religion, and the meditation circle was just one visible form of practice of the religion.

Just yesterday I had meditated in the shadow of the Great Wall of China, and today I would do so within the walls of the Forbidden City. I would practice with a delicious sense of subversion, knowing that no one could stop me, and in a spirit of solidarity with those just arrested. I do not close my eyes as I usually do, to remain unobtrusive, and yet a young man in military uniform stops talking with his comrades and watches me as I stand away from the group, looking out over the courtyard. Something about me has alerted his attention, but as I am doing nothing which could be deemed inappropriate, he loses interest and begins talking again with his friends.

As my breath slows and my focus of attention shifts from the outer world to the inner world, I can still see everything that surrounds me, but also, at the same time, can see with my inner vision. Never before have I experienced this, to be fully aware of the external world and internal world simultaneously, without effort. Perhaps it is this place, I think, this void, which produces a type of heightened perception.

There is an image, like a transparency that has been laid over my physical sight; I am seeing a woman lying on the ground. She does not move. She is dressed in an elaborate robe which is arrayed around her body. I know she has been lying there for some time. No one comes to her, she is utterly alone. The woman is lying next to a garden wall, a very high stone wall. Suddenly I see something rising over the wall, something flutters and rises…it is a kite. It rises higher and higher. The woman on the ground stirs, she lifts her head and sees the kite high above her, and she jumps to her feet. She is sobbing as she runs to the garden wall. I can see her shoulders shaking and heaving. She reaches up….*Oh please let it be him! Chen!!*

A shout rips my attention from the inner scene and back to the courtyard below, and it fades entirely as I watch one of the men in military uniform throw something to the ground, a small package. His friends are laughing, their white teeth gleaming in the sunshine. The sound startles me back, and now I am fully present here, in the cold. I turn to look for the others, they have moved on toward the next pavilion, and I hurry to catch up to them, wondering who the woman in the vision was, and why I had seen her there.

I follow to the entrance of a walkway, next to which is a sign indicating that the area beyond was the place where the Emperor's concubines and wives were housed. Apparently they were confined to this specified area and not allowed to roam freely in the Forbidden City, and only women and eunuchs were allowed to enter. Inside is a small courtyard surrounded on all sides by bedchambers and sitting rooms. In the center of the courtyard is a large, dark stone, encased in a glass box. A sign says that this stone symbolized the purity of the concubines. As I look at it through the glass I wonder, did it absorb impurities from these women somehow? The stone has a presence, an energy still emanates from it, unlike anything else in this place. It must have been witness to centuries of intrigue, drama, heartbreak....I feel a deep urge to touch the stone, to run my fingers over its variegated surface, but the glass prevents me, and I turn to wander around the courtyard, looking into the chambers, each one small, with a built in bed covered in silk cushions, the focal point of the room as it was the focal point of the inhabitants' lives.

They were called concubines, but they were slaves, imprisoned here to serve their master. The value of a woman was based solely on her ability to please one man; she was a commodity. How painful this must have been. I wonder how I would have adapted to such a system. Would I have gone along or tried to rebel somehow? It was a different time, a different society…would I have been conscious of the injustice, or was that mainly my modern-day sensibility layered over the past?

During my childhood, I had an innate and heightened awareness of unfairness and inequality, as many children do. But I had especially chafed at the rules which applied only to girls and curtailed my natural desire for freedom. Boys were allowed to do things which I was not, even though I knew them to be no smarter than I, and no more courageous. I fought hard, competing with boys in school, on the playground, and at home with my older brother. I resisted domination by anyone or anything, especially boys, and my mother always said that I had this type of fight in me from the moment of my birth. Where did that intensity come from? I had always wondered, as it seemed out of proportion to the actual limitations imposed on me by my parents and society, as if driven by a reaction to an experience which pre-dated my birth.

If there was an "I" that could remain intact through other lifetimes, if in rebirth it is possible to maintain a self with stable personality characteristics, and the self I know of as "me" were to live as a concubine in Imperial China, would I have suffered here, under this system, even if I had no knowledge of modern ideas of gender and freedom?

I listen hard as I hear the answer rise up from deep within: *yes. Yes, and more so.*

Everywhere we go, the Chinese people seem interested in us. There is an evident curiosity, and some even muster the courage to interact with us. They are especially interested in Maggie, a little Chinese girl accompanied by two tall, blond, blue-eyed American parents. Several Chinese women ask to hear her speak; others bring their own Chinese babies and children to hug her and touch her hand, or have their pictures taken with her. It is as if Maggie is a lucky talisman, as if a child who touches her receives some spark of her energy. It appears that this association with Americans or being an American is for most here seen as desirable, although it is difficult to tell. At the Great Wall yesterday when Alex and I were standing waiting for the others to appear, a group of high-spirited teenagers approached. One bold girl asked if she could stand next to us while her friend took our picture. Surprised, we agreed, and immediately two other girls jumped to either side of us before their young male friend snapped a picture. They were very excited about this, and chattered together, arms waving, laughing as they walked away from us.

"That was weird," Alex had said, and it was. The incident made me uneasy and I had a feeling somehow that we had just been had, though I was not sure what it meant. I got the distinct feeling we were the butt of some joke they were pulling, but could not tell if the punch line was benign or malevolent.

We leave the Forbidden City and emerge once again to

the sound of traffic and commotion in the heart of Beijing. A van is waiting for us just outside the walls, and we will go directly to the airport for our flight to Nanchang. The sightseeing for the trip is over, and from now on everything on the schedule will revolve around the babies, starting tomorrow morning when they are to be delivered to their new parents at the hotel.

During the ride to the airport I watch the billboards and traffic outside my window, and think of how tonight I will write in my journal and try to make sense of the vivid dreams and meditation experiences of the last two days. A Burger King sign looms above the roadway where modern cars whiz past our van. This admixture of past and present, East and West, has me disoriented, and I suddenly feel so tired, tired to the bone. All I want to do is sleep, and two hours later, when I am settled into my seat aboard our flight, I do sleep, but I do not rest. Someone is trying to tell me something, and finally, I start to hear.

*Passing through the gates of the Imperial Palace was as entering another world. The immense wooden gates, painted blood red, the color of luck, the color of the empire, opened to allow our carriage to pass into the cloistered interior, and when they closed behind us with a thud which resonated throughout the courtyard, I felt a sudden wave of panic, of claustrophobic fear, which overwhelmed me and caused me to claw my nails into the palm of Chen's hand. His own hand returned the pressure, and I turned to look into my friend's eyes, and saw there a vague specter, a ghost of a terror long ago forgotten. We did not speak,* for the air was filled with a noisy clamor, the bustle of court life which was indifferent to our arrival in its midst.

The carriage traveled on, through courtyard after courtyard, through a series of gates until it stopped before a high stone wall. In the wall was a set of double wooden doors, painted with flowers, birds and insects, and calligraphy which announced "Garden of the Emperor's Divine Seed." I watched as the Emperor's guard, quiet and withdrawn since our entry into the walled city, suddenly jumped from the carriage and with purpose began to direct a group of people gathered outside the wooden doors. Men and women stood there, and the man barked orders at them which caused a flurry of activity. The men in drab brown robes, tied with coarse rope, moved to one side of the doors while the women, dressed in the finest silks and headdresses, gathered on the other.

The guard put his head in through the carriage door, "Come out!" and I moved to rise from the bench but my legs, so long immobile and shaking from fear, gave way beneath me. Chen turned and caught my arm to steady me, and our eyes met, uncertain and questioning. "It will be alright!" I said, to myself, to Chen. And yet a dread had begun forming, a knot of amorphous fear, the source of which I could not name. The excitement of new adventures and dreams of a new life seemed far away, as far as my father's house in the village, as untouchable as dream mountains shrouded in mist. I stepped forward toward the lip of the carriage, took the hand the guard offered, and descended to the dusty cobblestones in my poor cloth shoes which had been made for me in the village.

Not yet summoning the will to lift my head, I let my eyes shift ahead, and saw the shoes which peeked from beneath the hems of the court ladies assembled before me. They were made of brightly colored silken brocades, upturned at the toes and with all manner of adornments. One pair in particular arrested my attention: they were made of blue and white brocade, piped with red. They were small shoes, the feet within must be bound in the traditional way, I thought, and I let my eyes come back again to my own dusty shoes, which covered feet that had been left free of that societal mutilation, thanks to my father's unorthodox ways and love of his daughter.

My eyes again lit upon the shoes that held those tiny feet, feet that would not allow the woman balancing upon them to run in the fields, to be free with the wind in her hair, to know how fast or how far her legs might take her. I felt pity for one so disabled, and I allowed my eyes then to travel up, past the hem of her skirt, to her small waist that was cinched with a lavender cummerbund, and on to her shapely bodice, which was held together at the throat with a silken frog closure. How beautiful the garment, like none I had yet seen....and my eyes felt a need to continue, to see the face of the one who wore such finery, for she must be the embodiment of female grace and elegance.

The skin was fine enough; the lips were perhaps reddened a bit unnaturally. But the eyes...when I reached the eyes of the one who had captured my attention, I saw a dark fathomless night, a place where unknown evil may live and breed. The black eyes stared back in cold fury as if I had personally offended the one behind them...and yet I had just arrived in this place, and had never seen her before. A chill went up the length of my spine as our eyes locked and I stood rooted to the spot where I stood, lost in the confusing hatred of her gaze.

Chen alighted from the carriage and stood beside me, so close I could hear his breathing, a bit shallow and coming in little bursts from his throat. The guard spoke harshly to him, "Over here!" and shoved him from the spot where he stood. I turned in surprise and started to voice a protest; but Chen looked stern and made a tiny movement with his head, no, do not speak; it is not wise. And I stood and watched as Chen was herded together with the men in the brown robes, and they began moving off and away from the women who were knotted at the doorway. "Goodbye!" Chen said, in a high thin voice that held a slight lilt in an effort to sound cheerful. His attempt to appear unfazed caused a hard lump to rise into my throat, and suddenly I could not swallow or breathe. I wanted to remain near him, the one soul in this place who knew my hopes and dreams. Surely we will be reunited in a short while, I reasoned, and this thought brought comfort to my heart and I turned to face the ones who stood before me.

I looked into each face now, and most carried expressions of bored disinterest, none a look of kindness; but none held the mean expression of the one with the brocade shoes. She stood there still, eyes fixed upon me, and when the guard took my arm to propel me forward and through the doorway that had swung open before me, I saw her figure from the corner of my eye as she fell in behind me and followed our steps with her teetering walk.

"You have entered the domain of the concubines," the guard said, and waved his arm to indicate the many chambers which lined the perimeter of the courtyard. "No men are allowed to enter but those personally chosen by the Emperor, and the eunuchs charged with serving the Emperor's women. Your friend shall never visit you here, it is forbidden. I will see you to your quarters," he said.

As we made our way across the open space, many other women came forward from the shadows of their chambers, to mark the coming of the new member of their ranks. How many there were I could not tell, but I felt their eyes upon me. There was a feeling of hunger, of despair in the air and I felt oppressed in the confines of *this place in which they and their sadness were contained. As we reached the center point of the courtyard, the guard stopped briefly our progress to address an older woman who had come to consult with him, and I stood by his side quietly, not looking about me, until again he motioned for me to continue with him.*

*As I made the move to bring my foot forward, I became aware of a curious resistance, and my mind whirled as I could not bring my leg to the spot I had intended in front of me, though my body continued its forward momentum and I knew I was falling, pitching forward, but could not extract my leg from its curious position in order to right myself. The sensation was one of falling into a great abyss; time slowed to a standstill, and I swiveled my head around to catch a glimpse of the guard's astonished face, of stone wall, of clouds and sky as I plummeted to the cobblestones.*

*A titter of laughter caught like wildfire and swept through the ranks of the concubines. It made a lovely low sound, like bells, and would have been beautiful to me had it not been at my expense. The flush of humiliation rose to my face and I lay there, not wanting to move from my lowly spot upon the ground.*

*The guard reached for my arm, and pulled me upright; he let me dust off my rough skirt before rising to my feet, and as I smoothed the fabric over my hips he turned, and hissed through clenched teeth, "You are not to interfere with her on my watch!"*

*He was speaking to the woman whose gaze had held hatred for me, the concubine who followed behind. I turned to see on her face an expression of barely suppressed satisfaction, and when she spoke it was with the acid drip of sarcasm in her voice. "Oh, but Jiang....how could she not have tripped upon those large, ugly feet?!! They merely got in the way of my own!" The concubine held her tiny foot forward from the hem of her gown, and turned the ankle slowly to show its stunted length.*

*The guard shook his head in dismissal of the woman and we turned to walk on, but I knew then that I must be careful in this place, that there were those that wished to cause me to fall to earth, to eat the dust of humiliation at the hands of my own kind.*

I wake to see Anna, Alex and the flight attendant who is standing in the aisle staring at me, waiting for a reply. I think she has asked me if I want something to drink, and I wave my hand no, I am fine, and they all look away from me, as I turn back to the window. I have just been dreaming again, and once more the setting was Imperial China, a palace there. It must be triggered by our visit to the Forbidden City, but it felt so real, what is going on with all these dreams? I check my watch. We have a little less than an hour before we land; I have time to write this down before I forget. I take out my notebook and begin writing in my journal, the journal which was meant to be a chronicle of my trip, but is now becoming a chronicle of a life being lived inside my dreams.

An attractive young woman dressed in a Western-style business suit meets us outside the airport. She is competent and efficient, instructing porters where to take our bags, and guiding us to yet another van which waits for us at the curb. She asks us to call her "Sheila," the Americanized name she has chosen to make it easier for us to address her. She never tells us her Chinese name, nor has Anna. They cannot be who they really are with us; they must alter their identities in an attempt to bridge the cultural gap for the time they are to spend as our guides. It must be a strain to do so, and several times I notice Sheila becoming impatient, as she reads us the itinerary and tries to explain the schedule for our time in Nanchang.

We drive a long way through open fields on a highway that could have been in any modern country in the world. The land is flat, and dull and dusty, uninteresting in every way, and I find it hard to stay awake as we drive, still half caught in the world of my dreams.

Sheila is passing out some papers for the adoptive parents to look at, and mentally I check out—it has nothing to do with me. Several moments and a few dusty miles later, I catch the tail-end of a statement that startles me back to attention: had she said the babies would be there at the hotel, today? All day long Anna has been telling us the babies would not be delivered to the hotel until tomorrow morning, and the parents had set their minds to a relaxing evening with nothing on the schedule. Anxious as they all were to meet their new children, a nice meal and some sleep were what they were planning for this evening. To suddenly think of dealing with babies in less than 15 minutes, just off a plane, hungry, exhausted and not prepared, was overwhelming. It is as if someone has thrown a switch inside the van, the air becomes electrified with anxiety. Judy looks as if she is hyperventilating, while Curtis rubs her back helplessly. Alex, sitting next to me, looks green. Her hands flutter as she rifles through her briefcase full of papers, though there is no paperwork to be done. The briefcase is a security blanket for her, providing structure to this experience. This paper for this day, this paper for that, an escape from the overwhelming emotions.

Until that moment, the idea of the babies has been an abstraction for me, just part of this trip but not the entire reason I was here. Now that meeting them is imminent, an excitement surges through me, a sudden happiness that feels like Christmas morning had felt when I was a child, just before seeing what Santa has brought. I can not contain it, I start laughing, and clapping my hands. Why, I ask myself, do I feel so excited, when I am not getting a baby? Probably, I reason, because the thought of being responsible for a baby for its lifetime is not intruding upon me as it certainly is for the parents. But still, the pure joy that wells in me is so unexpected—a vicarious happiness that feels entirely personal. In that moment I feel as if the babies are mine, too; and by the time we arrive in front of the hotel Jin Feng, I can't wait to see them.

I ask Sheila if they would be right inside the lobby when we walk in. She didn't know, she said. We walk inside the big glass doors, the new parents all hesitant and hanging back and I wanting to run in, to look for babies, for people holding babies. We look around, left to right, but the lobby is nearly deserted, no babies to be seen. Sheila gives us our keys and tells us to go on to our rooms; the babies will be brought there when they arrive.

The tension is palpable as we ride the elevator to our

floor, tight looks on all the parents' faces. The only one who smiles for me, the only one who seems to share my excitement, is Maggie, and she mugs as I snap photos of her just before she is to meet her new sister.

Each of the three families has a room along the same hallway on the fourth floor, and as we find ours, the bags are brought by the porter and Alex nervously begins to unpack the baby supplies she has brought with her. I can't stand it; I open the door and lean out into the corridor, trying to get a glimpse. Within moments I hear the elevator bell clang, and then, a group of people step off holding three babies, and my eyes lock upon the smallest little face, a baby, wrapped in a bulky padded suit with a hood covering her head, being carried down the hallway. I know instantly that this is the baby, the baby from the photograph. I don't even look at the others, though they are right behind in the arms of two other orphanage workers. Her face....I can't take my eyes off of her, there is something hauntingly familiar, and yet so strange about her. For one thing, she has the smallest nose I have ever seen. I can't tell, in this first moment, if she is beautiful or ugly. It is an unusual face, and I like it so much, it is so right and belongs to no other. She has big round eyes that hold the very serious expression of an old soul.

I hurry back inside the room and tell Alex that they are here, the baby is here. "You're kidding," she says, as if surprised.

"No, I'm not kidding," I answer, and go back outside into the hallway with my camera so that I can record this moment when Alex first meets her baby.

A man and two women, each holding a baby, stand at the doorway. Alex opens the door, and the man reads her last name from a sheet of paper he holds in his hand.

"Yes," she says, "that's me."

One of the women hands her the baby, the one I had known was hers, and the three walk away, leaving this child we had never met before forever in our care. Alex stands holding the baby in the doorway with an expression I can't read. She is not smiling, and she very slowly reaches up and pulls the hood back from the baby's head to reveal sparse black hair underneath. The two just look at each other, for several long moments, neither one flinching, a Mexican stand-off. And then, the baby starts to cry.

We go inside the room and close the door. The baby is crying very hard now, her face red, her mouth opened in a circle of fear. Fear. I had not been expecting fear. But now I know I should have, this baby has never seen us or anyone who looks like us in her life. We must look like aliens to her, with our big noses and round eyes and not-black hair. This was so obvious to me now, and I am sobered by her reaction, and by my own lack of sensitivity to this possibility. Alex tries giving her a bottle but she refuses it. Next she tries distracting her with a colorful toy, but the baby ignores it and cries harder. Alex hands her to me, but the baby does not calm down.

Alex lays her on the bed and begins removing the heavy padded suit. It is dirty, and it smells musty. Underneath, the baby wears a bright green cotton sweater and heavy pull-on pants. She is still crying as Alex removes each article and throws them in a heap next to the bed. As each layer comes off it becomes increasingly clear how small this baby is, how tiny. Alex takes off the baby's tee-shirt, and we look at her in silence as she lay on the bed in a diaper. She is so skinny, her arms and legs spindly and undeveloped.

"Oh my God," Alex says, "This baby can't be the age they said!" The agency had told her the baby she was matched with was 13 months old. I agree, she looks about the size of a seven-or eight-month old. Alex begins looking her over, takes off her diaper, turns her on her stomach. She smells; a closed damp odor rises from the bed. Across her shoulders and back is a red rash, and tiny scars. "What is this?" Alex asks, to no one in particular. Certainly, I don't know, but to see a baby in this condition makes me feel sick. I am used to big, robust American babies, and this is a shock. Alex seems stunned.

The baby lies quietly on the bed in front of us, not crying now, and looks back at us with an expression of grief and resignation. Neither Alex nor I say a word. I am thinking, Oh Jesus, Oh Jesus, there is real sadness in this world, and it is represented here in this room by this child. This is no blithe adventure, and the excitement I had felt just moments ago seems callow now in the face of this reality. Time stops as the three of us attempt to absorb our new realities, to find a way to accept that from now on nothing would be as we had thought it would be.

In the transparency of this moment, Alex's feelings vibrate across our silence. It does not feel like love, or compassion. It feels like disgust, and I can sense her judgment of this child as she fails to reach out to touch or comfort her, the naked vulnerable child upon the bed.

What happens when one is suddenly confronted with the sick, the neglected, the dirty? Either the heart opens, or it slams shut against the assault. Is this a choice, or a reaction born of a million prior choices?

What happens when love does not come?

What happens when it does, so unexpectedly that it takes your breath away, and leaves you with a heart that aches, and longs for justice?

Around and around we stroll the hotel hallway. Alex is on the phone with her husband, telling him about the baby, and I am trying to induce the baby into sleep by walking with her, by singing to her, by murmuring words she cannot understand. We finally succeeded in feeding her bits of ham and vegetables from the room service meal we ordered. The baby had been sitting in front of us in a stroller as we ate, and Alex held out a piece of food, just to see if she would take it. The baby literally lunged for the food, gobbling piece after piece until there was nothing left to give her. We looked at each other in horror, wondering how starved was this child?

After she ate we bathed her, and the terrified crying that we had managed to stop began anew. It had taken both of us to hold her in the tub, each of us trying to quickly soap the slippery, wriggling body and rinse her so that the ordeal could end. When I pulled her from the tub, the water was dirty brown, and I noticed the grime still embedded under her fingernails.

But now I hold her and she is quiet as we walk and walk. Finally she falls asleep in my arms, and I keep walking, thinking about her. Who is she? Who are her parents? Why was she given up? What woman bore this child through intense pain, only to relinquish her to the unknown? It is all a mystery, as if this baby has just dropped from the sky. No identity, no story, except the vague details which the orphanage had written on her information sheet: found at a train station on New Year's Eve. No note or any evidence of her family's identity amongst her belongings, which consisted of only the clothes she wore that night as she fell asleep, unsuspecting that when she awoke, there would be no one there, and she would be in a strange and frightening place, alone in the world.

"I'm so sorry, so sorry, little one" I say, over and over again. As I think of this, how scared she must have been, how desperate the cries in that cold empty station, a lump rises in my throat that I cannot swallow. I look down at the sweet face, so calm now, and I think, how could they, how could anyone…? Was it desperation, or cruelty? And I think that already, after knowing her for only a few hours, I could not, no matter what, set her down and walk away; I could not leave her to an uncertain fate.

After we had bathed her, Alex dressed her in a pink sleeper outfit that was way too big for her, and then propped her up on the bed with some pillows. The effect was pathetic, the too-big clothes swallowing her up, the propped up little body in an awkward position. I wanted to move her, but Alex just stood, looking at her without saying anything. Finally, she broke the silence. "Do you think she's pretty?" she asked.

The baby looked back at us with an expression of the deepest sadness, a mixture of fear, grief and incomprehension. I couldn't speak for a moment, what was there to say? Was she pretty? How could this possibly matter at this moment? Alex was judging her, this helpless sad baby, and I could tell by the question that she had already found her wanting.

I wanted to protect her, to shield her from this unfair and cruel judgment, and I answered yes; yes I think she's pretty. Yes, I think she may be the most beautiful baby I have ever seen. The relief on Alex's face was evident; the baby she was going to take was pretty, thank goodness. It was obvious that this was important to her, as important as anything else.

It was then that I had picked up the baby, and offered to take her into the hallway so that Alex could call her husband; but what I really wanted was to hold the baby close, and whisper some comfort to her as she fell asleep tonight, so that she would know there was reason to hope. We had walked around and around, and now back in the room, I place the sleeping baby into the small iron crib that the hotel provided. There are twin beds in the room and Alex unpacked some of her things and placed them on the bed farthest from the crib. "Here," I say, "you take this bed; you'll want to be close to the baby during the night."

"No, no," Alex says hastily. "This is fine, I'll sleep over here." She climbs into the bed, leaving me to the one next to the baby. In fact, the crib is pushed right up against my bed, so close that I can reach through the bars and touch her without having to get up.

I put on my pajamas and get into bed. A little light is coming through the pulled curtains, and I can see the baby lying curled into a ball near the end of the crib. I fall asleep to the sound of her breathing, even and deep. When I awake some hours later, after fretful, brightly colored dreams, the first thing I see is the little face, peering at me in the half dark through the iron bars of the crib. For the briefest moment, in that twilight before fully awakening, when I have not yet remembered where we are, or why we are here, I feel as if I am looking into a face I have always known, always dreamt of, or always wished for. And the first thought that swims up from the depths of dream time: *my baby.*

*That day began like any other. I awoke to the ringing of bells calling the monks to prayer. At dawn's first light they filed by in their orange robes, shaven heads bowed, moving slowly across the interior courtyard to assemble in the open air. Servants would then light the huge clay incense pots at the perimeter of the courtyard and the sweet smoke wafted to every corner of the palace. The chanting would begin and I watched the monks as they bowed and prayed, concealed behind the curtain of the doorway to my chamber. The light would start to come then, spreading throughout the sky. If I did not know better, I would think the light came at their call. The chanting transported me, I could* not help but float on the waves of its sound. It billowed up to the heavens and a part of me went there too, where it found peace. I began to long for this, to listen for the bells with eagerness, to fly from my bed at the first hint of the prayer call.

On that morning that began like any other, a strange incident occurred. As the chanting gained in intensity I felt a strong pull, as if I was being sucked into a tunnel, a tunnel of light. I could not resist but I was not afraid. Everything around me swirled and churned for what seemed like eternity. Suddenly I saw before me a face, a smiling face, and the swirling stopped. It was a face I had seen before, one of the monks that chanted in the courtyard each morning. I could still hear the chanting, as if in the distance, but I was so focused upon this face hovering before me that all else disappeared. The monk looked into my eyes with an expression of profound kindness. When he spoke it was as if the voice was disembodied, the lips did not move, the expression did not change. And yet I heard clearly, the kind monk speaking to me. He said, "And so, you are ready?" Without my thinking of it my answer rose up, "Yes, I am ready Master," but I did not know how or why I spoke thus. This seemed to please him, for he smiled broadly and said, "I will help you." And the vision evaporated before me.

I stood at my doorway for some time after the monks filed back to their chambers. I could not make sense of what had just occurred. Was I imagining things? Or dreaming, had I fallen asleep during the chanting? The vision was so real, I felt I could reach out and touch it. As the vision faded I felt weak and depleted, I wanted it back, I wanted to see the kindly face again. But no matter how hard I tried, I could not produce the image again in my mind. It had vanished like the smoke from the incense, leaving only a question. What had just happened to me, what did it mean?

It was then that my musings were interrupted by a commotion in the courtyard. I looked up to see a group of the Emperor's men in the distance, moving toward me. The men were dressed in the elaborate uniforms of the court, with long brocade robes and towering headdresses which gave them the illusion of being very tall from a distance. As they approached, I could see that the men were dragging someone, someone who appeared to be struggling mightily to escape from their clutches. Soon they were directly in front of my chamber doorway and they stopped for a moment as the struggle from the captive became more and more fierce. Several of the men had sticks and were bringing them down harshly upon the back, legs and torso of the person being dragged, but this seemed to do little to subdue his struggle. Then suddenly, the knot of men opened for a brief moment in the confusion and gave me a clear and unobstructed view and I could see that it was Chen. It was Chen my beloved friend being dragged, being struck, being taken somewhere against his will.

I stifled a scream as it rose into my throat, "No! What are you doing? Leave him be, leave him be!"

The group got hold of Chen's arms and legs and picked him up, and began running toward a doorway which had just swung open a short distance from where I stood. My mind froze in confusion. Why are they taking him in there? That was the doorway to the chamber of the eunuchs, that was the doorway beyond which no uncastrated male could enter. The eunuchs served the Empress, the concubines and the courtesans of the Emperor, they were the only males allowed to come into the closed confines of the inner court. Since we had arrived at the palace, Chen had not been allowed to visit me here; we could only see each other during my times escorted outside the inner court. What was he doing here?

The group pressed on, toward the doorway, holding aloft the

67

struggling Chen. And then, the slow horrible realization of what was occurring came upon me, and I began running in slow motion, screaming in silence as no one seemed to hear, "No, No! Stop, bring him back to me; Chen!" I could not see, the tears streamed down my face and I stumbled, falling onto the paving stones, looking up just in time to see the men shove Chen through the doorway, the doorway through which there could be no return. I heard the heavy thud of the door slamming shut just as I lost consciousness, lost my mind, lost my way in the grief of this cruelty.

How long I lay there I do not know. It must have been many hours, and yet no one came to tend to me. I was alone in the courtyard when I woke from what felt like a death, a death of the self that I once was. I drew my heavy robe around me against the chill of the descending night, and felt an overwhelming desire to see the kind face, the face of the monk in the vision, to lay my head upon his lap, to pour out the tears and grief that now seemed to be the only reality left to me. Sitting there on the ground in the half-dark and sharp cold, I heard the voice of the vision, the warm voice of the one I had called Master, and it said, "Come to me."

The next morning, I took a chance. Hiding behind the chamber doorway curtain, watching as the monks filed past after morning prayers, I slipped into line after the last orange-robed monk and followed through the ornately carved doorway of the palace temple. Inside, the smell of incense was overwhelmingly powerful. We moved through the main temple chamber and into a long dark corridor along which many doors opened into small bedrooms. The monks began entering these doorways, each to his own, and after a few moments I was left standing alone in the dim light, wondering what to do. At the *far end of the hallway I then noticed a light streaming through an open door, the only door which had not been closed after being entered by a monk. I started slowly down the hallway, a little afraid of whom I might encounter; how would I explain my presence here?*

*The thick stones of the wall felt as if they were closing in on me, I began to move more quickly toward that open doorway to escape this feeling of suffocation. My heart began beating wildly; I felt a nausea rise and a lightheadedness, a disorientation. I had to get to that doorway...to that doorway....*

*And then I stood in that light, streaming from an opening in the thick stone wall of that chamber. Bathed in this light was a figure, it was a monk who wore upon his chest a sash that was embroidered with many symbols and pictures which I did not understand. I looked slowly up, up into the face of the monk, and found it was the face I had seen in my vision the day before, the kind face I had longed for and had taken this chance to find. And then he smiled a smile of such warmth that I fell to the ground before him in gratitude and wonder. He was here, in the flesh before me, my vision, the one I had called Master. The one who had said he would help me.*

*"You have come." The monk spoke and in his words I heard meaning that I could not decipher. He seemed to have been expecting me, to know I would be here. How else to explain the open door, the look of greeting as I gained the threshold to his room? It was all too much, too much to think of now. I was suddenly so very tired that all I wanted to do was fall into a blissful sleep in his presence, to have him watch over me and protect me. I had felt so unprotected since leaving my father, so alone since Chen and I were separated upon our arrival here.*

*The monk leaned down and put his hand upon my head. A*

tingling feeling began from where he had placed his hand and spread down, to my throat, to my chest, until my entire body felt alive and quivering. The fatigue disappeared, and I sat up, my mind clear as it had never been. I looked into his eyes then, the dark eyes contained everything I needed, and I began speaking, telling the monk the story of my arrival here in the palace, of leaving my father's house in the countryside, of bringing Chen with me on this grand adventure, of my loneliness and fear. I told him too of my rising each morning to listen to the prayers of the monks, of that being my solace and peace in this strange, cold place. And finally, I told him of Chen, of the horror of what I feared had happened to my friend. And he listened as if he already knew.

"My child we have much work to do. All will become clear in time, and you will know the answers to your questions. But now, I want to tell you of something which will help you in your grief. Your friend has come to a crossroads, a place where his spirit must make a decision and a choice. Nothing is what it seems, my child, and everything that occurs can be used for growth if we so choose. All fear and pain are but illusions when you understand. And you can help your friend now only through the strength of your own spirit. What is it that you want? Go into the garden of your chambers and contemplate this question, go each day until the answer comes. When it comes, return to me, and we will begin."

And I reluctantly left him then. I would do as he said. I had nothing else, nothing else…and so for many days I went into the garden at sunrise and stayed until dusk, when the chill chased me to a fitful sleep on my small bed. Each day I asked the question of myself and each day I found no answer there. I kept thinking and wondering about Chen, where was he? Had he lived or died? I knew that to become a eunuch a man had to undergo a painful butchery, and that many contracted fevers or other illness or lost their spirit and became mere shadows. And this when they had freely chosen this path. What of Chen, who was forced into this drastic procedure? I knew him so well, knew he dreamed of a family and children, knew of his pride and hopes. I was sick with worry, so that each time I tried to contemplate the question posed to me by the monk, my mind returned to grief, to Chen.

I had many dreams in the night, I saw the monk's face, I saw Chen and spoke with him, I saw my father. And then one night I had a dream that caused me to sit up with a gasp, so vivid and alive was the experience. I saw Chen, beautiful Chen, and he was running in a field of flowers. He was laughing and joyous, and behind him rose a magnificent kite, a dragon, with a full tail of rainbow colors that whipped mightily in the wind. Oh, and he was happy! My Chen, what I wouldn't give to see you so again, and I sobbed and sobbed through that night, not knowing how I could go on, not knowing if I wanted to.

That night was eternal, and in it, I began to pray. I prayed for release from this pain, for salvation, for something to make sense. My pain was a wave so huge it could take me to heaven, I felt myself riding, spinning, falling, and all the time the question echoed, what do you want, what do you want?

And when I fell into that sleep that is beyond sleep, the sleep of exhaustion of all hopes, I heard for the first time an answer, so small and weak, and yet an answer nonetheless. What do you want, what do you want? I want to live, was the answer; I want to live.

The next morning when I entered my garden, the sun shone upon me and I saw all of nature in glittering illumination. This beauty astounded, how had I not seen before? And as I stood in wonder, I saw something rise over the garden wall in the distance. It was a kite, a rickety handmade kite, put together with found sticks and pieces of fabric. A tiny kite, struggling to gain the air, and as I watched, it fought its way up, and up a little more, until it caught a current and was lofted high, high above the palace wall. A kite. A kite! Someone was flying a kite, and it looked so much like the kites Chen and I used to make on our woodland adventures. He knew how to build them from almost anything he could find, my own father had taught him so.

I knew of no one who could build kites like Chen. And the dream then…I suddenly recalled the dream that had awakened me in the night. Could this, could it be? And then my eyes followed the kite string down, down to where it began, and it flew from the courtyard of the eunuch's pavilion, not far from my own, and I knew with unshakable certainty, that at the other end of the string was Chen's hand, guiding the little kite to heaven.

That day I returned to my Master, and the work began.

The baby is already awake, and looking at me through the bars of her crib, not making a sound of need or desire. I lean forward and poke my finger through the bars.

"Hello there, baby, how did you sleep?" I say.

Alex is just waking too, and she gets out of bed and comes over to pull the baby from her crib. Today the parents are scheduled to complete adoption paperwork in a regional office not far from our hotel, and Alex is uptight about it. She is thinking, will I have the right papers, what about the money? She seems far more focused on the administrative issues than on the baby, but I reason that this makes sense, if there is some glitch in the paperwork, the adoption could be in jeopardy.

I help Alex with the baby, dressing her and getting a bottle ready. There will be no time to write in my journal this morning, though the dream I had last night keeps entering my mind. It was odd, something about a kite? Anyway now that the baby is with us things will be different.

When we meet the other two couples in the lobby, it is obvious that the night for them had been long and sleepless. Curtis and Judy have dark circles under their eyes, and Louise and Jimmy were up circling the hallway most of the night with their little one, but they already seem like families, and we are not. This morning I am acutely aware that Alex, the baby and I are not a family, and I feel a twinge of doubt about my presence here.

We board a van outside the hotel and drive a short distance into the city. We get out and walk a few blocks down busy streets, a strange processional, three Caucasian women carrying bundles from which emerge three tiny Chinese faces. Many people stop to gawk or poke a companion and point our way. I am carrying the baby, as Alex is carrying the bulging, heavy briefcase that contains the vital adoption paperwork, as well as a sum in cash to be handed over to officials before the adoption can proceed.

The money has to be in new, fresh, unmarked bills— $5000. Alex was instructed to bring only $20 bills with no stray marks or creases evident anywhere on them, or the adoption could be refused. We had joked about this before the trip, how it made the whole exchange feel clandestine, like an undercover drug deal, or a payoff to the mob. The Chinese government insisting on thousands of dollars for a baby that someone had literally thrown away. What, or whom, was that money for, exactly?

We enter a cold, dark cement building and climb the stairs to the third floor, where we come to a large room filled with people, all adopting Chinese babies. Some speak French, they are Canadians; and there are a few from a Scandinavian country. But for the most part the adoptive parents are American. Alex goes off to check over the paperwork before she is called for the appointment, and I rock the baby and sing to her, give her a bottle, and watch as the new families are born. After the meeting with a government official behind closed doors, the parents emerge looking relieved and happy, and are taken to a corner of the room where their pictures are taken with their new babies. The babies are all so cute, and they all look so different, some chubby, some skinny, some with lots of hair and some with none.

It is a long time before a Chinese official comes to the doorway and announces Alex's name in a loud voice. Alex motions me to come over, and bring the baby. I move to hand the baby to her, but Alex says no, you come in too, and hold her while I take care of the business.

We enter a small office, empty except for a spare metal desk and chair, the bare window allowing the bright winter sunlight to shine in on the dust and grime. An imposing middle-aged Chinese man in military uniform is sitting behind the desk; he does not look up or acknowledge us when we sit in the metal chairs before him. There is silence as he rifles through the stack of papers. After some time he begins to speak, Anna is there to act as translator, and she poses the questions to Alex: "What is your income? What kind of house do you live in? Are there other children in the household? Who will stay home with the child? What type of work do you and your husband do? What is your education?"

I sit holding the baby, listening to this string of concerned questions and it makes me want to laugh. It seems odd, to be so fastidiously checking the backgrounds and resources of these people who had come from halfway around the world to adopt children that no one in China seemed to want, or be able to care for. The man is very stern, as if lecturing wayward school children. And he asks his last question, "Do you promise to never abandon this child?"

The question hangs in the air as I think of the audacity of this inquiry from a representative of a government whose own policies have caused the problem of abandoned babies in the first place. This is like a show, an elaborate stage play which we are supposed to believe is real. We are supposed to believe that they really care for these babies when millions are cast aside. The government has been trying to control raging population growth with the draconian "one child" policy; but didn't they know their own people, their own cultural biases? It seems like a willful disregard of truth, of reality. The bias toward male children here is an ancient cultural artifact; to ignore its power over people's choices has produced this disaster, has produced this orphaned child in my arms.

I kiss the top of the baby's head, so warm and soft, just as Alex answers the question, "No, never."

*I will never leave you.*

The one detail of the trip of which I am not absolutely sure just happens to be the most important detail, the moment in time when a new life began for me. I remember her words, and I remember not believing them. But like the amnesia that occurs around a traumatic accident, my memory of exactly what preceded the event warps and waves and I can't be absolutely sure when she said it. Time stopped then, and everything before and after was forever altered in my mind.

It must have been that day, the day she promised never to abandon the baby.

We had returned to the hotel, and I think I went to the gym for a while, or maybe took a walk. Everything is normal, moving along as planned, nothing amiss, except in hindsight, where I see all the clues.

The three of us are in our hotel room, it is late afternoon, or maybe early evening. We are talking, going about our business, and Alex is folding some baby clothes and laying them out on the bed while the baby plays quietly on the floor. "I'm so exhausted," Alex says.

"Yes of course you're exhausted," I say. "Anyone would be, such a grueling trip, and caring for the baby...."

Alex speaks in a flat, hard tone. "I can't do this."

I continue doing what I'm doing, maybe tidying the room or putting away clothing, it takes me some moments to understand what she has said, to begin to know that nothing will ever be the same.

Finally, it starts to sink in; I stop what I am doing. "Can't do this?" I ask. "What do you mean? I can help you, if that's what you need...."

"No. I mean I don't think I can take her. I can't take her home," she says, so resolutely, I know she means it. She can't take her, can't give this child a home. She can't save her, she can't save herself.

"But...but you have to, don't you? I mean, what else would you do?" I ask. My mind whirls, trying to figure out where I stand now in this strange incomprehensible new landscape, this inhospitable country of rejection.

"I'm going to turn her back in, send her back to the orphanage," she says. She has this all figured out, she has decided. She says it as if she is returning a blouse to a department store, no more or less of an emotional investment than that. A mundane transaction, an inconvenience, something to be taken care of; the tone of her voice chills me and suddenly a passionate need to stop this from happening takes hold.

"No, no!" I almost shout. "Don't do that! You can't do that." She looks at me evenly as I realize, she can do that, and she will do that, unless I can convince her otherwise. "I'll help you; I can take care of her for the rest of the trip, until you get home and you're feeling better. You're just tired and overwhelmed, you need some rest…"

"I don't want to take her home," she says, her voice flat and unyielding. She turns from me and continues folding the clothes, the little baby clothes that she will no longer need. I do not know this person; this is the part of herself she has kept from me. I have never known the person who is capable of this coldness.

"But,… *why?*" I ask. "Why can't you take her?" My voice rises in disbelief. "What's wrong with her? She's perfect!" And I realize at that moment that to me she is exactly that: perfect. I look over at her and see the innocence and beauty shining forth and I want to grab her, to run from this place.

Alex continues. "It's just not what I expected; I don't feel how I expected to feel. It doesn't feel right," she explains. It explains nothing. It is all about her; not one word of concern for the baby.

"But. I mean….so what?" I say, with a hollow little laugh. "You made a commitment; you can't back out of something like this now! You've got to think this through; you can't make a decision like this tonight, you've got to give this some time." The trauma this baby has been through already, in being taken from the orphanage and getting used to us, and now to send her back? What would that do to her? "I can help you….I would even take the baby for awhile after we get home, just until you're feeling better."

"But," she says, "What if I take her home and I don't feel better? I can't take that risk. I can't put my family through something like that."

An entire year spent planning for this adoption, and less

than 24 hours after she gets the baby she wants to back out? I can't grasp what is happening, it is unbelievable. Alex is the last person I would think would do this; she is ultra-responsible, not flighty in the least. It makes no sense, no sense at all, and I rationalize that she just needs some time and space, and she will snap out of this.

I feel no hesitation in saying, "If you get home and still don't want to keep her, I'll take her." There is no choice; how else to buy time? Alex looks at me intently, and immediately takes me up on it.

"You would? You would take her?" she asks.

"Yes. Yes," I say, "I would."

I want Alex to feel that she has some options, to not feel so much pressure to give the baby back right away. This is a passing thing, she will be over it in a day or two, and we will go about our lives the way we had planned.

"I'll take the baby out, why don't you call your husband and talk this over with him?" I suggest, knowing he will try to talk her out of abandoning the baby. She agrees and I pick up the baby, grateful that she can't understand a word we are saying.

I am shaking as I hold the baby, walking around and around the hallway, again. For well over an hour we walk and I talk to her, tell her it's going to be alright, and she falls asleep in my arms. I sit down on the floor with my back against the wall and hold her, sick to my stomach, feeling lightheaded. Suddenly, nothing in the world makes sense. This is the baby that was going to be my godchild; Alex had asked me to be her godmother the week before we left: it was an acknowledgement of the importance of the role I would play on this trip. I was going to be part of her life, and I was excited about that, and now it was all in jeopardy.

Last night I had bathed her, fed her, rocked her to sleep, and all day today I had held her and kept her close. She had already smiled at me, this morning when I changed her diaper, after we had made it through that first horrible night. It seemed like it might be the first smile she had ever smiled; I could see her watching me, mimicking me as she tried hard to pull the corners of her mouth into a grin to mirror mine. And when I bent to kiss her with tender affection, the look of surprise on her face made me certain she had rarely, if ever, been kissed.

And I had had dreams about her, several dreams about a dark-eyed baby, months before I had even seen her. The dark-eyed baby, in my terrible dream of forgetting, could that have been her? Weren't we connected, already, in some intimate way? How could I now just leave her behind, as if she had never been?

Alex comes to the doorway and motions for me to come inside. She says she is feeling better; her husband had calmed her down and helped her think through the situation. My relief must be apparent; she smiles at me and gives the baby a little pat as we walk into the room. Would I talk to him, her husband? He was still on the phone.

I put the baby down in her crib, still sound asleep. I pick up the phone receiver, my hand still shaking. I tell Alex's husband, when he asks, that I'm not sure what happened. I tell him that she is exhausted and needs some rest, and agree when he asks me if I will make sure she gets some sleep and that she keeps eating. I tell him I will take care of the baby; I'll do anything to help. And when he asks, "How's the baby?" my voice breaks as I answer, "She's beautiful."

His tone is worried; I can tell he is afraid this is not just a passing thing. He tells me that he never really wanted to adopt; Alex had talked him into it. Actually, he tells me that she had threatened him when he would not agree; threatened to leave him and take their son, and he was afraid she might do it. "And now this," he says. It is not the time to say, how could you allow this? It is not the time to say, this is insanity. I just say, "What do we do now?" and he answers, "Just get everyone home."

Just get everyone home. What home can this baby claim? The things we take for granted, like home, and parents, and identity and culture she will never be assured. Just the basic things which we hardly ever think about but which form the bedrock of our sense of self and our sense of safety in the world. Who is Alex to hand those things out to this child, and then take them back?

Alex and I then talk far into the night. For hours she spills out her fears and doubts; she tells me things about her childhood and her relationship with her mother, about why she had thought she wanted a child. She had wanted, she said, for someone to love her again, the way her son had, the way only a child can. The classic wrong reason, the worst reason in the world to have a child, so that he or she can love you.

Alex tells me things I never knew. In all the years we have known each other, we have never talked like this. I cannot remember a time when she betrayed strong emotions; she has always been of a controlled nature. But now, her pain is obvious: she truly does not understand her feelings, or what has happened. She is crying and reaching out to me, but I cannot be fully sympathetic because of the little baby sleeping a few feet away in the crib. That child is innocent, and totally vulnerable to Alex's feelings of confusion; should not at least one adult put this baby's needs first, above their own?

Alex is crying for herself, not for the baby, and my heart sinks further as the tangled web of her psyche weaves before me. I try hard to fit what Alex is saying into various psychological theories, but the pieces do not fit together in any sort of rational way. I am on the edge of an abyss, with no choice but to step off that edge, into the unknown, beyond psychology, beyond rationality, beyond the easily explainable. A child's life is at stake, as well as the long-term emotional well-being of my friend; if she leaves the baby here, would she ever be able to forgive herself? There is no question of this being my responsibility. I am here now, I agreed to come; and now the only question is, what can I do to assist in bringing about the best outcome? Because I already know the answer to the question, would I be able to forgive myself if I did not?

When she has finally talked and cried herself out, we try to sleep. I lay there in the dark, thinking about the baby, wanting to cry myself. Tomorrow we are scheduled to visit the orphanage; surely after we go there Alex won't be able to give her back. One more day of bonding, of getting to know this child, each hour that goes by will make it more and more inconceivable that she would relinquish her baby.

Her baby…it is then that I realize, Alex has never once called her by the name she had chosen for her. Not once. We have both been calling her "the baby." I had not noticed until now this lack of desire to claim her, to humanize her by giving her a name.

Whose baby was she, whose would she be? Who would name her, love her, hold her, dry her tears?

I would, Baby, if I could. And as I fall into restless sleep, Baby's face swims before me, tears like glistening pearls running down her cheeks, and drifting into a dream of lost happiness, I hear her calling, calling for her mother, the mother she has lost.

*My days in the palace began to fill with activity as the time appointed for the wedding ceremony approached. Nothing was left to chance; I was to be prepared as the bride of the Emperor according to ancient traditions and rituals. A virtual army of servants, ladies in waiting and courtesans assisted in this each day, some happily, and some with hatred and envy in their hearts. I could feel their spite as their hands touched me or my garments, and it caused me much anxiety. I could sense that a few of these would just as soon see me dead as become Empress, so that their place in the palace hierarchy could be preserved.*

*Fittings for gowns, cleansing rituals for my body, instructions in palace protocol, and rehearsals for rituals continued day after day. I became bored and tired of this very quickly, so much attention on things of so little importance. Each day I found a chance to slip away to meet my Master; he seemed to know just where to find me, sometimes as I turned a corner in a palace corridor, or when I crossed the courtyard to my chambers, or as I sat in reflection in the garden. Many times he would simply walk beside me for a time, and quietly say a few words, and then walk away again. And sometimes he would lay his hand upon me and I would feel an immediate infusion of energy which lasted for many days. I longed for these fleeting moments, and concentrated upon each word he spoke. He told me that meditating upon the light inside would lead to great insight; he explained how peace may descend upon the mind devoid of desire. He spoke often of compassion, of our connection to all beings, and of the great freedom that was possible for one who attained such knowing. Each day the teachings came, and I would hurry back to my chamber at the end of the day to write them down, and think upon them before sleeping, to try to understand.*

*One day there appeared in the doorway of my bedchamber a beautiful young woman, someone I had not seen in the palace before. "Mistress, I come to announce the arrival of your teacher," she said. I was confused; did she know about my Master? Had he himself sent her? But this did not seem to be his way, and he had told me many times that his teachings must remain secret. What could she be speaking of?*

*Just then the doorway filled with a presence, and before I saw her, I felt the warmth and kindness enter the room. A tall, exquisitely beautiful woman, of what age I could not tell, with glossy, long black hair that hung almost to the floor. The young woman who had announced her arrival moved about her, arranging her robes, and pulling back the doorway curtain so that she could enter my chamber. "My dear, I am here to begin the teachings," the woman said, in a soft but vibrant voice.*

*The teachings? I did not know of what she spoke.*

*"Did my Master send you?" I asked.*

*"Your Master? And who would that be?" she asked, a quizzical smile playing about her lips.*

*I could not answer, for I did not know the monk's name. By her answer I knew that she knew nothing of my encounters with him, and I must remain silent as to our work together. She seemed not to notice that I had not answered her question, and went on.*

*"The Emperor has sent me. He requires that all of his women be trained in the ways of the proper courtesan. As Empress, you must possess skills that will be pleasing to him and allow for beneficial marital relations. I am charged with teaching you the intimate ways of men and women, and we must begin now to ready you for the marriage ceremony. Come now with me, we have much to do." And she turned to leave my room, her assistant indicating that I should follow their lead.*

*As we walked through the courtyard I reflected upon what she had said. The intimate ways of men and women, what did she mean? I trailed behind her, admiring her beautiful robe. Her young attendant kept looking back at me and smiling in an encouraging way. Something about them made me feel safe, and I began to look forward to what may be in store.*

*The beautiful woman came to a carved and painted doorway, and stopped before it. The young attendant pushed it open, and the three of us entered into a glorious courtyard garden, a lush paradise, with birds singing and flowers in pots hanging from the walls, a profusion of blooms and blossoms and color. It was by far the most beautiful area of the palace that I had seen so far, and the scent of jasmine filled the air with a warm, musky scent. I looked around in amazement as I followed the two women through the garden, and* then into a large room beyond, a hall of light and beauty. The floors were covered in thick woven carpets, the walls with silk hangings and tapestry. The tall woman led us to large silk pillows arranged in a circle in the center of the room. We sat, and the woman folded her legs and sat in silence with eyes closed, breathing deeply and rhythmically, and I watched her and found my own breathing slowing, beginning to match hers without my willing it to do so. After a time she opened her eyes, a slow smile spreading across her face, and said, "The White Tigress welcomes you."

The White Tigress? I thought this must be nonsense. And yet, when she spoke this phrase, I immediately saw an image in my mind, a beautiful white tigress lying in a tree, her tail swishing lazily back and forth, content in her power. What did this have to do with 'the intimate ways of men and women', as she had said her teachings would do? I gathered my voice to speak, which I had not done since we had left my room.

"Madame, I know not of what you speak," I said. "You will be teaching me about animals?"

She laughed in a burst. "Yes, in a sense. But more than that. The teachings which I will share with you concern our animal natures, it is true. And yet, did you know it was possible to use the power of our animal natures to become like the gods?"

And with that she grabbed my hand in hers, leaned forward toward me, and began telling me of wondrous things, of impossible things, of power and love and beauty. She spoke on and on, and I was mesmerized by her words. Hours later when I had returned to my chambers and fell asleep on my little bed, I dreamed that I rode that White Tigress, through the sky, to the stars, to Heaven.

"The White Tigress seeks to become a passionate giver," said Madame. "Through the highest expression of love it is possible to attain immortality. Love is the elixir with the power over physical matters, including aging and death. We may develop the ability to reverse and even stop these processes, so as to continue practicing bringing love into the world for an infinite number of years."

I was enthralled by her words, they resonated deep within. For it had always seemed a shame to me, how quickly the body decayed and became old, how death approached just as wisdom and knowledge had been attained in large enough measure to apply it.

"When you learn the skills of the White Tigress, immortality flows to you naturally, along with youth and beauty. Have you not been told before? Be still, for I know you have not! A woman's power is great, and it has been hidden from her. It is the power of creation itself, a power that can be diverted, but never stopped. These teachings are secret knowledge, reserved for only a select few, those who by their skill can benefit a powerful male. In your case, the Emperor desires not pleasure alone, but superior children brought forth. The White Tigress teachings also accomplish this, as it raises the female practitioner's vibrations to a very high level, attracting special souls to embody within her. Those concubines and consorts who will not bear children for the Imperial lineage need not be taught to reach these exalted states, but only to become skilled in specific practices. You, however, must master the transformative states of mind, so that your children with the Emperor shall be pure and good and worthy of Imperial rule."

I thought of my Master, he also spoke of exalted states of mind. I wanted to ask Madame, is it the same? But I could not, for he wished his teachings to be kept secret. Madame continued,

"We will begin with the basic practices, and as you perfect these techniques, a reversal of the aging process will begin. As you are young, you will have little to reverse. In women, the process of aging and death begin with first menstruation, and we must return your body to that state, and reverse the blood to a nourishing circuit within you to revitalize your reproductive organs."

I remembered the day when the blood of my feminine self began to flow. The village women assured me it was a natural process. I had accepted their words, and now Madame was saying that I should not allow it?

"But Madame," I gathered my courage to speak. "How can I bear children if my female blood does not flow? When mine began, the village women said it meant that now my body was ready to make children, and that it was time to marry. They themselves have many children and know of such things."

"And, may I ask, what is the appearance of these women of whom you speak?" queried Madame. "Are they youthful, and vibrant, and filled with light? No? From this moment on, you must commit yourself to accept only that which comes from and supports vital life. There are many things the village women have told you which you will have to abandon. Are you ready to release that which is not true for your own highest good?"

I was stunned by her words. Not accept the elders' teachings? Before now, I would not have considered it a possibility, but suddenly, the truth of Madame's words shown bright and clear, a beacon to follow to somewhere unknown. It was true, the village women were bent and tired, irritable, haggard and sallow; none were youthful and vibrant past marriage. Madame herself was tall and moved with a lightness of body, her clear skin shown, her glossy hair swayed past her small waist. And what was her age? I could not say. From her bearing and wisdom it was clear that she must have lived many years, and yet, her body and face did not betray how many these might number.

"Yes, Madame," I whispered.

"My dear, what are you saying 'yes' to?" Madame gently prodded.

"Yes, Madame, I want that which is for my highest good alone," I said strongly, and with the beginning of something new in my voice.

Madame's lips eased into a smile as she said, "Then we shall begin."

Day after day, Madame shared with me more of the teachings. There was nothing of daily life omitted from the regimen, as Madame explained that nothing, not the slightest detail of our existence, was unimportant. Each action has the power to help or hinder our spiritual progress, she said, and taught me ways to optimize my ability to increase awareness.

For instance, I was allowed to eat only the purest of foods, and Madame explained that this was not for maintenance of the figure, but was a means to eliminate possible blocks to awareness.

"Poor eating habits lower your vibrations, just as good ones help to raise them. It is very simple. But in time you will see that maintenance of the body goes even beyond food sustenance. All physical manifestations are of spiritual origin."

"Madame, and what do you mean by spiritual origin?" I asked.

"Cause does not reside in the physical world," Madame said. "All cause has origin in the unseen world. Through the teachings I will show you how to work with your body as a tool. You will no longer confuse your body with your real self. It is merely a reflection of your whole self, which resides in spirit."

And so Madame taught me. It was all so new to me, and against much that I had been taught before. And yet, with Madame's kindness and gentle guidance, I began to experience the raising of consciousness which is the essence of the practice. As I grew in awareness through the practice of the teachings, the boundaries of my self expanded out, and eventually dissolved, and I began to know things of which I had no direct information. Knowledge would come to me whole and pure, as I made of myself a more perfect channel. For the goal of the practice, as Madame explained, was to become a conduit of the divine to manifest upon the earth.

In time she taught me that we can be in all places, that we may move about unseen to those whose minds are dim and undeveloped. Together we moved about the palace, into places of secrecy and intrigue; we stood undetected amidst sinister gatherings, witnessed intimate encounters amongst those of the Imperial Court. We used secret passageways, feeling along stone corridors for openings ignored or unremembered by others. Madame knew of all manner of hiding places in the palace, for it had been built with intrigue in mind, and Madame used the hidden places to help her students to gain knowledge of the ways of the court.

One evening she led me to a low dark corridor, I knew not where we were going. In time we came upon a small open room, and Madame moved some small stones in the wall and instructed me to look through. It was a bedchamber, an opulent room, unlike any I had seen in the palace before. "The Emperor's inner chamber," she said as I looked, and just as she did so a noise from inside the room caught our attention, and we turned to peer through the small openings in the wall.

We saw a concubine arrive, and enter the doorway, closing it tightly behind her. She was carrying a basket, with an odd assortment of items inside: a crimson silk scarf, a wide glass beaker, a peacock feather, and a jade ring. Madame whispered, "Now it is time for you to observe the Tigress secrets of delight."

Madame took my hand and bade me watch the scene unfolding in the room, and I turned my attention to the large bed in the middle, where the Emperor reclined, covered only with a thin layer of blue silk cloth.

The concubine kneeled beside the bed, and began taking the items out of the basket and arranging them within her reach. She was very beautiful, her hair arranged in coils about her head, and she wore a gown which fell a bit off her white shoulders, revealing the milky skin beneath. As she moved about, reaching into her basket, the Emperor watched her intently, sitting halfway up with his arms behind him, a smile of anticipation curling his lips.

When she had finished emptying her basket, the concubine turned her full attention to the Emperor upon the bed. With her left hand she reached for the silk coverlet and began pulling, slowly pulling, the smooth fabric across his lap. With her other hand she reached up to the shoulder of her own gown, pushing the fabric down her arm with deliberate motion, almost exposing her breast, and then pushed it back up a little, only to begin pulling it down again.

The concubine murmured some word I could not hear, and reached down and selected an item from her basket, the peacock feather. She used it to delicately reach every part of the Emperor's body, his closed eyes, his quivering lips; his chest and stomach, and down his legs to his feet. For some time the peacock feather traveled, until the Emperor seemed on the verge of losing control.

Using each of her tools in turn the concubine brought the Emperor to a state of uncontrollable frenzy, and at one point I thought the violent movement of his limbs might harm her, or his hissed utterances frighten her, and yet she continued. When the Emperor seemed almost insane with the stimulation, the concubine made a motion with one hand, and a door opened into the chamber.

A eunuch entered carrying a tray and came to the side of the bed where the concubine knelt before the Emperor. As she continued he reached for the glass beaker and brought it up to the tip of the Emperor's jade stem and held it there. The Emperor sat up then, groaned and grimaced, his lips pulled tight, and then with a burst released a large amount of whiteish liquid into the beaker which the concubine held, and fell back, spent, upon the bed.

The concubine handed the beaker to the eunuch, who held it aloft to observe it through the glass. He spoke not a word as he left the room, nor did the concubine speak as she gathered her belongings and pulled up her gown. I stood in stunned silence until Madame pulled at my hand, indicating it was time for us to go, and we left the way we had entered, passing through the darkness behind the palace walls.

"My dear, do not be frightened by what you have observed," began Madame, when we had reached her chambers. Since we had left the Emperor's room I had not spoken, my mind whirling and shocked to have witnessed the scene. My questions would not form, for I had no reference for what I had seen; so Madame began explaining that there were reasons for the practices I had seen the concubine perform.

"The goal is to provide heightened sensation so that the Emperor might produce copious quantities of the Imperial seed," she said. "The reason is that with the correct technique, the Emperor may use his seed to impregnate any number of concubines, without using his energy in relations with each one. All Tigress techniques seek to provide this heightened pleasure and stimulation, and always have a goal in mind. I myself initiated the Emperor into these techniques when he was about to enter manhood, I myself taught him the ways of the Tigress."

I was stunned by her revelation. "You, Madame? You.....and the Emperor? But...but..." My mind could not grasp the import of what she revealed.

"Yes, it is so. For how else would he know the ways in which one might bring a Divine Child into the Imperial lineage? How else would he begin to learn of love?" Madame's face held a wistful expression, and beneath its calm surface played conflicting emotions which I could not read. I knew then that no more questions about her relations with the Emperor were welcome, and I listened as she told me that I too must practice these techniques, but that my goal would differ from that of the concubine. For besides enhancing the Emperor's stimulation, I must learn to open to it myself, so that I might receive the divine essence in its purest form, and remain at the highest level of consciousness until conception of the Imperial child.

Madame warned me that learning to receive was the most difficult part of the task, and as I embarked on the practices, I discovered that she was correct. For a woman is taught to deny her own pleasure for the sake of serving a man, and thus denies her chance to reach heaven in her own right.

But the teachings showed me that a woman's pleasure is as holy as a man's, and that both must serve the other, their enjoyment in equal balance, for Divine Union to occur. I had asked Madame, and how is it that a woman learns to deny herself in such a way?

"Women teach other women, do they not?" she answered. "As mothers to daughters, as sister to sister... and it is through the female relationships that both the harmful and good of society is perpetuated. When competition amongst women ceases to exist, we may live in a world of heaven on earth. Women must learn to support and nurture the true loving nature and strength of each other; only then will they allow themselves to receive a man's divine essence."

I thought of my time here behind the palace walls, of both the kindness and the cruelty I had seen the concubines display amongst themselves.

"Madame, have you taught all the women in the Imperial Court; have you taught all the concubines?" I asked. "For there is one who....there is one who I cannot imagine having received this wisdom!" I thought of the concubine who had caused me to fall to the cobblestones on the day of my arrival; I thought of the many days since when she had attempted to interfere with me, or caused unease by glaring at me while I went about my preparations for the wedding.

"I have taught all," Madame replied. "But not all have accepted the teachings. Sadly, some choose another path...a path not of love, but of ego, and of this world. And they are the women who become bitter and old in time, and chafe against the realities of their lives."

"Madame, there is one....I am afraid of her intent toward me. She has caused me some minor harms and speaks ill of me to the other concubines."

"You speak of Ling Dao," Madame nodded in understanding.

"She has a heart turned to stone. She has been disappointed in love, and her standing amongst the concubines has been in decline for some time. She lives in fear, Mistress, for she knows not how to give...always remember that in dealings with her. Stand true in the light of love and all will be well."

Each evening I reported to Madame of my experiences, and by and by she began to speak of my first encounter with the Emperor.

"Upon your marriage to the Emperor, the two of you will become joined in Divine Union. You will seek to climb to the heavens together to retrieve the soul of your first holy child, and this can only occur through mastery of the mystical techniques which I have taught you. Until then you are to be guarded at all times, to ensure that no other man drop his seed in the Emperor's garden. It is by his will that you have acquired these skills, and in his eyes, it is for one purpose and one purpose only: to provide him with child. I must warn you that when a White Tigress reaches a certain level of mastery, any male she encounters will sense this and know it, and desire her for his own. So be very careful, and always on guard against this, as the power you now possess can be dangerous if used wrongly."

I then asked Madame, "And why was it I that was chosen by the Emperor for this task? Does he not have many women in his court and many others in his lands, who could provide him with child?" I had seen them there, and I knew that many women visited his royal bedchambers in the night.

"Yes, it is true that the Emperor has many women from which to choose. But like any other skill, only certain individuals have the spirit necessary to carry it to its highest levels. To master the teachings, one must be highly intelligent, of course; but she also must possess a fire within her, an unmistakable spark of the divine flowing from herself to others. It is this spark which the Emperor felt that day he saw you in the fields, and from this he knew that he must place you as the jewel in his crown. But not before I have polished and cut you and exposed your many facets!" Madame declared with a laugh. With her laugh my heart melted, Madame's sense of humor was a delight, and drew me again and again to her side. Madame believed in laughter, and with her laughter she made the coldness and loneliness of the rest of the palace bearable for me. As our days together went on, I began to love her; she became like a mother to me, the mother I had never known. Madame told me many things, things that were not strictly part of the teachings, but which she thought would be helpful to me, when I began my life with the Emperor.

"And what is he like, the Emperor?" I asked her one dusky evening, as I lay with my head in her lap, tired from the day.

After a silence, she answered, "He is very smart."

"Do you mean wise?" I asked.

"Wise? No, I cannot say wise. Wisdom is of the heart, and the Emperor has of yet to open his heart to wisdom. But as Empress you may help him in this. And you may be successful, so long as he does not know what you are doing," she answered, a mysterious tone in her voice.

"And how would I accomplish this, without his knowing? Will he not feel my intent?" I asked, for Madame had impressed upon me the importance of purity of intent in one's endeavors.

"Yes, exactly. You are learning well, my child. The Emperor, or anyone, will feel your true intent and react against it. And thus, it is your intent that must be of the highest order. Your intent must be for the good of the whole, for something outside your small self, and your relations with the Emperor. If it is thus, over time, the Emperor may slowly open his heart and feel compassion for all beings," she answered.

I absorbed her words, and was quiet for a time. When I felt that I had begun to grasp her meaning, I began tentatively to formulate my thoughts.

"In my heart, I know that many suffer. In my own village, there are people without enough food, or who have no roof over their heads when the harvest is meager. If the Emperor could feel and know of their plight, perhaps he could send food from the vast Imperial stores, or jewels from the treasure lining these walls. Is this what you mean? Is this what I should think of in my relations with the Emperor?" I asked.

Madame looked at me for a long moment. She had an expression which I could not read, and I thought, for just an instant, that I saw something like relief in her eyes.

"Exactly this," she said slowly. "China is a vast land, a land of uncounted souls. If your little village suffers thus, imagine that suffering played out across this great countryside! And imagine what an Emperor of compassion could do to help those suffering souls. You have been placed in a unique position, an opportunity that not many receive in this life. You, through your position, have the power to change untold number of lives. And what will you choose to do with this opportunity? It is up to you."

I inhaled her words. They came to me like a fragrance, the bracing scent of juniper, the sweet smell of lilies, the glory of truth revealed which has no form. I closed my eyes and envisioned those souls, and for a moment I was hovering above them in a robe of fiery red and gold, on the back of a dragon breathing fire. They reached up their arms to me; they reached up their arms...

愛

love

Before we visit the orphanage, we first must stop at yet another government office to attend to official adoption business, to satisfy another layer of government regulation. We left early this morning, and have been riding in the van for at least an hour already. The orphanage is in a dusty town a hundred miles from Nanchang, in Jiangxi province, a poor and rural area dominated by rice fields and farmland. From the window of the van I see women tending rice paddies, and men driving oxen with plows. Much of this countryside looks to have been untouched by time or the modern world. The houses are low-slung and made of mud and thatch; the people farm much as their ancestors did hundreds of years ago.

Alex is holding the baby and I have taken out my notebook, but cannot begin to write. So many dreams and impressions to record, and yet I am paralyzed by my feelings since Alex told me she doesn't want the baby. I am just hoping, hoping that today she will come to her senses. I look at the baby, decked out in a white knit cap and pink fleece coat, so innocent and unsuspecting that her fate hangs in the balance. I put my notebook away with a sigh, just as we arrive in front of a stark cinder-block building, on a busy street lined with people. A crowd gathers as we unload from the van, some in the back craning their necks to see us better. Judy says she has heard that sometimes parents of abandoned babies will gather here to look, to see if they can spot their child in the arms of an American couple.

The office of adoptions is on the second floor, and we climb the dark and dirty stairwell to reach it. We are shown to a sparsely furnished room, where we will wait until summoned, once again, by a government official. This meeting is more of a formality than the last; we are here only to pick up the official adoption papers that have already been processed. We wait, and I hold Baby, and I feel the tension start to release. Alex seems better today, less stressed; she is laughing a little with the others. Maybe the storm has already passed, and Baby is safe. By the time we meet with the officials, I am feeling almost giddy, and I even ask Anna to ask the burly man in a military uniform who stamps Baby's official papers if he likes his job. Anna speaks in Chinese to him, and a huge smile splits his face, and he nods vigorously. "Yes, yes," he says, "I like seeing the babies."

As we get back into the van for the short drive to the orphanage, I scan the crowd that has grown larger since we have been inside the building. I don't know what I'm looking for, but I am holding Baby, and maybe I will notice some spark of interest or recognition from someone there, and I will know that there was someone who cared enough about Baby to stand and wait, in hopes of seeing her again. Maybe her mother is that young girl there, in the back, with the new-born slung across her chest; perhaps her grandmother is that one, standing just in front, with the dirty apron; or maybe her father waits in the shadows, trying to appear nonchalant, but with an aching heart from so long pretending that his daughter does not exist.

But I see nothing, no such spark of interest, and we climb into the van once again. To reach the orphanage, we turn off the main road and onto a pile of rubble. To call it a road would be too generous. It is at most a path of rock, mud and gravel leading between the buildings, and the little van in which we are riding heaves and rocks and grinds its way along its length. We move slowly enough to make eye contact with people sitting on stoops, walking with large dirty bundles or riding rickety bicycles along the perilous roadway. Dilapidated houses, made of concrete, or cinder blocks, or mud, it is hard to distinguish the materials as everything—buildings, people, landscape, animals, sky—are bathed in shades of brown or grey. A small boy, glimpsed through a broken window pane which is framed by rusty iron bars, watches solemnly and without expression as we pass his grim, darkened house. I look very closely; this is where Baby would have lived, or someplace much like it, had her parents kept her.

The van pulls onto a paved plaza after waiting several minutes as a group of thin, tired-looking men pile enough stone onto the roadway so that we can pass. They watch us with severe, suspicious expressions as we step out of the vehicle and bundle the three Chinese babies into strollers and move toward the orphanage. There is silence among our group as we walk slowly in the chilly winter sunshine, toward what we fear seeing, and yet must see.

I am surprised to see ahead of us a shiny, high granite wall with large golden letters, in English, proclaiming "Love in the World" and "Life for Children." This wall must have been very expensive to build, and is so out of place here, where everything else looks to be in a state of collapse. Two days ago, I would have been sure this is cynical propaganda, built here at the entrance of the orphanage only to fool Americans who come to adopt. But I have observed here an intense need to be liked by us, a child-like desire to impress. Perhaps that's what this was, a sincere attempt to show their good faith where these children are concerned, that they are trying to do the right thing in an impossible situation.

The front of the orphanage is very well kept, too, with a paved courtyard and no rubble around. I am beginning to think this is not so bad, not half as bad as I thought it would be, and then I step inside, out of the hazy sunshine, and into a dark corridor, where I stand waiting for my eyes to adjust to the gloom. As I stand there I become aware that it is much colder inside the building than outside. It is the kind of cold that seeps into your bones, and permeates your mind, making your senses sharp at first, and numb as the freezing takes hold.

My first thought is that there could not possibly be babies in here, in this cold, but then I see them, just inside the doorway. At least 10 babies are lined up in wooden seats along the corridor, all swaddled in mismatched layers of clothing, unmoving and silent, their eyes trained upon us as we stand uncertainly in the corridor. A staff member in a white coat comes to greet us, and ushers us into one of several dark rooms just off the hallway. Inside the first room, row after row of cribs is pushed up against one another, filled with what looks like layers and layers of bedding. I walk along the rows and look more closely, and see that there are small dark heads inside each bed, newborns, infants, some sleeping and some awake, all silent, not a cry to be heard. In each crib one, sometimes two babies are kept, with one staff person to care for them all. There must be somewhere close to 40 babies in this room alone.

The room has no natural light, and in the mid-day is dark and cheerless. Concrete floors, tile walls, metal cribs and dirty linens comprise the harsh environment for the smallest, most vulnerable creatures I have ever seen. I peer into as many cribs as I can, trying to make eye contact, to send a silent message of futile and heartbreaking love which comes upon me with such power that it is suddenly hard to breathe. My chest fills up, something hard rises into my throat…one of the babies keeps reaching for my hand, whirling her arms like a windmill as if to propel herself forward and into my arms.

I lean over her, noting the downy softness of her spiky black hair, and see the hope that is visible in her keen, shining eyes. She still believes, I think; still believes in the goodness of human beings. It would be so easy to just pick this child up, to carry her away from here and make a place for her in my life. It would be the natural thing to do. The unnatural thing is leaving her here, leaving any of these babies to their uncertain futures. Her child's mind must sense that if she could make it into someone's arms, it would be against nature to put her down again, and that is why she seems to be willing herself into mine.

"I'm sorry," I whisper to the unnamed child. "They would never let me leave with you. There's red tape, regulations, money to be exchanged…a process." How could she understand this lunacy, when I did not? I touch her cheek and move away, and from the corner of my eye I can see her still waving her little arms, not giving up, not giving in.

The visitors are allowed to view just three of the nursery rooms on the first floor of the orphanage, and they are identical, with rows of cribs, an unrelenting chilliness, and unbroken silence. I ask Anna if she will translate some questions I have, and we approach one of the staff members, a middle-aged woman in a white coat, who is overseeing the babies in the corridor.

"How many babies are here?" I ask. Anna speaks my question in Chinese, and the woman responds.

"Three hundred babies come here each year," she replies through Anna.

"Three hundred?" I think about this. "How many of those get adopted?" I ask.

Again, Anna speaks to her and she responds.

"Maybe one third" comes the answer.

One third. If each year 300 babies are brought here, and only 100 of those ever leave, what happens to the rest? Where are they? 200 babies times just 5 years is 1000 children! I didn't see, or even more tellingly, hear, any evidence that there were 1000 children here.

"How many die?" I ask.

Anna hesitates, and looks at me for a moment before she poses the question to the woman in the white coat. Immediately the woman shakes her head, speaking harshly.

"She won't talk about that," says Anna.

"Well, what happens to the ones who live, but are never

adopted? Will she talk about that?" I ask, irritation in my voice.

Anna translates the response, "They live here, in the orphanage, are educated, and trained for some type of work."

It is clear that the woman is very uncomfortable with this line of questioning, and so is Anna. I am exhausted thinking of this, what could all this mean, what happens to these children? And this was just one orphanage in one small provincial town. China is a country of over a billion people...I had read somewhere that the U.N. estimates that over a million girl children are "missing" from the population each year; a million children that are abandoned, aborted, or killed outright, just for being female. When I had read that statistic, it was just a number; now that I had seen real, flesh and blood examples of the statistic it became another matter entirely. My mind and heart felt oppressed by the magnitude of human suffering represented by that number, and the question it gave birth to: what is to be done?

And the work they are trained for, is that military service, or back-breaking factory labor? Perhaps they are left to end up falling into a life of prostitution, service in a brothel; there will certainly be a need for more of those as the skewed demographic gets worse and all these male children grow up and have trouble finding wives. I think of the beautiful baby I have just touched, she of the desperately waving arms...

Now Alex hands Baby to me. Several times already during our time here she has found a reason to give her over to me, and at this moment Baby's warmth and weight is a comfort to me, she is a symbol of hope, however small. Surely now that Alex has seen this place, and what she would be sending her back to, no question could remain about taking this child. To give up the chance to bring one of these lost children home? I can't conceive of it, and I rejoice for Baby even as I grieve for those left behind.

Some strange, unexpected connection has been forged between me and these children. Though I have only known Baby for a day and a half, she seems an intimate part of me. And the babies I have seen so briefly in their cribs just now...I am sure I will see their faces in my mind for the rest of my life. We cannot just slip in and out of each others' lives as easily as we assume.

Maybe it's the nature of this trip, the heightened emotional atmosphere around the adoptions, or it could be the attention you must give to things when you are outside your natural habitat, things which would ordinarily go unnoticed. Whatever has allowed me a glimpse into the true nature of our effect on one another, I know now in my depths that each and every interaction, however brief, between two human beings leaves an indelible mark behind.

I take Baby into the room where she had been housed for the first year of her life. The staff worker in white takes her from me, and Anna says that she has been Baby's caretaker for most of the time since she was brought here. Baby has been silent and solemn, but content in my arms while I carried her about this place. But upon being picked up by the caretaker, she becomes visibly upset, her eyes dart to mine, questioning. The woman puts her down in a crib and says, through Anna, that this is Baby's crib. Baby looks dejected, her sad eyes wide, her mouth drawn down at the corners. I can almost hear her thoughts....are you leaving me here? I reach down, not being able to stand even a brief troubling of her heart. She puts her arms around my neck and I pull her from the tiny prison and walk away with her, out into the corridor.

Many of the babies are still here, in the unusual wooden chairs that keep them sitting upright and yet unable to move, like walker chairs without the wheels. Again, a staff member takes Baby from me, and puts her into an unoccupied seat. Immediately, Baby begins reaching out, toward the hand of the child sitting next to her, lifting as high as she can out of the constricting device until she is leaning over, and begins patting her neighbor's arm, and trying to touch the child's face. I watch in stunned silence. My god, I think, she is trying to comfort this child. It is clear these babies have learned to communicate with and draw strength from each other; they must, it is a matter of survival, for there is no other source.

Anna announces it is time to go, and I pull Baby from the chair and hold her up in front of her friend. "Say goodbye, Baby; maybe you'll meet again some day," I tell her, and her little arm waves a bit as we walk toward the doorway, followed by the lonely eyes of that silent child. The others in the group are already moving out to the plaza, but I hesitate inside. I notice Alex is sitting on the steps outside, her head in her hands. She seems distressed and yet I linger, there seems to be something I should do, some commemorative act to perform before carrying Baby from this place. This is a highly symbolic moment in an experience that is full of symbolism, and I hold Baby close, her head next to mine. I notice a doorway, one half propped open to reveal a courtyard behind the building. I step to the threshold, which faces out into a trash-strewn, overgrown yard surrounded by the high walls of the orphanage building. In contrast to the front entrance with its pavement of beautiful stone, this weed-choked wasteland tells the true tale of this place.

Baby and I stand looking out over the forgotten field. I feel an enormous hot pressure rise in my chest, and all the emotion I have been holding back comes surging forth, my heart pounding, my head throbbing as the sadness of this place overwhelms my ability to keep it at bay. Baby is calm and alert, as if she is waiting for something. I whisper a prayer of anguish, the anguish I feel for these children we will leave behind. Where is this pain to go? I cannot keep it inside me; I cannot take it outside these walls. Silent, fervent prayers must go somewhere. Who else to pray to then, but Mary, the iconic mother of us all?

"Mary, oh Mary," I plead. "What about these children?" The tears are pouring down my face now, hot and urgent. The enormity, the enormity of this…what human being could turn on their heels and walk away? And yet, I will do just that, I had to do just that. I had witnessed something that will haunt me as I sit at my kitchen table drinking coffee in suburbia, as I watch the privileged children at play in the neighborhood park; I will want to tell the mothers there about all these children lying uncared for in metal cribs, longing for any type of human warmth or contact. But how will I do so without guilt? I am walking away, too.

But then I remember, when I walk away, I will be holding tightly to one of these babies; one warm beating heart saved for the world. I close my eyes against the ugliness that is this potential garden, and against the human potential wasted inside these walls.

Instantly, a scene of powerful beauty fills my mind. The field before me is no longer a wasteland, but is transformed into an oasis of flowering trees, and lush grass. The sky is no longer colorless, but deep clear blue. And then, thousands of glowing white doves swoop down from that sky, through the dilapidated courtyard, and into the dark cold rooms of the orphanage. The peaceful glow of the doves fills the room, their breath warms the air. Above each crib alights one dove to protect the sleeping child below. The Virgin Mary hovers above all, her arms outstretched, glowing with unearthly light. "I would not forsake my children," she says. "I have been here all along."

I open my eyes as this image fades from my mind. I am overcome with gratitude for the vision that let me see past my own despair. How long have I been standing here? Am I hallucinating? If so, it seems a supremely sane response to such tragedy. I am oddly comforted by this vision, the burden on my chest is gone, my mind is peaceful and still. I know now that it is time, and I walk out into the hazy sunshine of the plaza. I feel a lightness, a certainty, that my being in this place is not an accident.

What has just transpired seems to confer upon me a complete responsibility for this child. I walk carefully across the cobblestones, knowing that in my arms I hold a treasure beyond price, a jewel found twinkling in a pile of rubble.

*My Master and I now met less and less, and yet, his voice inside me grew stronger each day. Every teaching I received from Madame was responded to, elaborated on and confirmed by this voice, and it became as if the two were somehow fusing together into a beautiful tapestry of thought. I felt the Master's presence with me always, especially at the times when I experienced an exalted state of consciousness, where my mind released itself from the confines of the body.*

*Up and up I would float until I was hovering above the scene, my body lay below me on the bed, and yet it was not me. How could I be in two places at once? Here, and yet not, there and yet not? When this occurred I felt blissful, as if nothing yet remained to be done. But as soon as I returned to awareness within my body, a gnawing feeling of incompleteness would resume. And what did this mean? I wanted to ask Madame, but I could not tell her about my meditation practices with my Master. Shall I go to my Master, I wondered, even though he had warned me of the danger of doing so? I could not put down this burning question, and so I resolved to go to him, to receive guidance, to find answers.*

*Early the next morning the bells calling the monks to prayers began to sound. I waited in my little bed until the chants of the monks in the court began to dwindle and fade, and I knew they would be returning to their chambers. Once again, I slipped through the temple door as I had done the day of my first meeting with my Master. I found myself in the long corridor lined with doors, each closing in turn as the monk who resided there entered, one by one. I waited in the cool darkness until I was alone and as before, one doorway remained just slightly ajar, as a thin edge of light shown through the opening. I made my way down the corridor until I stood at the Master's door. It surprised me to hear the quiet murmur of voices bubbling together from behind the door. I had not considered that my Master may have a visitor there. As I stood not knowing what to do, I heard a short burst of laughter, a warm and happy sound, a sound I could not mistake, a laugh I knew so well.*

*In my surprise, I did not think. I reached out my hand and pushed at the door, I had to see, to confirm that what I had heard was true. And as the door swung open I saw them in the center of the room, standing close, heads bowed toward each other in intimate exchange, both smiling as one smiles when they are in the company of one they love with special feeling. I stood not moving or speaking, and for several moments neither Madame nor my Master seemed to know of my presence. I saw him reach out his hand and touch her cheek tenderly, and as he did so she turned her head, toward me and my intrusion, and I felt a brief wave of horror at my curiosity.*

*And then she spoke, "We've been waiting for you. Come in!" The relief I felt must have radiated from my face, as they both moved to embrace me then.*

*"Oh Master, oh Madame! Please pardon my intrusion, I did not know, did not know…" I cried. As the shock subsided at seeing my teachers there together, I began to feel such joy and exhilaration at the discovery that I burst into tears of happiness.*

*They each spoke in reassurance that they had indeed expected my arrival. "We have some very important things to tell you, and* we called you here so as not to be overheard by the servants or others within your quarters. Please sit down so that we may begin, we must hurry," my Master said, leading me to a cushion where I sat with them upon the floor, listening eagerly to my teachers' words.

"The Emperor will place you under guard tomorrow at dawn, as I have informed him of your readiness for marriage and the Divine Union to occur. We will no longer have freedom to meet, as my official duties in your training have been completed. Our continued meeting would arouse suspicion in the palace, and we must avoid doing so for our work to continue," said Madame.

"Madame, we are not to meet again? I could not bear it! And how am I to know of my progress in the practice? And Master…" I turned to his kindly face. "Why have we met so seldom these past days? Am I to be without your guidance as well?" I asked, my voice catching in my throat.

"My child, you know by now that I am always with you. You only have to raise the vibrations of your thoughts and intend to contact me, and we may continue to meet. It is vital that your skill in this be honed, as our meeting in the conventional way would violate palace doctrine. As you know, women are only to be instructed in certain areas, domestic arts and beauty rituals. Women are never to be given knowledge of the mystical fire, that power is reserved for the use of men alone, men such as the Emperor and the priests and monks of the temple," he explained.

"But why?" I asked. "Why for men alone? I see no harm in women practicing the meditation and exercises you have taught me— they make me feel at peace, they are for me alone; it hurts no one."

"Ah, little one….you view this from the point of view of one who has no worldly power to protect. You see, when those who gain the insight of the higher vibrations seek to use it for the maintenance of personal power, they must also seek to keep this knowledge from those over whom they wield that power. And the power of the mind is the most potent force in creation. Even your own skills, so recently developed, could topple an Emperor. Do you believe this?" my Master asked, looking at me intently.

I pondered his question. I thought of how I felt when I experienced awareness outside my body. I thought of the vision of the people of China, their arms outstretched to me.... "Yes, Master. Yes I do believe it," I answered.

"That is good," he said, relief evident on his face. "You must begin to accept your power or you may never use it for good. There is much to be done, much to be done for China. And you will soon be elevated to a position of unique influence at this time, a time of change throughout the land. Already the earth is trembling with the cries of the people, already they reach out for a new way. There has been much violence and hardship and there are many with nothing to lose. Even their lives they do not fear losing, as the experience of nothing would be preferable to this prolonged experience of misery. Those with nothing to lose are the most dangerous, and that energy must be channeled at this time for the good of China. Otherwise, all that is good and true will be swept away in the torrent of anger that will erupt and will have to be rebuilt again in another time. And it may be much more difficult rebuilding the good later than trying to save it now, but the good shall be gained, that is sure. For all moves toward perfection and unity, in time."

His words alarmed me; I had not realized the scope of the unrest in our lands. "Master, what am I to do? I am but a virtual prisoner within these walls. I cannot freely come and go; I cannot help these suffering people directly. Only through my relations with the Emperor may I seek to send them aid, as Madame and I have discussed. She has explained the way in which I might do this," I said.

"Yes, you will have great influence through your association with the Emperor," Madame said. "And yet, as Master Liu has spoken, there will be more, much more available to you. This is why it is of utmost importance that our contact be maintained, and in this way it shall be: I have arranged for my beloved assistant Shiu Lin to be placed in your service, as of tomorrow. She will be with you at all times and be your confidant in this endeavor. Shiu Lin will have direct access to me so that she may relay messages of importance between us. You may tell her all and everything, as she is an initiate in the highest levels of my order and knows of the importance of this work. It is my hope that you will also love her as a sister, and that you two may become comfort and strength for each other."

I thought of the lovely face of the young assistant who had brought Madame to me that first day of our meeting, who had sat with us as Madame imparted the teachings to me. I could indeed imagine her as a sister, someone with whom I could share my experiences and the teachings, which had become the most important thing to me. I bowed to Madame, and thanked her for this gift. Madame beamed in response. "I am pleased," she said softly. "I am pleased."

"Much more will become clear in time," said my Master, who I now knew as Master Liu from Madame's reference to him, the first I had heard his name spoken. "I, too, have made arrangements to facilitate the continuance of our work. As I have said, we shall not meet in person. But in order for you to gain a better understanding of those you may seek to help, you must find a way to venture outside the palace walls. There exists a place just outside where the hungry of this city are fed by the generosity of the Emperor. Each day the crowds come to accept the gruel and bread which is provided by the leftovers from the palace food stores. It is here where you may see for yourself that which I have told you, and there is someone there you must meet. My brother, himself formerly a monk within these palace walls, serves the poor and hungry of this place, and knows much which he will share with you. The Emperor and other members of the Imperial family sometimes conduct ceremonial visits there, to enhance their standing and gain the good will of the people. If you will it, you may arrange a visit there, and speak with my brother of the work. He, too, is to be trusted, as his heart is pure even though his temper is sometimes hot!" laughed Master Liu.

"I will do as you have said, Master," I answered. I wanted to see this place of which he spoke. My own village, though poor, was quiet and all helped their neighbors, and gave food and shelter when one of theirs fell upon hard times. I could not conceive of the violence and desperation of those with nothing to lose, those who must be fed with the hand which threw away food at the palace. "And what shall I say to your brother, when we meet?" I asked.

"Tell him you are there to help him, and that you have known each other before," he answered. And though I did not understand what this meant, I knew that I would speak in this way, when I met Master's brother, the one who helped the poor.

As Madame and Master Liu bade me farewell, tears welled in my eyes, and I fell to the floor and threw my arms around their legs and cried, "Be with me always!"

Curtis and Judy's baby cries all the way from the orphanage back to Nanchang. For two hours, nothing calms her. She is crying tears for all of us, a sadness we cannot express. Even Maggie is silent and subdued; there are no songs from Sunday school, or telling jokes with Curtis. She sits in the back of the van with her parents and new baby sister, watching the countryside roll by, with a blank expression on her face. Earlier today her mother had in a very matter of fact way told us that the orphanage where they had gotten Maggie, in southern China, was far worse than the one we had just seen. The babies slept in wooden crates, and only straw covered the dirt floor. Just like a manger, I thought, and flicked my eyes to Maggie's face, which had gone suddenly mask-like and immobile. A wall had gone up inside her, protecting her from this information. It was too much for a six year old to contemplate.

Alex and I don't speak during the ride back, she had told me when I saw her outside the orphanage on the plaza that she was feeling sick, nauseous. Back in the van I had given her a granola bar and some water and that had helped, she said. I am holding Baby, who is calmly chewing on a shortbread biscuit, her eyes big and bright. She is quiet, so quiet and self-possessed. I talk to her without speaking, she answers me without sound, we are sharing some private psychic space where I can feel her every feeling, and she mine. I watch as rice paddy fields flow by outside the window.

Fatigue is starting to take its toll on all of us now. The grueling trip, the sleepless first two nights with the new babies, and the visit to the orphanage have left us drained. But compared to the others, I am feeling energetic, probably because of the 15 hour sleep marathon two nights before. When we arrive back at the hotel, I offer to let Alex rest while I take the baby out into the city with Jimmy, Louise, Maggie and Livvy, their new baby.

Before we leave the hotel room, I put Baby into her stroller and prepare the diaper bag with her necessities: bottle of formula, snack, blanket, diapers, wipes, toys. I had never cared for an infant before, and yet oddly, I knew just what to do for Baby. I am in high spirits as we get ready to go, though I can't explain why. When we leave the room, Alex is lying in her bed, head totally under the covers, drapes drawn against the light, and we go quietly so as not to disturb her sleep.

Jimmy flags down a taxi in front of our hotel, and the six of us pile in, Jimmy and Louise want to go to a department store they know of, one they visited the last time they were here, to adopt Maggie. The city is teeming with life: people riding bicycles or pushing carts with children in them, cars and trucks zigzagging through the streets, horns blaring. People are everywhere, so many people. I had thought Nanchang was a small provincial backwater, but I asked Anna and she said the population was 3 million. There are high-rise buildings, modern vehicles, and a beautiful promenade along the river. And yet, as the cab enters a traffic round-about, I look over to see a dirty peasant man, holding a stick twice as tall as he is, driving a huge pink sow and her six piglets around the circle, merging in with the vehicle traffic. It is so funny and unexpected, and Maggie and I start to giggle together uncontrollably when I point it out to her.

Most of the buildings are dingy and run down, with lines of laundry hanging from almost every window.

Underwear and socks hang next to dead ducks and sausages left out to cure. When my mind adjusts to these strange juxtapositions, I feel a strange exhilaration, a raw energy picked up from these streets, where life is being lived at its most unrefined. I like the ragged edges that are showing here, and I look around with avid enjoyment at the spectacle outside my window.

We drive across town, it takes about a half hour before we pull up in front of a large square building set behind a wide paved plaza, a row of red banners flapping happily above the entrance. Lots of people are milling about the plaza, and as soon as we open the doors and step out of the cab, we are thronged by a crowd trying to catch a glimpse of the foreigners who have just arrived on the scene. There is no understanding of respect for privacy, or personal boundaries. People crowd right up to us, looking straight into our faces with no smiles, with no acknowledgment of our right to space so that we can maneuver our way into the building. It is a surprise to suddenly be in such close proximity to so many people. Until now, we have been protected from onlookers by Anna, by the walls and windows of the van, by the controlled confines of the hotel. Now we are in their midst, with nothing to buffer us from each other. They look at our clothes, listen intently to us speak, watch how we handle the babies. Some women come up and pull on the pants leg of Louise's baby, and pantomime their displeasure that she is not dressed warmly enough. The Chinese bundle their babies in layers and layers of warm clothing, with no skin showing, and Louise's baby has only a thin jacket and skin is showing between the trouser leg and the top of her sock, a parenting sin.

Jimmy and Louise move away quickly toward the entrance, and I start to panic, I am still struggling to open the stroller that Alex brought for the baby, I can't follow. The proximity of these strangers, none of whom look like me or can understand me if I speak, frightens me. I am afraid I will lose Jimmy and Louise in the crowd and not be able to find my way back to the hotel. What would I do, lost alone in this city with the baby? I can't even pronounce the name of our hotel.

Finally Jimmy notices I am not behind them, and pushes back through the crowd and takes my arm, leading me and Baby through the sea of people and into the department store. We wheel the babies around the displays of merchandise. People stare, and I wonder what they are thinking. Are they resentful of these Americans adopting Chinese children? Are they supportive, just curious? I stop with Baby in front of a jewelry display case and look at the jade jewelry arrayed inside. Maybe I should buy Baby some jade for her to keep, what would be nice? I indicate to the salesgirl behind the counter that I would like to see a tiny bracelet, a circle of smooth jade with a golden clasp. I have seen other babies wearing these bracelets; Anna told me they are for protection from evil spirits. I look up and the salesgirl looks at me, then down at the baby in the stroller, then back at me again. Struggling for the right words, she stammers, "You, baby?"

For the sake of ease, I answer "Yes; my baby."

"Lucky baby, go to America," she says. "Lucky baby." She

says this wistfully, without smiling. Yes, yes. Lucky baby.

Lucky Baby and I wheel through the bedding displays next, then the shoe department, and then cosmetics. The beauty counters are presided over by a larger than life-size poster of Cindy Crawford, hawking Revlon. She is ubiquitous, it is impossible to evade her image even here in Nanchang, China. What good, I wonder, could the image of Cindy Crawford possibly do for these women? Couldn't Revlon use Asian faces to sell its beauty products to Asian women? It would just be the courteous thing to do, especially here, where a tube of lipstick might cost the equivalent of a week's wages at the shoe-string factory.

I am in a daze, a fog of surrealism. Is this happening, am I in China, wheeling a baby around a department store? Did Alex really ask me last night if I would take this baby? Take this baby, raise this baby….Lucky Baby, how lucky would that be for you?

I lean down to look Baby in the eye. Her big, round eyes, accentuated by the knit cap, are deep, dark, somber. Her face is all eyes, all windows of a soul I cannot fathom.

*We will be together again.*

"So," I whisper, "Is it going to be me and you then?" I am trying this idea out in my mind, to see how it feels. I am asking her, I am asking myself, what would it take, could we do this? We look deeply at each other, the question already answered.

At dawn's first light I heard a rustling outside my door. It was very early as the bells had yet to sound calling the monks to prayer. Quiet voices spoke briefly, and as I rose from bed I heard footsteps as they retreated across the courtyard. Drawing back the curtain from the doorway, I glimpsed a man dressed in the military attire of the Emperor's Imperial Guard, as he disappeared into the doorway which led to the inner chambers of the Emperor. He was tall and broad shouldered, as befitted one of his high rank. His headdress confirmed his status of most high advisor to the Emperor. Just before he disappeared through the doorway, he turned his head slightly, just enough for our eyes to meet. If he was surprised to see me there, he did not betray it; for all I saw in that brief glimpse was a glimmer of regret before he was gone, as he continued on his way without hesitation.

I was startled to hear next to me a cough, a clearing of the throat. I looked around the curtain to see another man dressed in military attire, this one not nearly so decorated as the retreating man's. This man stood straight and still beside my doorway, chin high, seemingly determined not to acknowledge that I was there. I looked into his face. It was the same man who had come to retrieve me from my father's home that day, who had not spoken to me throughout the entire journey across the countryside to the palace. And now he was to be my guard, the one who would watch my every step and hear my every word until I had conceived the first child for the Emperor.

Things were different now. Just a short time ago on that wordless journey I was afraid, timid and unable to find my voice. I had not attempted to break the silence which he had imposed, not even to ask what kind of life he was taking me to. But now, after my experiences with the teachings, I knew no timidity in speaking with men. I had been trained in ways to excite a man through my speech, through my ideas, and through my mind. And I knew that all men are at least a little afraid of women, and that only when that fear is eased can true exchange take place.

I stood before him. I breathed in and out in a technique taught by my Master, waiting for right timing to begin my words. He shifted his body slightly, and still I waited there. Again he moved, his eyes flicking down, almost to my face. I continued to wait there, like a tigress in her tree, no need to pounce. The tigress knows that what she wants will come to her, and so she is able to wait forever.

He cleared his throat once, twice. His eyes again came down, this time to my face. We locked eyes and I held his there for a time before I spoke. As I held his gaze, I let the energy of my heart release outward to envelope him, surround him, comfort him. He did not move his eyes away then, and so I spoke.

"And what is your name?" I asked quietly, softly.

Before he could stop himself he had answered, "My name is Jiang." The ice had been broken, the tables turned. Our exchange would be on my terms now; he had willingly compromised his orders not to speak to me, his prisoner. Jiang blinked as he looked at me, sensing something had happened, but not knowing what. I continued to release light from my being and I could see him relax a bit, and accept, this is the way it would be.

"My prayer, Jiang, is that you find your post an enjoyable one," I said as I touched his arm lightly, feeling the energy pass between us, making an exchange. "And would you be so kind as to tell me, who was the man I saw retreating from my door?"

"He is the Emperor's Most High Advisor, to whom I report.

His name is Han, and he is a fierce warrior," Jiang replied, rushing his words, obviously in awe of the one he called Han.

"And tell me Jiang, if this 'Han' is such a fierce warrior, why is his duty to post guards in front of my door? Why is he not in battle, serving his master in the way he knows best?" I asked.

Jiang licked his lips, looking quite nervous at my question. "I do not know all," he said. "I merely carry out the orders of Han. And yet I do hear…that the Emperor has called him here for a special purpose, to mount an incursion against the people, those who would challenge the Emperor's rule. Han is the most trusted of his men, and has been loyal and brave. And yet, as I have heard, Han has refused to carry out the Emperor's order to attack the people in the far land of revolt, and the Emperor has posted him in charge of the palace until they can come to agreement in discussions," said Jiang.

I absorbed this. The man who was my guard's master, who held my own fate in his hands, was charged with carrying out violence against the very people of whom my Master had spoken, just one day ago. "He is refusing to do so? Can you speak to me of why?" I asked, trying to appear nonchalant.

"This I cannot say, Mistress, for I do not know. This is a question for Han alone, and neither you nor I will have occasion to ask," replied Jiang in a haughty tone.

At this I gave a laugh. Not have occasion to ask? I intended to have the occasion to ask, and very soon, as the answer could be of grave importance to Madame and Master Liu in their work. "Well, I thank you, Jiang. Could you please share with me just one more thing: Will Han your master be nearby to these quarters in coming days? Shall I see him again?" I asked.

"He is to come each day, in the early light, on his way from his chambers to meet with the Emperor," replied Jiang.

I nodded, and thanked him. "And now Jiang, you may be at rest, for I will be inside for some time engaged in preparation for the wedding day and shall not venture out until morning. I look forward to seeing you then."

Jiang bowed in acceptance, and I let the curtain fall across my doorway. At my desk I took up my pen and began to write. I wanted to record Madame's and Master's words of yesterday, so as not to forget. And after that I would retreat to my garden to visualize my future meeting with Han, and get the answers I sought. I must know why this man had refused the Emperor's orders. What kind of man could do so and still retain the Emperor's good grace? I closed my eyes and let his image come to my mind. I saw him in his military dress, ready for battle. And then a swirling mist obscured him from my sight. In a moment the vision cleared and I saw him sitting, legs folded, eyes closed in meditation, a giant lotus opening petal by petal above his head, streaming a glorious light. I opened my eyes and began to write. Tomorrow I would make my chance, but now I must prepare, I must wonder and dream, I must answer yet another question: who is he?

I rose before the light. Shiu Lin helped me to dress, choosing a beautiful gown of amethyst silk, coiling my hair into an elaborate design atop my head. "And Mistress, of what importance are today's activities, that we should prepare so carefully?" she asked.

"Shiu Lin, I only know that today could be of importance, not that it will be. Perhaps I will have more to share later, after I have returned," I answered. I could see the concern upon her face, and I touched her cheek and thanked her for her assistance. "We shall talk in the garden at dusk. And now I leave and ask you to pray for the *success of my venture."*

*Shiu Lin nodded and I pulled back the doorway curtain to find Jiang standing at his post. He appeared sleepy, and he startled a bit, widening his eyes, at the same time straightening his posture into rigid alignment. "Good morning, Jiang. I thank you for your service through the night, and I ask, will you accompany me on a walk through the palace grounds this morning, as I am stiff from sitting inside my chamber all of yesterday?"*

*Jiang nodded, asking "And where would Mistress like to walk?"*

*"Oh, just around the courtyard here a bit. Perhaps later I will venture to the temple to provide an offering as well," I answered. I began walking, with Jiang following a short distance behind. I breathed deeply of the cool air, as the light began to creep into the edges of the sky. I knew that soon the bells would sound, the monks would converge upon the square, and I would be forced to retreat. I tried to be discreet as I scanned the corners of the square, looking this way and that, so as not to miss seeing Han should he pass this way. After some time walking I had reached the far corner of the courtyard just as the first prayer bell sounded, and I thought with some alarm that my opportunity for that day had passed. But just then I saw a figure emerge from a corridor, walking purposefully in the direction in which I stood. It was Han, and he was dressed not in his military attire, but in loose clothing suited to martial arts practice, the exercise of warriors. He carried on his back a long pouch that clanked when he walked—I could hear it from across the courtyard as he came closer and closer.*

*Just then the monks began filing into the square as well. Waiting, waiting for right timing...I kept my attention on both Han and the monks, and just as I sensed a question rising in Jiang, my guard, I saw Han enter a doorway, and I knew where I must go.* In a few moments the area had filled with monks, making it clear that walking here would be impossible now.

"I would like to enter here," I said, as I reached the place where I had seen Han enter, and before Jiang could respond I turned into the corridor, and increased my pace so that he must hurry to catch up to me.

I had entered another series of courtyards, open to the sky, surrounded by more chambers and high stone walls. I had not been in this place before, and I saw no one as I walked along, looking curiously into each courtyard, trying to appear casual in front of Jiang. Where had Han disappeared to, and what was this place? Just as this question came to mind, I passed the opening to a large, sunlit lawn, surrounded by stone walls, and in the center of the lawn stood Han.

I stopped with an intake of breath. He had removed the upper garments he had been wearing before, and now his torso was bare, exposing a magnificent physique, muscled by the exertion of battle, and the long years of practice of the martial arts. In his right hand he grasped a long glittering sword, and he was poised with it extended out from his body, holding perfect position, eyes closed in concentration, breathing deeply.

Jiang wanted to protest, he pulled at the sleeve of my gown, trying to move my body back, behind the wall, so as not to be seen by his Master. He did not dare speak as he would then call Han's attention to our presence. But I stood as if rooted, there was such power in this sight, the sight of a warrior at peace, and yet holding the tool of violence in his hand. I watched his movements, following his every turn, glimpsing the agility with which he wielded his sword. Something began to move inside me, in the area of my heart. It swirled there in harmony with his movements, and I reached up *instinctively to put my hand there, in protection.*

*Just as I did so, Han turned, and opened his eyes. This time, there was surprise in them, but the warrior did not flinch. He held his position for a moment, absorbing the new information of a change in his environment, and then his arm fell, dropping the sword.*

*He began striding across the lawn toward us, and I could see Jiang become more and more nervous as he approached. I felt compassion for him, and sent a small winged prayer out, asking that he not receive punishment for allowing me here. Before Han even reached us, I began, "It was my doing....I did not know my way, and came upon you here...please forgive us for disturbing your practice."*

*Han did not respond until he stood directly before me. Now that we stood so close I could see that his eyes held depth and kindness, and the hint of a smile played around them. "Mistress, I am relieved at the interruption for today, I had not the passion for my sword that one must have to complete the practice well," he said.*

*I returned his smile. "No passion for your sword? Yes, I see how this could be difficult for a warrior. But for a man, I should think this may be a relief. Am I correct?" I asked, looking Han directly in the eye.*

*Han looked back at me for a long moment, a sad expression suddenly coming and then going again, to be replaced by a quizzical look which held there. "And Mistress, how could you guess how a man might feel?" he asked softly, looking down, taking his eyes from mine.*

*I waited and did not respond. I waited as I had with Jiang, for the right timing of my words. The swirling in my heart that had begun as I watched Han's movements grew stronger, and I released it into the gap between us; it was for him. When it had reached him*

I knew it, for he lifted his eyes to mine. In those eyes was a look so stark and naked, a look of grief and pain such as I had not seen. And I said then, my voice gentle as a breeze, "That is what I should like to ask you, Sir."

Jiang, who had been standing by silently during our exchange, made a sound of strangled protest. "Jiang, you are dismissed for the day," Han spoke, in the tone of one who must be obeyed. "I will oversee the Mistress and escort her back to her chambers. You are to take up your post when we return."

I did not see the expression on Jiang's face as he turned on his heel and made his way quickly down the corridor, but as Han turned again to face me, I saw the hint of a smile and I knew that for him, these roles they played were a game, just as for Jiang they were an absolute. We stood looking at each other just as the last waves of chanting from the monks in the outer court drifted to heaven.

"Let us walk," he said, and we began that journey that two begin who know: we hold time, love and beauty in our hands, and there shall be a time when all veils shall fall.

Shiu Lin was waiting just inside the doorway when I returned in the soft light of early dusk. She rushed to my side, excited and happy. "Mistress, you won't believe what I have seen! In my prayers, in my visions something wonderful has happened to you! Please, tell me, where have you been today?" She grabbed my hand, pulling me into the room. "I have been waiting for hours, please don't delay!"

I raised my finger to my lips to indicate caution, and stepping back I pulled the curtain aside. There stood Jiang, already returned to his post outside my door. I let the curtain fall and bade Shiu Lin follow me, into the garden just beyond my chamber. There we sat upon the low stone bench, and she whispered to me of what she had seen. "Mistress, I saw a tree," she began, with breathless excitement.

"A tree, Shiu Lin?" I asked. "And for this you are so excited?" I laughed.

"But it was not just a tree, Mistress. It was a tree of blazing light, reaching high into the sky. I could not see the top, it was so tall. And you stood before it, and received its blessings as they fell. I cannot describe the beauty, it is beyond this world."

The smile left my face as I envisioned the tree of which she spoke. "And what were the blessings, those that fell to me?" I asked.

"I don't know, Mistress, I only know that there were many, many blessings. At first one only fell; and then another, and another...and then more and more fell, until it was like rain! And you stood, with your arms outstretched, to receive them. Oh, Mistress!" Shiu Lin blotted the corners of her eyes, her tears had gathered there. "What has happened today, that you should receive such gifts?"

I envisioned that of which she spoke, the blessings falling like the rain. "Shiu Lin, I cannot say myself why you have seen this vision. I can only say, I have come to know someone of an extraordinary nature. A man....but not just any man. He is a warrior, an important figure in the court of the Emperor himself. He has many resources at his disposal, and of this we talked throughout the day. Shiu Lin....you know of the work of Madame and Master Liu. This man, the one called Han, can facilitate this work. I just know it is so, and will be, in time. His heart is opened, and he is willing though he does not know it yet!"

Shiu Lin clapped her hands in delight. "Mistress, I know of this man. Is he not of the highest military order of the Emperor? And how did you meet? How was it that you were able to speak to him at length, and with Jiang there...." asked Shiu Lin.

"I willed it so! Jiang had told me of Han's reluctance to perpetrate an attack upon the people of the land, despite the Emperor's orders to do so. I just had to know why this was so. I saw him cross the courtyard this morning, and I sought to follow him, and we spoke then. Jiang was dismissed at service for the day, while Han himself escorted me."

Shiu Lin's eyes shone with interest. "And what did you find, Mistress? You must tell me, as I can go to Madame, tonight, and tell her of this occurrence."

"What did I find? I found a man of highest mind, Shiu Lin; and one who also feels great pain. He is alone in his thoughts and feelings within the court, and it was in our speaking that he found comfort. He will not attack the people as he feels the order is unjust. He feels compassion for those who would revolt, as they are in need of bread, of work and shelter. He explained to me of all he has seen, and now I must see for myself. Shiu Lin...he has agreed to arrange for me a visit to the place where the Emperor feeds the hungry. I must go there, as Master instructed me to do. In two days time, we will make a ceremonial visit there, and you must accompany me."

"I will do so gladly!" exclaimed Shiu Lin. "And now I must be off, to tell Madame of all you have said!" Shiu Lin hugged me and rushed from the garden, leaving me to my thoughts.

I sat for some time there, among the roses and sweet smelling jasmine. Han's face came to my mind again and again; I heard his voice, heard him speak the words that touched my heart. Something moved in me, and I felt again that which I had felt as Han and I sat together in the dappled sunlight of the pine grove. I felt that I must help him in some way, that I had been called to do so.

I closed my eyes and breathed in the night air. Its coolness made me alert to all sensations, to each thing inside and outside of me which could be reached by my awareness. I breathed and felt my mind clearing of all thought while I focused with attention upon a light inside, and the light grew larger and more luminous with each breath, until at last, I saw it, my Master's face, just as he had said. I could reach him when I wished.

"Master," I said without speaking, with my thoughts, "I want to tell you of my meeting today."

"And do you think I do not know of it?" came the answer, from inside me, like a thought.

"I should not have doubted it! But what does it mean? Master, who is this man, the one they call Han?" I asked.

"You know in your heart who this man is. He is one who will work for the good, and that is all you need to know. You have come together because of your desire to help the people, and you shall have opportunity to do so in time. Please be patient, and follow your heart's guidance in this," replied the master.

"Master, Shiu Lin told me of a vision she received today, a vision of blessings being bestowed upon me. Can you tell me of this? What does it mean?"

"My child, each decision that you make carries with it the seeds of joy, or the seeds of despair. You have made a choice which will be of a magnitude undreamed of by you at this time. The blessings are yours by this choice, and will be kept for you forever in the vaults of heaven, and rain to you on earth as such time allows."

I felt a chill ripple throughout my body at these words, words I did not fully understand, but did not doubt. Pulling my robe around me more tightly, I left the garden to spend the night dreaming fitfully

133

*upon my little bed, dreaming of legions of angels, and a small black-haired baby, who reached out her arms to me.*

After leaving the department store, Jimmy, Louise, Maggie and I, and the babies, take a taxi to a riverfront hotel that is rumored to have the best American-style hamburgers in the city. The lobby is decorated for Christmas, with a tall fake evergreen trimmed in red velvet bows. Christmas music plays over the speakers in the almost-empty dining room, reminding me for a moment how far we are from home.

The waiter takes our order, "ba-sgetti" for Maggie, and burgers for the rest of us. We talk then; Jimmy tells me about their life at home, and what it's been like to raise a little Chinese girl in a small town. He asks me why I came on this trip, and I tell him a little bit about my friendship with Alex, but I don't feel like going into detail. Right now I am confused about her, and I can't let them in on what has been going on. Luckily the food arrives and we dig into our "American" hamburgers that taste exactly like soy sauce.

I feed little bits of the burger to Baby, and she gobbles them up, one after the other; she is ravenous. When we run out of burger, she eats rice, noodles, vegetables, anything I offer. My appetite is nowhere near as robust as hers. I am glad to see her eating, gaining strength with each passing hour, the thin thread connecting her to life becoming more and more substantial.

And then I understand. Until now, I have not been able to identify exactly what I had seen in Baby's eyes that first night. Something like grief, I had thought, or sadness, though neither seemed quite right. Now I knew, she had been just barely hanging on to life.

Baby would not make it if she went back to the orphanage. Her will to live would not survive a return to those conditions. Surely, infants too can reach a point of not wanting to struggle anymore. To be in a world with no love or warmth, hungry and cold all the time, where no one cares particularly about you....surely at some point they give up, not willing to fight for such a harsh existence any longer. How many of these abandoned babies just wither away after a time?

Removing her from the only place she had ever known had clearly been a shock. But after two days of someone holding her, feeding her, singing to her, and keeping her warm she had already begun to blossom, to fight her way back to life. To send her back now to a life of deprivation would be a cruelty beyond belief.

All my stated reasons for coming on this trip were swept away with this understanding, and I knew my true purpose was to prevent that cruelty, to stop that cycle of pain in at least one life, and with this chance I had been given, to redeem my own.

It is dark when Baby and I return to the hotel room. Alex opens the door, a look of pinched exhaustion on her face. She tells me she has not slept at all, or eaten, since we've been gone; she is feeling worse and worse. She says that after we left, she lay in bed and couldn't stop her mind from whirling, from turning the situation over and over in her head.

She is feeling panicked again, and she just can't get past the feeling that this isn't right, that taking the baby is a mistake.

"I can't do it," she says. "I can't take the baby."

I sit down with Baby on the bed. I had expected that when we returned, Alex would greet us feeling rested, feeling better, ready to put this all behind her. Now it was obvious that her doubts were not transitory misgivings. Two days have gone by, with no real attempt to bond with the baby.

I sit in silence for a long moment. Alex still could not express exactly why she felt she couldn't take Baby, but I knew the reason. She didn't love her; it was as simple as that. As unbelievable as it was to me, she did not love this child, and felt that she never could. She should not have her, I thought, it is correct that she not take her to a life with no real love.

"Will you take her?" she asks.

Will I take her? Last night, when I had told Alex that I would take the baby, I was trying to be helpful, to give her some breathing room until her doubts and fears subsided. It was easy to say, then. I didn't really believe it would happen. But now I know she is beyond deciding whether to keep this child; she will not.

The question, Will you take her? hangs in the air between us, and everything I have ever aspired to be, all the lessons I have ever learned, all the pain I have ever felt crystallize around it, transforming it into the real question: Will you love her?

"Yes," I say. "I will."

The day dawned when I should make my visit to the marketplace, outside the palace walls, to the place where the hungry came to be fed leftovers from the house in which I lived. All morning I felt an irritability, a tightness in my stomach and a feeling of impatience. Could we not go quickly without so much ceremony? The carriages must be prepared; I must be dressed in the stifling embroidered robes of the Imperial Court. Those who would carry my sedan chair must be summoned and instructed, and a retinue of guards from Han's service employed to protect the entourage. "There may be violence in the marketplace, Mistress, and we must be prepared to defend the Imperial Bride," said Jiang, when I asked him the purpose of so many men to accompany me.

Finally the preparations were complete. Shiu Lin helped me exit my chambers, holding the curtain and lifting my heavy robe as I walked. I felt choked by the high collar, the stiff fabric and the cinched waist of the garment and longed for the freedom of my simple white robe which I wore always in my chambers. Shiu Lin saw my distress, and murmured reassurances as we made our way to the outer court where the carriages awaited. Jiang followed behind, silent as usual, but with an air of gravity which I had not detected in him before. As we reached the staging area for the processional, he let out a gasp: a long line of men in full military dress stood circling the carriages, holding weapons and bristling with anticipation. I felt his surprise ripple through me, and felt a twinge of fear. Why was all this protection necessary? In what danger was I in meeting my own people?

Han stood apart from the scene, surveying his men, speaking orders calmly to the underlings who scurried to and fro. He turned at our approach, and our eyes met. In them I saw again the fleeting look of regret I had seen that first morning when he left my door. He bowed slightly, and in a voice of strength called out, "Make way, for the Emperor's Bride approaches!"

He spoke thus, and the line of men parted before me, leaving a path to the doorway of a red lacquered carriage, the Imperial flag flying from a staff high above. A eunuch in a simple wrapped garment held open the door, and Shiu Lin helped me step inside, following behind and shutting the door. The windows were covered with curtains which moved in the breeze, and as the wind caught the light fabric, I saw, standing just below the window, the top of the head of one of the eunuchs who would be carrying my pallet. Just then he looked up, and I was looking into the face of Chen, my beloved friend, who I had not seen since that day of horror when he was carried to the place of no return.

"Chen!" I let out a loud sound that came from the depths of my being, and moved to grab the ledge of the window, just as the carriage moved forward with a lurch.

"Mistress! Please sit down, you will be injured!" I heard Shiu Lin say as I hoisted myself up from the low bench and leaned through the window opening, almost catapulting out as the carriage moved.

"Chen! Chen! It is you! Oh Chen, we must speak!" The tears were pouring down my face as I choked out the words, I could not believe it was him, my friend, that I was seeing him again, at last. Chen looked up into my eyes. I saw tears there, tears that mirrored my own. But through his tears he smiled, a smile of such delight, of such beauty, that I smiled in return, and reached out to touch his hair, to stroke it will all the tenderness of a mother reunited with her long lost child.

"I will come to your chambers upon our return," he said. "I have completed my training and am to serve at the discretion of the Empress following her wedding." He had a twinkle in his eye, a look of happiness, a look that said 'We are together again, just as we planned.'

I sighed, and just then Shiu Lin tugged at my arm, pulling me back inside the carriage. I turned to her and did not say a word, but put my head into her lap and sobbed and sobbed for the lost dreams of Chen. The carriage continued on its journey, and after a time the sounds outside the window became louder and more raucous, voices rising and falling, sounds of activity swirling around us. I became quiet and listened, the sounds were so new. I had lived in a small village in the countryside, a peaceful existence. And the palace was a hushed place, with sounds echoing through the endless open courtyards and chambers, always seeming far away and diffuse. But these sounds were so close—life moving at a whirling pace, a city with so many souls all eager to be heard. I sat up and leaned forward to pull the curtain away from the window opening. What I saw astounded me, at first my eyes could not make sense of the jumble of activity. All manner of people moving about the streets, carrying baskets and bundles, pulling carts and pushing oxen, holding children, arms filled with laundry. People cried out, people laughed…and all seemed intent on completing their tasks, only partially aware of our processional streaming by. The buildings looked dirty and some crumbled into the street, which was pitted with holes and guttered by brown water. The eunuchs who carried me were constantly forced to side-step the pits and craters so as not to fall, spilling me and Shiu Lin into the street as well. I felt the bobbing and swaying of my carriage and it was as riding waves upon the sea.

Shiu Lin grabbed at my hand as the cacophony grew. Shouts filled the air, vendors selling hot nuts, tea, meat, rice, fruit and live ducks lined each side of the roadway now. We had come into the market, the place where life was lived, bought and sold. I held the curtain fast; I could not take my eyes from the sight of this riot of color and movement. Though I had become used to the quiet and order of palace life, a thrill stirred in me, goose bumps raised my flesh. People coming and going as they pleased, selling that which they had grown or raised or made, and buying that which they needed and wanted…no one to tell them what each moment of their lives must be. The energy and excitement surged in the air, and I felt sadness at the thought that I would never again be free.

Just then the carriage pulled alongside a long, low place, more like a shelter than a building, with a thatched roof and open sides with benches and tables arranged in rows along its length. The processional came to a halt. Outside this place a long line of dirty people—men, women and children—stood like docile animals, waiting for something. Each held a bowl or chopsticks in hand, each looked miserable in his own way. I scanned their faces; a few looked up but most kept their eyes trained upon the back of the shelter in expectation.

A bell sounded. At once, the line of people surged forth toward something I could not see. They pushed each other, men shoving women, women knocking into children, pushing forward into the shelter. Cries of desperation were heard, the wail of a child took on the high pitch of fear. Other people began streaming in from all sides, people who had not been standing in the line, but now sought to take advantage of the disorder provoked by the sounding of the bell. I stood half up in the carriage, putting my head through the window opening to better see the melee taking place. Fighting had broken out….some men had formed a knot of flailing limbs, grunts and shouts rose from their midst, and then someone was thrown from the throng and onto his head in the dirt. A small stream of blood oozed from a gash in his head, and he did not move. No one came to his aid as the crowd surged further into the shelter.

Uniformed men had now arrived and surrounded the building. Some moved forward and began hitting those in the crowd that they could reach with their long sticks. As they were hit the victims fell, holding heads or arms, crying or cursing or sitting silently in dejection. A woman, holding a baby, tried to move forward around the outer edge of the crowd. A man turned and pushed her, causing her to bump forcefully into one of the uniformed men. I saw him raise his stick, raise his arm high, and bring it down with force upon the upper shoulders of the woman, and she fell, her baby tumbling a few feet away from her in the dirt.

"Stop!!! Stop this at once!!!" The cry came from somewhere deep inside, the power and volume of my shout caused all eyes to turn toward the carriage, where I had flung open the door and jumped into the street. A stunned Shiu Lin still sat inside, clutching at the curtain. The eunuchs stood with mouths wide, unsure of what they were witnessing. And the military guards began looking toward their officers for direction, and none came. The officers were looking at me in surprise, Han among them. I saw him from the corner of my eye as I moved toward the baby that still lay on the gritty street.

All was quiet around me as I reached the tiny baby, and stooped to pick it up. Covered in dirty rags and the grime of street life, the baby was small and dark, and I could tell that its body was skin and bones beneath the cloth. I held it to the stiff bodice of my robe and felt it stir, moving its arms and legs a little. I stroked its head as I moved toward its mother, who lay sobbing on the ground. She lifted her torso up with one arm, the other arm hanging limp and useless by her side. I bent to her, holding the baby out to show her it was not injured, and placed it on her lap.

The crowd around us began to stir and awaken from its surprise. Han and a group of his men had come forward and now stood around us. He reached down and held my arm as I rose from the ground. "Mistress, you should not be outside your carriage unprotected. The guards must surround you at all times to ensure your safety," he said.

I jerked my arm away. "And what of the safety of this woman, and her child?" I asked, indicating she who still sat, babe in arms, upon the ground before us. "Who shall provide for that?" My cheeks were flushed with anger, my breath coming in gasps.

I leaned forward and held the woman's injured arm. "Can you stand?" I asked gently, and she nodded her head, and began to rise slowly, holding her child carefully, from the ground. Her tears had dried; she now looked up into my face in wonder. With my arm around her shoulders we walked forward and the crowd parted, opening a path into the shelter. "And why are you here?" I asked her, my voice barely above a whisper so as not to frighten her, or the child.

"Mistress, I come here each day for food for my child, and a little for myself," she answered shyly, not looking into my eyes, her humility not allowing such direct contact.

"Where is your home, your family? Do you have no husband to care for you? No parents, no siblings? Why must you come to this place, where there is such danger?"

The woman hung her head in sorrow, the weight of her cruel life pressed down upon her. "My husband has died, killed in the fighting in our village. I was with child, and my family, my parents were too poor to feed me. My husband's family took me in for a time, until the birth of my child; but when they knew the child to be merely female, they turned us out and so I came here to this city, where I beg each day for a few coins to bring here. I buy gruel for us and return to a small shelter I have made, near the river outside the gates, and wait for the next day, when I make my way here again, to receive of the Emperor's generosity," she answered.

I felt the anger rising at her story, the story of pain and suffering endured by so many countless women. "The Emperor's generosity? Do you not know that the Imperial stores hold ten times the food needed to feed the court and its people? Do you not know that much goes to waste, and that they only bring here what is left over from their feasts? And you say you have no food, nothing to give your hungry child? Many grow fat within the palace walls, I have seen so myself."

The woman looked at me with disbelief, trying to absorb my words. "But is not the Emperor of divine birth? Has he not been chosen to rule by the Gods themselves, does he not provide for his subjects to the best of his ability?" she asked, a puzzled look upon her face. "Could a God allow his people to starve, while he himself grows fat?"

I looked at her and saw her confusion, her pain. Moving my hand down her arm from her shoulder, I grasped her hand in mine, and as I did so, I slipped a large jeweled ring from my finger, and pressed it into her palm. Just as she looked down to see what she now held, Han forcefully pulled me apart from the woman, who continued moving forward toward the meager sustenance being ladled from large pots into their upheld bowls.

"Mistress, you should never speak thus! It is dangerous for you to be heard calling into question the policies of the Emperor. Do you not know this?" Han hissed into my ear.

I pulled my arm away, once again resisting him. "And I should *say nothing, while women and children starve?" I hissed back, hot with temper. "These people, all of them here, hungry…how many more, throughout the countryside? And is this why they revolt, to ask for a better way, to feed their wives and children?"*

*I felt a light touch upon my arm then, and I turned to see the face that was unmistakably the brother of my Master, as the familial resemblance was particularly strong between them. He smiled.*

*"Mistress, I am glad you have come. May I show you where we feed so many, so that they might live?" His voice was low but had an urgency, and his calm manner held a barely disguised intensity in check. I sensed his deep feeling immediately, it bore the frequency of anger, of righteous indignation at injustice. And then I grabbed his hand and brought it to my cheek, knowing it was just as Master Liu had said, that I had known him before, and that I would help him.*

*"Show me what you will," I said, and we walked together amongst the hungry, amongst those without hope, amongst my people.*

I take Baby out into the hallway, around and around on our well-worn path, while Alex calls her husband and tells him that no baby will be coming home. Did I actually just agree to take a baby? Just like that? I've taken longer to decide about buying a pair of shoes than I did to decide this, the most important decision I have ever made. Why was this so easy, why no fear or hesitation? I search inside myself for some shred of doubt, and find nothing, nothing but an open feeling, a spaciousness in my heart, clear and deep, a cloudless blue sky. In the moment I had said I would take her, I felt the most sane I have ever been in my life. An exquisite balance between head and heart, neither driven by emotion nor halted by thought, it was the most pure 'yes' I had said to anything, ever. A drink of pure water for my own parched and thirsty soul, I drank it down, yes, yes, to life. Yes to love, with no guarantees.

My hand shakes as I wait for my husband to pick up the phone. I have no idea what he will say, how he will react to this. I am scared because I know that no matter what he says, I have to bring this baby home. He picks up the phone, his voice traveling a ridiculously long distance across tiny wires. He says hello, and I have never been so happy to hear his voice. In the four days since he left me at the airport, I had lived a lifetime.

"What are you doing calling? I thought you said we wouldn't talk until your birthday, when you are in Hong Kong!" he says.

"Well..." my hands are shaking, my voice is shaking, my stomach is fluttering, how do I say this? "This trip is not going as planned..."

"What happened, is everything alright? What's wrong?" He is serious now, he can tell by some tone in my voice that I am barely hanging on, that I am about to cry.

"Alex doesn't want this baby."

I hear myself say it, out loud, and it sounds awful, like I've just spoken an obscenity. There is silence. "...doesn't want this baby" echoes across the miles between us. I know that he hears this instantaneously, but it is as if there is a lag before the full impact hits him.

Silence. Silence. Silence. The moment draws out, an eternal moment, living another lifetime in just this instant. This is where questions might spontaneously arise, like "why not?" or "what happened?" but there is nothing, no questions. Silence.

"We'll take her," he says.

A feeling I have never experienced before, a spontaneous, mindless joy, floods over me. I am sobbing and laughing and babbling into the phone, "she's beautiful, the sweetest thing ever, she's perfect for us, I know you will love her…"

"I already do," he says.

"But how? Why? How can you just say 'yes' like that, you haven't even seen her, you know nothing about her…."

"I know you. If you say this is the right thing, then it's the right thing. I trust you," he says, and it changes everything. This is trust bought with years of my life, years I sometimes thought were wasted. What is trust worth? In this case, a baby's life.

"Whatever else you do in life, it will never be better than this," I tell him, and it is done. There are logistics to be discussed, we don't even know if legally it's possible to do this; and yet, our relationship is complete in this moment, and there is a feeling that together, we can make this, or anything happen.

*I slept in the carriage through the return journey. I felt overwhelmed by what I had seen, as if I now carried an unseen*

burden, one that weighted my shoulders and hung upon my heart. What was to be done? Though I had seen, I did not know, and my sleep was anguished by the question.

When the processional arrived at the palace, Shiu Lin helped me from the carriage and held my arm as we walked toward my chambers. I spoke quietly with her, telling her of my feelings, and she murmured her agreement and sympathy with my thoughts. "But what is to be done?" I asked, knowing as I did so that she would not know, and she did not. But I knew from the teachings of Master and Madame, that even asking a question can set into motion those forces which would provide the answer.

In my chamber, we readied for bed. My hair was uncoiled and a light shift placed over my head, the fabric draped and billowed around me and I felt so free after the constriction of the official robe. Just as I lay upon my little bed, I heard quiet voices outside my door. Shiu Lin went to the curtain and pulled it aside to look out. She laughed and pulled her head back into the room, her face a happy smile, and said, "Come in!" as she held the curtain open, and there stood Chen, holding a bird in his outstretched hand. It was a dove, a beautiful white specimen, and it perched upon his finger with a dignified air.

"For you, Mistress!" said Chen, and I leaped from my bed and ran to embrace him, while the bird sat calmly and without fear at my approach.

"Chen, I am so glad you came as you said! I have worried so about you! I saw what happened, the day they took you away....Chen, I am so sorry, so sorry for the pain it has caused you, it is my fault!" Chen patted my arm, and tried to shush me. I went on, "It was my doing, I brought you here! You would be in the village and safe now, with Lo Ming, were it not for me insisting that you come." I spilled the words forth, and Chen waved them away with his free hand.

"Mistress, let us not speak of this now. It was not your fault, and what is done, is done; neither you nor I, nor God in heaven, can change it now," Chen said, stroking my cheek. "I come to you so that you may see and know that I am all right." I grabbed his hand and put it to my lips.

"Oh Chen, how did this happen? Why, why?" I whispered.

"We will speak of this another time. It is of little importance compared to what I have learned. I would not trade it for any treasure, or even my freedom...for now I know, that nothing can be taken which is of any value in heaven. The self lies beyond the evil acts of men....this self they cannot touch. And I want you to know, that which has grown in me is of the light!"

I felt such joy at his words, for now I knew our paths in spirit had not diverged, we flew toward the same God, the same heaven. I looked into his eyes, they glowed with life.

"And now I come to help you, for your wedding is to be two days hence, and the Emperor shall meet you on the eve before the ceremony, and you must be ready."

His words made me forget for a moment the events of the day. "My wedding is two days hence?" I asked, startled at the news. I had not thought it would be so soon, for I had received no word from the Emperor since my arrival in the palace.

"Indeed, it is to be so. The Emperor desired for the wedding to be held on the first auspicious day following your completion of the training. Madame has apprised him of your great and unrivaled progress in the practice, and he is understandably anxious to take his bride," Chen said, a rueful smile upon his face.

"But why should the Emperor wish to meet me before then,

will that not bring bad luck to our union?" I asked, puzzled by this break in protocol. Tradition held that a bride and groom not meet until the wedding ceremony, and already our union was unusual for the way in which the Emperor had chosen me for his bride.

"The Emperor will bestow upon you the Imperial Jewels which can only be handed from himself to his bride. They are to be worn at the ceremony, and will be yours to use to enhance your reign as Empress. The Imperial Jewels are said to have been brought from heaven by a dragon breathing fire, and possess the dragon's breath in crystallized form. They are said to make any woman who wears them more beautiful, and any man who touches them more wise. And thus they are for the Emperor and Empress alone, as this power has been divinely given for their use," Chen explained.

I thought of the ring I had passed just today into the hand of the woman at the market. A little piece of heaven brought to the hell she lived on earth. Chen had lifted his arm and was cooing at the bird.

"Chen, what of this bird? Have you brought it for me, I should love to keep it!" I held out my finger and the bird jumped from Chen's finger to mine, and gripped it tight. I laughed and cooed in delight at the bird, and its feathers ruffled and he returned my sounds.

"Yes, it is for you! It is one of a pair, and I possess the other…we can release them each day, and they shall meet in the sky!" Chen beamed with satisfaction, happy to give me his own precious gift.

"Oh Chen, I shall treasure it. And now, I must speak to you of what we have seen today, in the market. Surely you saw it too…the woman and her baby, so cruelly beaten and discarded." Chen listened with a grave expression, nodding and rubbing his chin.

"And what is to be done?" I asked the question again, for how could knowing of the plight of these people not lead to a desire to help?

"Mistress, I do not know. Let me ponder this question and what you have told me. We shall meet tomorrow morning. I shall release my bird and you shall release yours, just as the bells sound for morning prayer. After an interval we shall meet in the courtyard, and watch as they return to us, from the sky. I have spent many months training them thus, and look forward with delight to the fruition of my plan. And then I shall help you prepare for your meeting with the Emperor, and your elevation to Empress the next day."

"Oh Chen, I am so happy to have you with me. And thank you for my bird, for it represents to me the freedom I have lost, and the hope that I shall regain it again, someday."

And with that, Chen bade me good night. The next morning in the courtyard I stood next to him awaiting the birds' return from their release in the sky, and with eyes raised toward heaven, it came to me, what could be done.

The white wings of the doves glowed against the blue background of sky, they soared above our heads, and as they neared, I saw attached to each a small pouch, used to transport messages across the land.

And I knew what could be done....

The palace filled with activity. Later that morning, I could hear people scurrying about, moving to and fro in the courtyard outside my chambers. Shiu Lin helped me to dress, tying the sash of a crimson robe embroidered with hundreds of tiny gold bumble bees. I loved this robe, and kept running my hands over the stitches that formed the bodies of the insects. The gown had been made especially for this day, the day before the wedding, when there would be official functions and ritual ceremonies to attend.

When she had finished my coiffure, Shiu Lin pressed a thin piece of paper into the palm of my hand. "And what is this?" I asked.

"It is from Madame," she replied. "She asked that I give it to you before you are wed. But you are not to read it until tonight, just before you sleep."

I tucked the small folded paper into the sleeve of my gown and prepared to leave my chambers for the temple, where a ceremony would be held asking for blessings to be bestowed upon the future bride of the Emperor. I pulled back the doorway curtain, and with a start, stepped backward in surprise on to the feet of Shiu Lin, who followed closely behind. I had been expecting to see Jiang as usual at his post. Instead, Han stood beside my door, straight and tall, his military bearing impressive and far superior to that of Jiang. I thought then, here is a warrior, and Jiang is but a soldier; the two are like different species of men.

"Mistress, I have come to accompany you to the temple," Han said evenly, not betraying a hint of emotion.

"You, to accompany me? But what of Jiang, can he not do this slight duty? Or Shiu Lin, she is right here. There is no need for you to trouble yourself, it is only a short distance," I said, waving Shiu Lin forward.

"Mistress, on this important day I should like to have the honor of escorting you to your official engagements. I have dismissed Jiang, and ask Shiu Lin to be at her leisure as well," he said, hesitating a little.

I looked at Shiu Lin. Her expression gave away little of her thoughts, though I knew she must note the unusual nature of Han's actions. "Mistress, I shall await you in your chambers," she said, and bowed slightly as she let the curtain drop before her.

I stood alone with Han, on the threshold. Looking into his face

I could see little to tell me of what lay behind his request. Was he angry with me for my actions in the market yesterday; was he seeking a chance to chastise me? Or perhaps inform me of some type of punishment I may receive for speaking as I had? Already Shiu Lin had informed me that many in the palace were talking of the events of the day before, especially the concubines and courtesans who wished to see me stumble. The consensus among them had been that my behavior was grossly out of line with official decorum, and with societal mores against women acting independently. Shiu Lin had shared with me some of the spiteful things that she had overheard, but had not done so to hurt me. She had wanted me to beware, to caution me that I was being closely watched. This I knew, but chose to ignore; for there seemed far more important things to consider than my reputation amongst such as these.

"Shall we go then?" I asked softly. Han nodded, and we began walking across the courtyard toward the temple pavilion. During the walk, Han spoke of trivial things, the weather this day, the many activities taking place in the palace, his many duties associated with his post.

I was perplexed. If he was not angry, or had no particular reason to speak to me, why had he requested to escort me? We reached the temple, which was filling rapidly with members of the court and the monks. We entered the rear door where I was shown to a seat of honor upon the dais.

Han remained standing at the door, and did not accompany me inside. "I will be here waiting for you when the ceremony concludes," he said, and as I sat waiting, looking out at the sea of faces filling the benches before me, I thought of him standing there, a warrior with nothing to fight for.

Chanting began, incense was lit and the temple became filled with the smoky sweet smell and grew warm with so many bodies pressed together. All eyes were upon me, I could not escape the attention of so many minds projecting toward me. As the chanting swelled and the incense swirled, the mass of faces began to whirl before me. It was as if I could sense the thought and intent of each person present, and each soul wanted something from me...the feeling was of being grabbed and pulled, pulled under, as a drowning person pulls under the one who has come to save him. I put my hand to my head, what do they want?

The ceremony dragged on, the chanting beat in my ears and the incense made me nauseous. When the prayers began for the Emperor, for the life of the Emperor, for his health and longevity, I saw a black noxious cloud form, and it began to engulf me in its sinister gloom.

I felt I was falling, but I was stumbling from my chair, moving toward a door, any door, through which I might escape. The pounding would not stop, I could not see, and how I reached the door I do not know; but suddenly, the light and air poured through an opening and I stood blinking and choking in front of Han, whose face went white as he reached for my arm and pulled me through, the door slamming shut behind me.

I fell into his arms, unable to stand. He lifted me, easily carrying my dead weight swiftly and with purpose away from the temple. I must have lost consciousness in those minutes, as the next thing I remember is being placed gently upon the grass, and looking up into the boughs of an ancient pine tree which played with the sunlight streaming through its branches. I fell into sleep; for how long I do not know. When I awoke Han sat just beside me, still and grave. The sun was lower behind the pine trees' branches, and I felt that I had been somewhere far away and would never again be the same *as I was before.*

*"Where am I?" I asked, struggling to sit upright, looking around me. Behind me stood the grove of pine, ancient and noble. Before me was a pool of dark water, ringed with blooming water lilies, reflecting their blossoms in its depths. Butterflies played at the edges of the water and bees hurried from blossom to blossom. On the far side of the pool stood a lovely pagoda, its graceful lines echoing its own reflection. I felt peace, a peace I had not known since my days in the forest near my village, when Chen and I would pick berries and mushrooms, happily losing ourselves in the beauty of nature.*

*"You have come to Black Dragon Pool, Mistress. It is to be yours...this reflecting pool has been reserved for the Empress since ancient times, and as you will become Empress tomorrow upon your marriage, you may enjoy its peace and tranquility now, when it appears you so badly need it," said Han.*

*"I shall become Empress tomorrow," I repeated, and at those words the fear and nausea gripped me again, and I remembered what had happened in the temple.*

*I stood up abruptly. "I cannot do it," I said, looking Han full in the face.*

*Han jumped up, alarmed. "You cannot do it? But, what do you mean?"*

*"I cannot become Empress," I said, and moved to go past him. As I did so, I wavered and lost my balance, and crumpled down once again to the soft grass, still weak and exhausted. Han steadied me, holding my arm and guiding me back so that I lay upon the ground, the crimson gown pooled out around me.*

*"You must become Empress, it is too late to change that. The Emperor would not take kindly to being jilted by his chosen bride,*

of that I can assure you. And what could you be thinking, to want to turn aside this honor?" Han asked. He reached forward and pushed aside a lock of hair from my forehead which had escaped my coiffure. His fingers brushed my skin and I felt an energy linger there; a warmth, a tenderness.

"In the temple, I saw a black cloud descend upon me. If I become Empress, I will not survive it, I will not survive," I answered, shivering from the remembrance of the darkness in that cloud.

Han was silent for a moment, carefully considering my words. "But of course, as Empress you will have everything necessary to your well-being at your disposal," Han said, trying to reassure me. "You are overwhelmed with the enormity of the wedding preparations now, but that will subside. And besides, I shall help you, should you need anything, anything at all."

His face showed an unmistakable sincerity, a softness toward me which took me by surprise. "You shall help me? But why? Why should you trouble yourself with my needs?" I asked, urgently, grabbing his hand where it lay in the grass before me. "And why should you choose to accompany me today?" His hand was dry and warm, and I felt him jerk slightly at my touch, not expecting it to come. Han looked at me with luminous eyes as I held his hand there, on my lap, not letting go.

"Mistress," he began. "What happened yesterday, in the market...."

"Yes, yes I know; you are angry with me for my words, for my bold usurpation of authority!" I interrupted him, eager to explain. "But you must know, I did not think ...I merely acted with an instinct of care for the woman I saw there, with the child."

"But that is just it!" Han cried. "You acted, not from tradition or with a thought for acceptable behavior. You acted from the heart, *and with courage. And in that moment, I thought of you as I have never thought of a woman before: I saw you as a warrior, a kindred spirit to my own. And I thought what a fine Empress you would make, and vowed to be in your service."*

I was struck silent at his words. A man such as Han, pledged to my service? But what could this mean? How could he protect me, in what way could he help? I was to be married tomorrow, and had seen the black cloud descend; and yet Han was reassuring me that all would be well.

I lifted my head to reply and saw his face before me, so close I could feel his breath upon my cheek. "We must go back now," he said. "You are expected in the Emperor's chambers."

Han brought his lips to mine and gently pressed them there, and I did not move. My heart pounded in my chest, and all else was silence.

I want to call Antoinette, but I didn't even bring her number; why would I call her from China? But now I want to get her insight on these strange events, events that will change my life, one way or another. Baby is asleep and Alex is in bed, so I tell her I am going to make a phone call, and go to the lobby where I can have some privacy.

The week before I left, I had talked to Antoinette, and she had reminded me to take her phone number with me. Why had I not done it? I am standing in a phone booth, wondering how to get her number, when I see it, in my mind's eye: her number right there, and I pick up the phone and dial, and within moments she is on the other end of the line.

I tell her, "Oh, Antoinette, you are not going to believe this..." and I begin explaining how this trip has become an incredible journey.

"She asked me to take the baby," I finally say.

There is silence on the other end of the line. I wait, and become aware that this is not the silence of surprise, but that she is praying. I get the feeling she has been waiting for this.

"And what did you say?" she finally asks, quietly, expectantly.

"I said I would. I agreed to take her," I answer, and I hear her let out her breath on the other end, a great sigh. "Oh, God," she says. "Remember when I asked you a few weeks ago if you wanted me to come on this trip with you? I knew something of significance was going to happen, I just didn't know what."

It was true. She had offered to come, and it had seemed so strange to me at the time. Antoinette did not know Alex at all, and this trip really wasn't about me. She didn't explain why she felt she should come, and the issue was dropped and we didn't speak of it again, until now. And now I wonder, what had she known, what did she see?

"Antoinette, that's not all; I've been having dreams, strange dreams while I've been here, almost every night. I can't put my finger on it, but these dreams are all about China—maybe it's connected somehow".

"Have you written them down?" she asks. I tell her I have written some, but since Alex told me she didn't want the baby, I haven't been able to. "Write them down, and call me back if you can," she says, and I agree to call her back;

just talking to her has made me feel much better. But one thing she said sticks in my mind and causes concern: she told me to pray for protection, for myself and for Baby, until we are safely home, until we are out of China.

That night I lay in bed in the darkened room. My mind leaps from thought to thought, from mundane concerns about diapers and bottles and cribs, to sublime visions of our new family unit. My friends and family will think I'm totally nuts—I go to China and bring back a baby! No one would be expecting this, I wasn't even expecting this. Am I crazy? Wouldn't a normal person have some doubts, some hesitation? But I have none.

I want to meditate, to see if any insight will come. Breathing deeply and sinking deeper into my self, into the calm center I have learned how to find, into my heart. I can feel it beating its steady rhythm, never failing me, always there to be found. Breathing, breathing, I let go of the rim of consciousness, I fall in…into that secret place, where everything is known.

Something emerges, out of the darkness, I see her shining as she comes forward, and she is holding something in her arms. It is the Virgin Mary, and she is holding a child in her arms. Beside her stands my own mother, smiling with uncontained delight. They are looking at me, and Mary moves forward, she hands the child to me. She hands the child to me, and I look down and it is Baby, the child is Baby, and Mary has handed her to me. I look up, into the Mother's eyes, and she lifts her arms once again and places a wreath of white flowers upon my head. And she speaks.

I am giving her to you, she says. I am giving this blessed child to you.

The image fades and I am stunned with happiness; I am in awe at what I have seen. My mother has been dead these past six years, for six years I have been without her. And now she has come to my inner sight, to comfort me, to show me that all is well, and to confirm that no more questions need to be asked.

When we reached my chamber doorway, the sun had slipped below the palace walls, splashing pink and crimson red into the sky as it sank. Shiu Lin jumped up when I entered; she had obviously been waiting anxiously for my return.

"Mistress, where have you been?" she cried. "All have inquired of your whereabouts this day! You have missed important events, and I have been saying you were taken ill. Since your mysterious disappearance from the temple this morning I have been sick with worry, you are to meet the Emperor tonight! We must prepare, look at your gown!" Shiu Lin held the stained and wrinkled fabric in her hands, and looked quizzically up at me. "Mistress...." Shiu Lin did not finish, but looked from my face to the dress and back again, a look of realization dawning on her face. She dropped the dress and turned quickly away, saying, "We must ready you for your audience with your future husband," in a voice that was strange and thick.

Shiu Lin brought forth a gown of royal purple, adorned with a sash of yellow silk. The neck was high and the bodice unadorned, so as to showcase the Imperial jewels when they were bestowed upon me by the Emperor. The dress was to be merely a canvas for the jewels, and yet I loved its simple lines, the austerity of its cut. When I looked into the reflecting glass that Shiu Lin held before me as she arranged my hair, I thought the sharp outline of the dress perfectly complemented a kind of sharpness I now saw in my own features, a distinctness that had not been present before. It was as if I had suddenly been brought into focus.

I brought the glass down and looked up at Shiu Lin. "There is much I need to tell you," I said, speaking for the first time since entering the chambers. I turned to her and held her hand, and she kneeled before me and put her arms around my waist, hiding her face from me. "Do not say, Mistress, do not say! For it is clear to see that you have succeeded in taming a dragon," she said.

"Shiu Lin, it is my heart which has been tamed. We shall speak more upon my return this evening," I said, patting her soft cheek and wiping a tear that had fallen there.

We stood then and embraced, and left the chamber, followed by Jiang. As we walked in silence, I centered my breath as Master had taught; I sought to calm the nerves that had suddenly come, an unease about this encounter with the Emperor. My breath came in rhythm with my steps, I walked slowly and deliberately.

What awaited me? I remembered the Emperor as I had seen him in the fields that day, high on the back of a black steed, but could not recall his face. I breathed more deeply, and cleared my thoughts. And there, after a time, was my Master's face before my mind's eye, though I was walking and looking with my physical eyes. Never had I achieved this dual sight before, the inner and outer worlds perceived simultaneously. It felt strange, but also familiar, as if this perception had always been there, on the edges of my awareness, and I had just not noticed.

*My Master before me smiled as always. "Master, what awaits me?" I asked in thought, and heard in answer, "The fate which you choose." And before I could ask him to clarify, my concentration was broken by the commotion caused by our arrival at the gate of the Emperor's pavilion, and I lost his image in the confusion of activity. The heavy gates were swung open and we entered a city within a city, the Emperor's domain, where all revolved around him and acted at his command.*

*A sedan chair appeared before me, and Shiu Lin helped me to step into it, and it was lifted by two large men, and they began to carry me forward through the street. It was dark, and I could make out only the shapes of buildings and things, and see a few faces illuminated by torchlight. We moved toward a very tall pavilion in the distance, its red roof visible even in the twilight. Its hulking mass dominated everything around it, making shadows of the other structures within the compound. When we finally reached its entrance I was helped down by two elaborately dressed women, both beautiful with a terrible aloofness, and neither spoke to me while they led me into the pavilion. I got the sudden impression that they did not like me, though I had not seen either of them before. We walked in silence down a wide corridor, at the end of which was a golden door, embossed with the shapes of all manner of symbols, animals and dragons. The doors were three times as tall as any man, and with difficulty they were swung open, and we stood in the entrance to a hall that was so large it was as if without beginning or end.*

*In the center stood a platform, with many steps leading to a high golden throne. The women indicated I was to walk forward, toward this platform, and toward a figure I could see sitting there, though I could not make out the features of the one on high. I came* nearer and nearer the steps, and when I reached them began to climb, not looking up, holding my gown aloft, watching each step and carefully placing my foot upon it. I did not count the steps, though it seemed an eternity passed before I reached the last and final one beyond which there were no more. I placed my feet together on the level platform, and letting my skirt drop I looked up into the face of the one who sat upon the throne.

I did not bow. I said nothing as I looked into his face. It was a face that may be called handsome, and youthful, when in repose. But my heart saw something else, even as he spoke words of warmth and welcome, and held out a large tray with jewels of every imaginable type arrayed upon it. An attendant slipped a large emerald necklace over my head, the heavy pendant fell upon my bosom, and I listened as he spoke of the rarity of the gem and his pleasure at giving it to his bride.

I reached up, to touch the gem. Lifting it away from my chest, I looked into its depths, its surface finely cut to create a fire inside the stone. Life was there, encased inside the rock, it moved and sparkled, looking for a way out of its prison. And then I saw a spark of this living fire jump across the gap between its heart and mine. It lodged there, deep within my heart, and the spark started a fire where before had been darkness.

In shock and surprise, I looked up to see if the Emperor had witnessed this extraordinary happening, but he had not. He continued speaking of the jewels as if they were mere objects, possessions, when I knew now they contained mineral fire, life essence. I closed my fist around the stone and held it to my breast, to guard it, to keep it close. I did not wish the Emperor's eyes to fall upon it again, for he had no sight for such things. I felt pity as I said, "Sir, I thank you for the gift of these gems in honor of our union in matrimony," and he nodded, pleased.

"And so tomorrow...we shall be wed," he said, feigning a casual tone. "You shall be mine."

The hair on the back of my neck rose and bristled at his words. How could I be 'his'? How could one human being possess another? He saw the jewels, which contained living essence, as possessions, devoid of life; he saw human beings, which contain the God force, as possessions, also. One can only belong to another through love, and we had no love between us.

"We shall be wed," I repeated his words back to him. "But surely His Highness already owns enough 'things'?" The emperor lifted his eyes in surprise, searching mine for evidence of impertinence. I continued, "Can we not be joined for a greater purpose than to satisfy passing desire?"

The Emperor sat up with a start. The expression on his face went from surprise to quickly flashed anger, and on to a searching, and finally, a deep interest held there. He looked straight at me, his eyes shallow and opaque. Here was a challenge, in a life devoid of personal challenges, and I could see him decide to take it up, rather than to smash it.

"And what might that 'greater purpose' be?" he posed lightly, trying to appear amused in effort to hide the true interest beneath. "Is not bringing forth the future rulers of China great enough?" The Emperor seemed to be trying to banter, to indulge my naiveté, to undermine the seriousness of my statement with cynical amusement.

"Yes," I answered, "such is an important task. And yet, I see so much more..." The Emperor gave a slight guffaw before recomposing himself. I ignored this evidence of his arrogance and went on, "There are people suffering in this land, are there not? Could we not join together in an effort to change this, if even a little?"

The Emperor stifled another small laugh, and then sighed, a deep breath of resignation. "There have always been, and shall always be, those in poverty, those who suffer; and those who would not respect my rule do not deserve my assistance."

His fatalistic philosophy completely absolved him of responsibility for those who suffered under his rule. It has always been....it shall always be....what was there to be done, if this was so? But it was a selective fatalism, and did not determine his own behavior; for he had stated that his assistance to his subjects depended upon their unquestioning acceptance of his dictates, not upon his obligations to them as Emperor.

"We do what we can," the Emperor quickly added. "But my charge is to protect the Imperial lineage, first and foremost. It is ordained by the Gods." His irritation mounted as he strove to justify his position.

I said nothing as I stood there before him. I thought of what he had said, and understood; the Emperor cared for nothing but himself, his power. It was as Madame had said, he was not wise; but perhaps if, as Madame had taught, I hold the highest intent in mind, he will begin to see....

I thought of the unity of all things, and saw in my mind the people of China, prosperous and free. I saw the Emperor ruling with love and compassion for his people. With these thoughts held in my mind I spoke, "Certainly your highness may ordain what you wish in your kingdom, just as the Gods have ordained you ruler of it."

The look he gave me then, as he took my hand to lead me away, was one of such passive helplessness, I almost reached out to embrace him in reassurance that his power indeed lay within. But I said nothing, and descended the stairs to return to my chambers one last time, before being married and brought to my quarters here, *within the Emperor's domain.*

*Walking across the courtyard on the way back, I felt something slip down from my sleeve and brush my hand. It was the paper which Shiu Lin had pressed upon me, from Madame, which I had all but forgotten. She had instructed me to read it tonight, just before sleep, the last sleep before I became Empress. But I opened the thin paper then, and read by the light of the torch held by Jiang, written in beautiful calligraphy which is poetry in itself: "Know in your heart that love conquers all."*

*I folded the paper and held it clenched in my hand. Closing my eyes, I said a prayer that my heart open to love. And I saw the flames that had been ignited by the gem spark flare up, and up, until all within was light, heat and warmth, and all dross was burned away in the purity of that fire.*

*And I vowed then to love the Emperor, to love the potential in him for good, so as to conquer that ignorance which breeds fear and destruction, and keeps the suffering immobile in a hell of their own making.*

*The day of the wedding dawned clear and bright. The light of early morning had a magical quality, making it seem as if the world had begun anew in the night. I sat in my little garden for the last time and in my reverie, I thought of Han and the reflecting pool. I could see again how the image of his face swam on the surface as we both peered into the black depths, just before our time there together had ended. Could it have been just yesterday? Time had become a stranger to me, a concept I could no longer hold in my mind. Since my experience in the temple, it had stopped, sped up, overlapped and expanded, as if time itself was now driven by my consciousness, rather than my* awareness being confined by it. Time no longer held me prisoner.

The wedding ceremony was to be a day-long affair, with my official installation as Empress in the evening at its close. There would be a magnificent feast, and much revelry. And yet I felt not joyous but filled with a grave acceptance of this fate. For my meeting with the Emperor last evening had impressed upon me the difficulty of the task which awaited, to open a closed mind, to reach a cold heart. I felt the weight of this burden, which I had chosen for myself.

With my friend Shiu Lin, I prepared to become Empress. I had asked her to pray with me, and grabbed her hands and pulled her to me when she entered the garden to fetch me to dress. Together we stood, and called out to our God for assistance; not the Gods of which the Emperor spoke, the many Gods who ordained his rule, but the one true God, the God of all, he who loved all his children as equals, not one above the others.

Shiu Lin told me she saw a column of light descend to surround us, and gold crosses had rained down from the air. Her spiritual sight was masterful, and had been honed through many years of practice in the mystical arts, work she had done under the gentle guidance of Madame. And though in that moment of my distress I could not see that of which she spoke, I felt something rise in me then, some force that could not be denied, and I dropped Shiu Lin's hands and turned to run from the garden, my hair uncoiled and trailing, Shiu Lin's voice pleading my return.

I ran to the courtyard, Jiang was not at his post, but I was far past my chambers before I even realized that I had left unimpeded by my guard. Flying through the streets and corridors in my simple white gown, no one realized it was I who was to be Empress today, and no one tried to stop me. I ran and ran for an eternity, my breath coming in jagged gasps, warmth rising in my chest, my heart about to burst. I thought of how I used to run, in the fields near my home, and the freedom it was, the freedom I had lost.

Sobs erupted in short bursts; I felt as if I might break from their force, or suffocate from the tight constriction of my throat. Please, please help me, help me, I asked, over and over again, of whom I do not know. My prayers were birds that beat their wings against the sky, trying to get to heaven, straining desperately to reach the One.

Finally I reached the gate which led to the garden of Black Dragon Pool, a secluded place where no one came, where no one ever came to witness the great beauty in which it lay. Beyond the gate something of priceless value awaited, and I must reach that spot where I might be saved. Heaving open the heavy black lacquered gate, I fell inside and lay for a moment, spent with exhaustion. The wind moved gently through the trees, it sang to me of peace. I felt my breathing slow and my heart become calm as it caressed my skin and tickled the grass on which I lay. I lifted my head slowly, the reflecting pool was just ahead, not far away, I must go there, I must find an answer in its depths.

I have no memory of walking toward the water, but at once I was there, as if transported by my wish alone. On my knees at its lip, I leaned over and parted the tall grass at its edge. I saw a reflection rippling there, a face; but it was not mine! My mind froze in confusion.

I could not make sense of what I was seeing. I looked hard and concentrated to bring the vision into focus. A face...it was...it looked like...and the moment I realized my prayers had been answered, I whipped around sharply, and there behind me, peering into the pool, stood Han.

He did not speak. But as I moved toward him, as I went to him, I could hear his thoughts; I could hear the words that poured from his heart. I never knew such sounds existed, such words of beauty and love and tenderness. They rippled over me, through me, around me until I was bathed in the sound of love. When finally I spoke to him, my words were the echo of those silent and holy declarations.

The void of his silence gave birth to a passionate force within me. It rose up, a fiery river, up my spine, up and up to the crown of my head, where it plumed out and gushed forth, enveloping us both in its energy. We could not escape, we did not want to, for to deny this was to deny creation itself, the beautiful, the holy. I did not deny it, but accepted it, danced with it in the morning light, and let my pain be its fuel, which it burned with hungry delight. And as we spiraled upward, together before God, I knew that in this was perfection, in this was truth. I prayed for all good that could come from an act of pure love, and was answered with a taste of heaven.

When we left that place, hand in hand until we reached the heavy black gate which led to the world, we peered again together into the depths of the reflecting pool, and I noticed floating in the center, a lotus.

It had not been there before, but now had opened and spread its petals to the sun. A blessing, a pure white reflection of the divine, it floated there serene and unassailable, forever perfect.

The next morning, neither Alex nor Baby is awake when I rise from bed, dress, and go to the hotel restaurant in search of breakfast, and coffee. For the first time in two days I am hungry, and I fill my plate with eggs, bacon, bread and fruit from the buffet and sit alone at a small table. Everything tastes so good, like I am eating for the first time, but it is really just that I'm eating for the first time while being happy.

And I am, happy. The thought of bringing Baby home fills me with curious delight, with exhilaration, and all night I was in and out of sleep, thinking about Baby, how my life would change, how I had not known before how much I wanted it to change. It wasn't until I had said that I would take Baby that I realized how much I wanted her. I had taken a leap of faith, and my heart had opened up like a parachute, and I had made a safe landing, firm on solid ground.

A pure thing, happening by chance or by grace, had taken me by surprise and run around my defenses. I would have to give her everything, my whole self, and what would that be like? Always before, in matters of love, I had held back, been cautious; not giving to the full extent seemed wise and prudent, the smart thing to do. Now it seemed stunted and sad. The longing I had always had was for this, this one pure thing. Whatever happened now, whether she came to me or not, I would always have that moment, the one moment I had said Yes and meant it with my entire being.

I still could not believe it, but oh…if the planets and stars whirled into alignment, if all obstacles crumbled, if there was a God, a benevolent God, and Baby were to be mine, the life we could live together would be a different kind of life than I had ever known.

I finish my breakfast and walk slowly across the lobby, engrossed in thought. It crosses my mind that many obstacles still remain and that the odds are against all the pieces of this puzzle falling into place. And yet I feel so strongly, so surely that it is done, that I will have Baby, and that no matter what arises she must be with me.

I glance at my watch, I have been gone a long time, almost two hours now, I had not realized. Going up in the elevator I wonder how Baby slept, is she awake yet? I cannot wait to see her again, to spend another day getting to know her, the baby that is going to be my child.

Letting myself into the room, I know immediately that something has changed. I open the door and feel the bustling energy in the room, see that the drapes have been pulled back to let in the morning light, the beds have been made and Alex is moving around purposefully, tidying up her belongings. Both she and Baby are dressed, and Baby is sitting on a blanket on the floor, playing with a rattle. Something in the way Alex is moving, something in the energy, something even in the cute outfit she has put on Baby tells me, last night was a dream, a foolish fantasy.

I stand just inside the doorway, reluctant to enter, a dread rising up and with it the force of self-recriminating thoughts, you-idiot-how-could-you-have-let-yourself-want-this-how-could-you-have-thought-this-could-really-happen-my-god-you-actually-let-yourself-believe-you-would-get-this-child-you-let-yourself-love-her unleashed in my mind.

Alex turns and sees me there, "Oh, I'm glad you're back!" she says, cheerfully, terrible in her cheerfulness. I wish she was a little bit sheepish, it would at least allow me to manufacture some compassion for her. But no, not to be, even that is taken from me, with the terrible cheerfulness.

"I've been up for a while now, and I can't believe it, I feel so much better today! You know…(Why do I already know what she is going to say? Terrible knowing)…I don't know why I was feeling like I couldn't take this baby. Today, I feel like I can do it!"

As if nothing had happened. As if she had not asked me to take this baby, to change my life, to commit in an instant. As if I had not said yes.

As if she were not my child.

"But I want to try it for today and see what happens. It doesn't mean that I'll definitely keep her."

She wants to try it for today, and see what happens. She wants to try it…what, what in God's name could she be thinking? So if it doesn't feel right today, I suppose she'll let me know tonight, so I can go through another night of emotional upheaval, and then the next morning, maybe she'll feel better again…and on and on. Every alarm bell in my psyche is clanging, be careful, be careful. Don't even give off a whiff of resistance to this, and don't try to reason with insanity.

I take a deep gulp of air, calm down, calm down. Some instinct takes over and I hear myself saying, "Well, I'm glad you're feeling better, that's great." Deep breath. I smile and wave at Baby, playing happily on the ground.

"I know, it is amazing. It's like I'm a different person! I guess all I needed was a good night's sleep," she exclaims.

I guess. She continues to prattle on, something— something about what to do today or eating breakfast or something. I'm not listening, deep in counsel with myself.

What to do? There is only one option, I am so deflated and depleted right now that I have to get out.

"Alex, I just have to say…..I'm feeling pretty drained after all this. Last night was emotional for me, I mean…my husband and I made plans to change our lives! And now all of it is in doubt, so I just need to step back, step away. You and the baby need some time to bond, and I can't just keep taking care of her for you. I can't stay engaged, wondering if you are going to want the baby or not want the baby. You need to decide. I'm going to spend the day by myself and let you be with her."

Alex said that she understood. It is odd, chilling, how easily she has accepted her own change of mind. I would say change of heart, but I am certain now, that her heart still remains closed. I am certain because of the cavalier way she is playing with our lives.

I start moving around the room, putting on my running clothes, getting my backpack together: books, notebook, pen. I can't wait to get out. Baby keeps trying to get my attention; I can't even look at her. It breaks my heart. I am abandoning her, leaving her with this woman who is not even sure that she wants her.

On the way out of the hotel I stash my backpack in the office off the lobby. Emerging into the hazy sunlight, into the dust and noise of the city, I am relieved. I feel relieved of an oppressive burden, the desires and dreams I had been nurturing before I walked back into the room this morning. Those dreams had evaporated, burned away with Alex's words.

All that remains is a distilled essence of love, love for that baby. I start running along the promenade, beside the river, people staring, turning their heads as I pass by. I don't care, I just want to run and run and run, to go deeply into that essence of love.

Oh, God, please, please, let her go to the right place, please let her be happy. I am sobbing, tears welling into my eyes so that it is hard to see, what could I do? I am powerless; I have never felt so completely at the mercy of events. There is something I can do, someone I can love, and will I be allowed to? My heart is burning, I can feel the heat rise up in my chest, and a band grips and tightens there, making it hard to breathe.

I am running, running to free myself from this pain, from the limitations of my fear, running to put my mind at ease, in order. Thoughts bubble up from the depths, clearing a path through the confusion in my mind. Old snatches of prayers, words of wisdom, something to hang onto: Make me a channel of your peace *I plead*; Faith can move mountains *I will move mountains, to bring you to me*; We are *all one there is nothing that exists that is not yours*.

Beautiful words, words of comfort. One of my favorite poems comes, whole and shining, a Rilke poem that I had memorized during another searing experience, long ago,

> *Whom will you cry to, heart? More and more lonely,*
> *Your path struggles on through incomprehensible*
> *Mankind. All the more futile perhaps*
> *For keeping to its direction,*
> *Keeping on toward the future,*
> *Toward what has been lost.*

*Once. You lamented? What was it? A fallen berry*
*Of jubilation, unripe.*

*But now the whole tree of my jubilation*
*Is breaking, in the storm it is breaking, my slow tree of joy.*
*Loveliest in my invisible landscape, you that made me more*
*known*
*To the invisible angels.*

I run for miles with the Rilke poem, he understood so completely. My slow tree of joy is breaking, my fallen berry of jubilation, unripe. My pain starts to ebb in the flow of his words, in the camaraderie of his voice. I wonder about the invisible angels, what do they do? Perhaps love attracts them, like moths to a flame. If that is true, then they must be around me now.

With that thought I feel a chill run the length of my body, the breath of angels rippling across my skin. I slow down, stop running, there is nothing to run from, and nothing to run to. I will just float on the waves of life for awhile, and see what happens.

*From that moment on, the lotus was always with me. It floated above my head, slowly rotating, emitting light from its center and sparkling dust from its petals. I could see it there, whenever I chose to turn my attention inward towards it. Even during the wedding ceremony, and throughout my royal ascension to Empress, it rotated there, a source of comfort and strength, a secret talisman which conferred upon me a protection from all things not of love.*

*Much of that day passed as a blur, for the lotus which was born* of the love which Han and I had shared held my attention as the activity swirled around me. A wedding, but it was not mine…I had been joined to something beyond this world in the garden of the reflecting pool. An ascension to Empress, but it was an illusion, for I had already been elevated in the realm of spirit. These were formalities, games only, meaning nothing without the concomitant soul experience. And no one else seemed to notice that the transformation in me had already taken place.

But the "I" which was joined to the Emperor, the "I" which received the title Empress, spoke the vows and accepted the crown, that "I" was only fulfilling a duty, was only following the rules of that game which had been laid down. The fullness of my self rested in an expanded awareness of life and light beyond this world, beyond what is readily seen. And there I rested, in peace.

At the end of the day of revelry and ceremony, the Emperor and I were to retreat into his chambers to consummate our union. Even this did not disturb me, for the presence of the white lotus would ensure my protection, would ensure that only that which was of love could approach. For that was all I would accept.

The Emperor enjoyed the way that I spoke. It was for this reason that our first night together passed in harmony despite the lack of consummation. In his stately chambers, upon the luxurious platform hung with silks and tapestries that was his bed, we talked far into the night, until the dawn began to appear at the windows. I made him laugh a little, and at this he was surprised. For generally the Emperor was of a serious nature, and held little to be of humor in the world. At times when he spoke, the muscles at the side of his mouth would draw tight, bringing the lips into a grimace, involuntarily and against his will, exposing the inner turmoil of his existence.

He was a learned man, and his education in books and science was vast. The Emperor was surprised, and pleasantly so, to learn that first evening that I had been educated as well, at the knee of my beloved father, and that I could speak with him about literature and history, that I knew geography and a little science as well. He began excitedly and proudly to tell me of his experimentation in alchemy and medicine, for this was his true interest. The Emperor became truly animated when he spoke of the potions and combinations of plants which had produced unexpected results, and of his forays into surgical techniques and healing remedies. His teacher had been a court doctor who was revered throughout the kingdom for his unorthodox and successful healing methods, and as a young boy, the Emperor would watch as he attended his patients, and over time, the interest grew into a passion. It was interesting, and I followed his explanations, asking questions and making comments, some of which spurred him to new flights of thought and query.

As dawn crept into the windows, he said "I have never known a woman such as you," and left me with a kiss on the cheek, to begin another day of performing duties which did not interest him, but which maintained the loneliness of his sterile power.

That first morning in my expansive new chambers, Shiu Lin rushed excitedly into my bedroom, "Mistress! You are to receive a visitor today, and you shall be quite pleased! We must dress, for the visitor will be here very soon." She opened the window curtains with a flourish and bright sunshine flooded the room.

"But Shiu Lin, will you not tell me whom to expect?" I asked playfully, knowing that she was delighting in keeping this a surprise.

"Oh no, Mistress...you shall see for yourself shortly!" and she brought forth a new gown from the wardrobe, and placed it on the bed. The gown was of purple silk, elaborately embroidered with flowers and insects along the hem and sleeves. By tradition, each day as Empress I was to wear a new gown, every one more exquisite than the last. After the wearing the gowns were to be destroyed, so that no one else could wear the garments which possessed the divine essence emitted by the Empress.

After dressing and the fixing of my coiffure, Shiu Lin and I waited in the garden of my chambers, a garden ten times the size of the little space outside my former rooms. We walked there in delight, pointing out to each other the plants and flowers, the beauty of the design, the glory that can be when nature is touched by the hand of man. The soft bubbling of a fountain and the twittering of birds accompanied us as we moved about, and I told Shiu Lin of my first night with the Emperor. She looked at me quizzically, but before she could ask me her questions, we were interrupted by a court page, announcing the arrival of a visitor. The young boy disappeared inside the chambers, sweeping his arm in a gallant gesture as the visitor came through, and I saw that it was Madame, my beloved teacher.

"Madame!" I shouted joyfully, and rushed to throw my arms around her in delight. She was beautiful as always, skin glowing and long hair gleaming, dressed in a pristine white gown of soft flowing fabric. "I had not been expecting you! Why have you come? Did you not tell me we could no longer meet? What has brought you to me?" I held her hand as we walked further into the garden, toward the bubbling fountain, where our words might be more private.

"I have come because of the importance of what has happened to you," she replied, indicating that I should sit beside her on the stone bench beside the path.

"Do you mean becoming Empress? But you have known I should be so for some time," I said, not understanding.

"No; I do not mean your becoming Empress. There is something far more important which has occurred, do you not know my meaning?" she asked, looking searchingly into my face.

Just then, the image of the lotus came into clarity in my mind, the white blossom revolving above my head in divine serenity. Madame knew!

"Madame, I…" I began, searching for words to explain, not knowing how to say what had happened at the reflecting pool, for I had never heard of such a thing occurring, had not known a power like that existed.

"My dear, but you do not have to explain. I know what has happened, I knew as soon as the lotus was brought into being. The power is too great to go unnoticed by those who can see such things," Madame said, smiling gently.

"But Madame, what does it mean? I have never felt such feelings, and the white lotus…why has it come?" I asked, finally voicing the questions I had held inside me.

"The white lotus is born of an act of pure love. Only by your choice have you brought it into being. As a trained White Tigress, you had at your disposal a power that could grant you many things in this world. With that power, you could destroy or even kill a man, gain dominance over other women, or suppress others free will. Such is the danger of the teachings. And yet, the teachings can also be used as a catalyst to an experience of love so great, that desire for all worldly power is transcended. It is this which you have experienced, this which you chose. And by this choice you allowed the energy of pure love to move through you as a channel onto this earthly plane. The White Lotus is the symbol of this love and the enlightenment which it brings."

I knew her words were true, I felt a shiver of knowing pass over my skin as she spoke, But one question remained, and I queried her, "But Madame, why did you not tell me of the possibility of attaining the White Lotus? Why did you not explain to me that there was more, beyond the White Tigress teachings, and that I could attain this high level of experience?"

"Because, my dear, this choice must be of the purest intent, and uninfluenced by thought of attainment," Madame said. "I could not tell you, or it would have ensured you would never attain the White Lotus. It must be an expression of pure free will, a desire for the highest love alone." Tears welled up in her eyes, and she reached for my hand. "And in you I am most proud."

I hugged her tightly against me, and felt the tears roll down my own cheeks. "Madame, I have been blessed to have you as my teacher and I thank you for all that you are." And then Madame hurried away, Shiu Lin at her side to show her out of the garden.

When they had gone through the doorway, I sat on the bench and closed my eyes. I saw Madame and Shiu Lin standing in front of me, hand in hand, and above each of their heads revolved a white lotus, so pure and bright that I knew the light was not of this world, but of Heaven.

One day not long after Madame's visit, Shiu Lin rushed into the garden where I was sitting in meditation amidst the flowers and birds. "Mistress! There is much commotion in the palace! There has been an uprising....a riot; just outside the palace gates! There has been violence, for the Emperor's men have tried to disperse the crowd which chants and throws rocks and stones against the gates. And there is one who has been arrested, and brought to the prison inside these walls. It is the one you met at the shelter, the one who is the Master's brother! They have shackled him and brought him to a dungeon cell and claim he is the cause of unrest, that he has fanned the flames of disenchantment with the Emperor's reign."

Dismay rose in my heart, for once accused of seditious acts against the Emperor, very few escape with their lives. A public death in the square was a likely outcome, with little or no hearing on the truth of the accusations, or the justness of the punishment. My mind whirled with the news, what to do? I must try to save him, the man who fed the hungry and longed for justice. "Shiu Lin, I must go to the Emperor at once. Help me to prepare."

I dressed in a robe of sky blue silk, emblazoned with red dragons, and donned a sapphire ring, which glittered its deep blue light upon my hand. We hurried from my chambers, Jiang trailing behind, ever more watchful of me since the day of my wedding, when I slipped away to Black Dragon Pool before he could stop me. I did not tell him where we were going, and he grumbled a bit as we made our way through the streets toward the tall red pavilion where the Emperor conducted the business of the realm.

When we reached the steep staircase and I began to ascend, Jiang made to protest. "Mistress, you may not enter! For the Emperor has not summoned you thus!" he exclaimed. I ignored his entreaties, and Shiu Lin and I continued to quickly mount the steps, and Jiang had no choice but to follow in our path.

We came to the massive golden doors through which I had passed on the night the Imperial jewels were bestowed upon me. I looked up, noting the intricate embossed decoration, and my eyes fell upon a symbol at the very top of each door which had escaped my notice before. It was a caduceus, two snakes intertwined around a staff, the symbol of healing, the symbol of alchemy. Alchemy, the process of changing one thing into something better, a transmutation. I thought of the Emperor's great interest in the healing arts, and wondered, would he choose to transcend the limits of merely physical effects, or seek a greater good?

The doors slowly opened as we approached, as if by magic. In the center of the cavernous hall, the Emperor sat high upon his golden throne. He did not notice our entrance, as there were many others inside awaiting an audience with the Emperor.

"The Emperor will not have time to see you, Mistress; he is busy collecting tax offerings from the representatives of all the villages across the land," Jiang whispered. I waved him away with my hand, enthralled by the event I was witnessing.

The Emperor sat, bedecked in silk and jewels, his plump white hand reaching from the sleeve of his robe to accept bundles of food, money, gifts, incense, and even live animals from the brown hands of villagers, nails crusted with dirt, wearing simple grey or brown garments, heads bowed low. The Emperor wore a slight smile of smug content as he accepted the fruits of their toil, secure in his right to demand this payment. All around him, the bounty of their labor piled high, hours, days, and months of people's lives represented there, never to be regained.

I felt a roiling in my stomach as I thought of the hungry in the market shelter, the woman and her baby, those in my village who suffered. What right did he have to take this bounty, when those forced to give it could not at times feed themselves, or their children? At once I felt myself surging forward, toward the staircase which led to his throne, and I was suddenly before him, his eyes showing startled surprise, confusion at my presence.

In a moment, he recovered his composure. "And to what do I

owe the honor of this visit from the Empress?" he drawled. "Surely, it must be of utmost importance or she would not deign to disturb me in my duties." His voice held a thinly veiled edge, a threatening element of quiet sharpness. It did not frighten me, but made me angry, and that anger smoldered beneath the surface of my words.

"I apologize to His Highness for disrupting this..." and I paused, looking around the great hall at the people assembled there; at the piled offerings received from their hands, "...this spectacle." I turned my eyes back to his; they revealed a feeling of unabashed entitlement. "But there is something of grave importance for which I must beg your attention. For there has been an injustice done to one whom I know to be of highest integrity, and I know that His Highness would desire to remedy the situation at the earliest opportunity."

His eyes softened at the allusion to his desire for justice. "An injustice? Of what do you speak?" he asked, his voice less strained as he considered my words.

"A man has been arrested, one who formerly served the court within these walls for a time, in the temple. He now serves those who suffer, by distributing the Emperor's generous food offerings from the palace stores to the hungry. I have met this man, and I know him to be of honor, seeking only to help those who cannot help themselves, while at the same time serving the Imperial Court through his works."

The Emperor leaned back in his chair; it was such a slight thing, one person arrested. Already bored with this talk of injustice, he asked, "And why has he been arrested if he is a man of integrity, as you say?"

"I am sure there has been a mistake, and I come to ask that you order his release immediately, so that he may resume his duties to the Emperor, and continue to facilitate your generous giving of food to the hungry," I responded.

I could see that my words had affected him, that he liked the idea of his own generosity. The Emperor's face relaxed, he held out his smooth hand, examining the large rings on his fingers. A slight smile pulled at his lips, his eyes held a far-away look.

I felt the weight of the ring of sapphire upon my own hand, felt its smooth contour with my finger. I could almost feel it vibrate there, feel the energy of its essence emanate from its depths. I became suddenly aware that my Master's face was before my mind's eye, and for a moment turned my attention there, and heard him say "This stone shall give you strength in your task." The image faded as I returned my attention to the Emperor's face, and at the same time I reached up with the hand which held the ring, placing it over my heart, letting its powerful light shine forth.

I saw it catch the Emperor's eye as he looked up to speak, and he said "I will order the release of the one you have requested. There is much turmoil at present in the land, and any who serve to facilitate the Imperial will are much needed now." And with that he clapped his hands and ordered the release, in a loud voice so that all in the hall should hear that the Emperor wished to release such a man to freedom.

I thanked him and turned to go. As I descended the stairway my Master's face again appeared before me, and he was smiling a smile of amused delight. All in the hall watched me go out, the air buzzing with excitement, my own heart singing with relief.

For a time I sit in the café in the hotel lobby, drinking tea, writing in my journal, thinking. Why did I feel such a profound sense of grief, what had I lost? Nothing, really. I had come to China for an adventure and for two days I had thought I might bring home a baby. For two days my world changed, and I had embraced that change, and now my arms were empty.

The Indian sage Krishnamurti says that fear is the gap between the known and the unknown. Moving from one to the other causes so much fear to arise that the chasm is hardly ever crossed. If all you have ever known was unhappiness, grief and despair, then happiness, joy and life will be the unknown. This situation had been so unexpected, had happened so suddenly that I was catapulted across the gap, fear had never had a chance to take hold.

Now I am on the other side and have taken a few steps down the road of happiness; I realize I cannot turn back. I have to be done with the discontent, the depression, forever. I have to give up my old crutches and start walking forward toward life in every moment, no matter what happens with Baby.

Wasted time, years of it, given to sadness, questioning, fear. I must have made a choice, somewhere deep and subterranean, that I would allow the move to happiness, that I would allow it now. Why had that happiness never occurred before now? We choose, we choose and then events confirm; events confirm and we choose again, a never ending process of creating our realities. Eventually those choices form a pattern of a life, and that pattern exerts an irresistible force upon all subsequent choices. It becomes more and more difficult to make a true change. And yet, it can be done. I have just lived it.

And now, what does this all mean? I am in uncharted territory, on my little road of happiness…a traveler without a map. But I think of Antoinette, and I know that I must talk to her, that she will understand this. I go to the phone booth off the central lobby, dial her number, and she is there in a moment, on the other end of the line. I tell her what has happened, that Alex has changed her mind, that I had been overwhelmed with grief, but that I am finding peace somehow.

"It was absolutely the right thing," she says, "to step away. I have been in prayer almost constantly since your last call, I can't tell you everything now, it's better if I wait until you are back safely. But I need to ask you, have you done any prayers or meditation since we spoke last?"

"Yes," I tell her, "I was meditating last night and I saw the most extraordinary thing. The Virgin Mary came to me, my mother was there too."

"What happened, what did she do?" Antoinette asks.

"Well, she handed me the baby," I say.

Antoinette sits in silence on the other end, for a moment. And then she says, "I don't know how to tell you this."

"Just tell me."

"That is your baby. You are meant to have her," she says.

The invisible angels are back, I feel a chill ripple my skin.

"I know," I say. *I know.*

I already know.

When I finish talking with Antoinette I walk back out

onto the bustling street outside the hotel. I am seeing it for the first time, I have been so distracted by the events unfolding in our little world that I have not really looked, not really seen. Now, it comes into focus. I breathe the air, feel the vibrations of life around me. I look into people's faces, and what I had perceived before as a vaguely hostile attitude now appears to be an attractive seriousness, a dignity. A small woman carrying a large wicker basket nods, and smiles shyly. A young mother holds her little boy over the curb as he urinates from the split pants that are worn by babies in China, and laughs. A young man dressed in a neatly pressed white shirt and pleated trousers opens a door for me, and bows slightly.

I enter a small grocery store around the corner from the hotel. Walking up and down the aisles is a revelation. Bright, colorful packages with mysterious contents, unusual fruits wrapped in tissue paper, personal products for Asian skin and hair (no Cindy Crawford here). In the cookie aisle, I spend half an hour studying the different boxes and bags, curious about what might be inside, which ones would Baby like? Everything is exotic, fresh, exciting.

I tote my basket to the check-out line, and lay the merchandise I have selected on the counter: an apple, a banana, two small plastic bowls with pictures of Chinese children playing, two boxes of cookies, a bag of powdered baby formula, an orange drink. A young woman works the antiquated cash register, says something to me in Chinese, and I shake my head to indicate my lack of understanding. She points to the numbers displayed through the window of the register, the number of yuan the products cost. I hold out a small roll of paper yuan, she looks through the bills and selects two, and some coins. I thank her, having no idea if she took the correct amount, and not caring. Leaving the store, eating my apple, feeling the breeze on my face, enjoying a sense of ease and well-being, feeling for the first time since this trip began like myself. What has changed in me has brought a new world to my sight; love has grown and now determines how I see.

I return to the hotel just in time to shower and change clothes before we leave for the airport for our flight to Guangzhou. Alex is on the floor with Baby on her lap, reading through a stack of official papers she will have to submit at the U.S. Consulate tomorrow. Baby is trying to play, to engage Alex's attention, and Alex sighs, shifts her weight, tries to avoid the baby's waving hands. Every now and then as I move about the room, Baby and I make eye contact, and I send her a silent, surreptitious greeting... hello, Baby. Everything is going to be okay, Baby.

We drag our luggage to the lobby, and load it into the van, and again the three families and Anna climb aboard. Traveling from Beijing to Nanchang had not seemed arduous, but now, we have the babies. Strollers, blankets, diaper bags, food and bottles, in addition to the huge pieces of luggage, must be negotiated through the airport check-in. Passports and tickets are being checked two and three times, while babies fuss and cry.

Waiting in the gate area, Alex keeps sighing, deep heavy exhalations of breath, as she shifts Baby from one hip to another, or walks around the orange plastic seats. She seems annoyed, but I attribute this to the frustration of traveling. I am feeling strangely elated, talking with the others in the group, playing word games with Maggie. Free of turmoil, and free of projecting disaster or paradise scenarios into the future, I can enjoy exactly where I happened to be, which is in an airport in China, with a group of people in the midst of an amazing journey. I am the witness.

The stewardess for China Air calls our flight number, and we move toward the boarding gate with the other passengers, a mass of businessmen dressed in identical dark blue suits, pressing in close, pushing toward the gateway. All the seats on the flight are assigned, so it's unclear what the rush is. We squeeze ourselves onto the plane, find our row, and sitting three across, Alex in the window seat with Baby on her lap, I take the middle seat, and Anna sits next to me.

During the short flight, Anna and I talk. I ask her about her family, her job. She tells me that she has a husband and young daughter, six years old. She has studied at the University of Beijing, and had earned the equivalent of a Master's degree there. I ask her if she would like to visit America, and she says yes, she would; but it is difficult to obtain a visa, and she thinks she may never get the chance to go.

I tell Anna that I think all the men in China look mean. She wrinkles up her nose, and squints her eyes. "You do?" she asks. Yes, I say, they all have such stern expressions; I hardly ever see a man smile here. Anna tells me that no, they are not mean; they just don't show any deference to women, it's the way things are in China.

Anna struggles against her natural shyness and ventures a question: "Do all American men beat their wives?" she asks, almost apologetically. Now it is my turn to wrinkle my nose and squint my eyes in surprise.

"No!" I laugh. "Where did you get that?" She says that this is what they are told, in China; that all American men beat their wives. I want to ask exactly who it is that tells them that, but don't. Instead I say, "That's news to me. I wouldn't be married to one if they did!" We giggle together then; Anna covers her mouth with her hand, like a little girl who has just said something naughty might do.

During the flight Alex sits with her head slightly turned, looking out the window at a bank of clouds. Baby keeps trying to get my attention, touches my hand, leans over to try to get into my lap. No, Baby, I say silently. I'm sorry Baby, but I can't pick you up.

I want so badly to reach over and grab her, pull her to me. But I know that if Alex senses any sort of longing in me for the baby that it would interfere with the emotional process in deciding about her. Antoinette and I had talked about how there was almost a perversion in the way that she had handed Baby out to me, and then so casually pulled her back, at worst toying deliberately with my emotions, at best showing a crass insensitivity.

Until now I had been inclined to give Alex the benefit of the doubt, to be understanding about her emotional turmoil concerning the baby. Antoinette, however, had introduced an idea I had not considered, that Alex was doing this deliberately, that she was being cruel. "But why?" I had asked her. "Why in the world would she do that?" Antoinette didn't answer and I knew that she was holding something back; something she had seen and was not willing to tell me now.

And then I thought of something Alex had said, the night she told me she couldn't take the baby. She had told me that she was jealous of how attached the baby had become to me in those first two days. I protested then, told Alex that it was natural for the baby to become attached to me; I was the one caring for her, in this strange and frightening new situation. And I had pointed out to her that it had been she herself who had kept her distance from the baby, that the baby had not rejected her. But then she had said that what she was jealous of was my happiness with the baby, my feelings for the baby, because she did not feel that way.

My antenna had gone up then, it had seemed so irrational. What was really going on here? And when Antoinette told me of her suspicions about Alex's true motives, I remembered the hard look on her face when she had talked of her jealousy, the cold tone of her voice. It may be true, I thought, that Alex is being deliberately cruel, but I have to hold to the one thought that seems of the highest order, and not be distracted; and that one thought is for the happiness and well-being of Baby.

How could she not fall completely in love with Baby, I keep thinking, over and over as I watch the two of them together. Please love her, I keep thinking, if you are going to take her, please love her. And yet a part of me feels that she should not have her, that her love for Baby would always be imperfect, a house built upon a shaky foundation.

I lean back against the seat and close my eyes. It is night time now, the sky beyond the window black, the lights on inside the cabin. Suddenly I am very, very tired, and I want to sleep, but cannot. I had lost something that I had never had. I was missing something I had not even known that I wanted. What should I do now? Start my own adoption proceedings, come back to China and get a little girl of my own? But it was this little girl, this one....and even though I knew that what Antoinette had said was true, this baby was meant to be mine, for reasons I didn't understand; even though I felt so strongly Baby belonged with me, Alex was the one who had meant to adopt her, and I had no power to make her mine.

I feel a strange sensation of falling; I shiver and open my eyes. Alex is looking at me, looking right into my eyes.

"It's happening again," she says.

I am confused, disoriented. "What?" I say.

"The panic. I'm feeling panicked, like I have to get away from her," she says, desperation in her voice. She is holding Baby away from her body, at arms length on her knees, as if pulling her close would be painful.

I look at them in silence. What does she mean? I had thought everything was going okay; Alex had seemed fine with the baby today.

"I can't do it. I really can't. I know that for sure now," she says.

And when she says this, I realize that I had known that

this would happen, deep down I had known.

"What do you want to do?" I ask her, the question vibrates in the air between us, resonating with a power that had come through me as I spoke it. The power was from a source beyond me, a source which was now calling for her answer, the answer.

"I want you to take her."

There. It was done. Alex had spoken it three times, three times denied this child. When Peter denied Jesus the third time, the cock had crowed—the cock was crowing now. Baby was not her child, could never be her child.

She was mine.

Guangzhou is a far different type of city than Nanchang or Beijing. It is warm, semi-tropical, with neon lights, commerce, western-style buildings. Even at ten o'clock at night the city is bustling, traffic clogging the roads. During the ride from the airport I watch eagerly through the window as the city unfolds. Signs for McDonalds, Motorola, Sony, even Starbucks line the streets, and something in my gut unclenches, a recognition that we have returned to civilization.

The van pulls up in front of a very large building, the luxurious White Swan hotel complex, which is connected with the U.S. Consulate. The hotel is famous, having been used over the years as a showcase for powerful Western visitors. Richard Nixon, among others, has stayed here, and the service is geared toward satisfying the discerning traveler.

The hotel is technically on an island, separated from the rest of the city by a ring of water, but joined to it by footbridges and pedestrian walkways.

Anna tells the parents that they have to take the babies to have their pictures taken for the visa application, and it must be done tonight, immediately, so they are ready for the appointment tomorrow morning at the Consulate. Everyone is tired, there is grumbling about this; but there is no way to avoid it, it must be done. Alex takes Baby, and I check into the hotel and find our room, a lovely room with a dramatic view of the churning river below. Even now, after ten p.m., barges travel the waters here in this busy port city, and I watch as their hulking silhouettes move past in the darkness.

Now that I have a few quiet minutes to myself I think about calling my husband. He doesn't even know about Alex's change of mind this morning, or her abrupt reversal tonight. He has no idea of the emotional turmoil of these past few hours, and I feel the need to talk to someone, confide in someone, be comforted by someone.

When he answers the phone I can hear in his voice a distance that was not there last night, a business-like attitude that catches me off guard and makes me sink into the exhaustion I have been fighting, an exhaustion that has taken an entire lifetime to build. No relief, no relief.

He says, in his brisk Washington-way, that he and Alex's husband have had a meeting with an attorney earlier today, that they discussed the situation, and that he gave them some strong advice, which he thinks we should heed. "He says we can't do it. There is no way we can adopt this child."

The exhaustion. I can't answer him, so suddenly has it come upon me and doused my spirit. The exhaustion of dreams denied, always denied.

"Hello?" he says, not sure I am still on the line.

I have to pull energy from somewhere to speak, and finally I do, "Why not?" I ask, with no anger or emotion at all in my voice, I hear the flat tone and think, I will never be the same.

"He said we may run into trouble with immigration. If Alex goes through with the adoption in China, knowing she is not going to keep the baby, the INS could charge her with fraud. For us to try to adopt the baby after you get back here would be a red flag, they might think it was planned."

Planned?! It is so absurd, why would I have someone else adopt a baby for me?

"The lawyer was absolutely adamant that we should not try to do this. If the INS were to go after Alex for fraud, she could go to jail. We can't put her in that position, I won't do it. I don't see any way we can do this," he says, with finality.

"But what about the baby?" I ask. Why does everyone keep forgetting about her?

He continues talking, about the regulations, the INS restrictions, legal opinions, and reasons why it can't be done. My mind rejects every word he says—I don't even listen to the details. I know with every cell of my body that Baby will be mine.

"There has to be a way," I say, ignoring his certainty that this is impossible. There is always a way.

"Look, I know you really want this, and I'm sorry, but it's not going to happen. Your emotions are clouding your thinking right now, I understand that. But I'm telling you, we can't adopt her, and that's just the way it is."

Now, I am angry. 'That's the way it is' just was not going to cut it here. I am angry at him, angry that he accepts this verdict so easily. I say, "I have never thought so clearly in all my life," and I had not. I tell him that the only cloudy thinking is the lawyer's, and his, and that he doesn't understand what is happening here.

"There has to be a way. There has to be someone else you can call, someone who can help us. I refuse to give up based on one person's opinion, this is too important. I won't rest until we've exhausted all the possibilities, every one of them," I say, my voice rising in defiance.

"I have been afraid of this, that you would get your hopes up, start thinking this was going to happen and then it doesn't work and you are disappointed. You have to know the odds are not good on this, you have to know it's not likely," he says.

It may not be likely, I think, but unlikely things happen all the time, all the time. The odds are against people winning the lottery too, and yet people do. Wouldn't the odds be better if we don't give up, if we explore all possibilities? It seems so obvious to me, how can he not see this?

"I know that, I know. Alex already changed her mind today, twice! Do you think I'm not aware how many obstacles there are? It's excruciating, but what should I do, give up? I can't do that, I would never forgive myself, never," I say.

He says he will think about what to do next; he is at least going to reconsider the idea that this is impossible. I tell him I will call him again tomorrow and just as I am hanging up the phone, Alex walks into the room with Baby, and I tell her about what he has said. She immediately wants to call her husband. She is concerned, so I take Baby from her and start dressing her for bed.

It feels so good to hold her again. I take off the pink dress that is too big; I stick her arms and legs into the one-piece sleeper suit that has little pictures of lipsticks, hairbrushes, compacts and purses on it. Cosmetics on a baby sleeper, why? I look at the label; all it says is "Made in China."

Baby has her bottle and her blanket, and I take her out to the hallway to walk until she falls asleep. The hotel floor has two hostesses to attend to the guests every need, and as soon as we open the door they approach us and coo over the baby. One of the hostesses says that she sees a lot of Americans here adopting Chinese babies. "You like her?" she asks hopefully, indicating Baby.

"Yes, I like her; I like her very much," I say.

"She have good life," the hostess says. Yes.

Around the hallway we go, the baby falls asleep easily tonight, and I take her back to the room and tuck her into the wooden crib next to the bed. I had not noticed when we first arrived, but the room has one King-sized bed, instead of two smaller beds, and Alex and I will have to share it tonight. Alex is still on the phone, asking her husband pointed questions about the meeting with the lawyer, her voice rising as she demands answers.

"That's ridiculous!" I hear her exclaim, as I head out the door in my running shoes, looking for the hotel gym, somewhere I can clear my head. The hotel is huge. I wander through a labyrinth of hallways, through the lobby, following the signs to an outside terrace to the entrance of the glass-walled gymnasium. There is an attendant at the door, he hands me a towel and leads me inside. There are only two other people here working out, as it is late. I choose a treadmill in the far corner and get on, start to walk. The treadmill is set directly in front of the full-length glass wall, and I can see the dark river beyond the window, the lights on the barges strung like Christmas trees moving slowly up and down the waterway.

I can see myself in the reflection of the glass also, superimposed over the image of the river beyond. The effect is that in the image, it looks as if I am walking on the water. A barge goes by, and I am walking on its deck. It passes and I walk on the water again. The treadmill speeds up, now I am running, and always when I run, emotions lodged deep in my tissues start to release, to ripple up to my chest. My chest becomes tight, my heart constricts, warmth spreading up to my shoulders and neck.

Grief. Again, for a short time, I thought Baby would be mine. Again, a major obstacle arises, and I am thrown back on myself. A test....a test of what, my strength? Stamina? I don't know, I don't know. You never get what you want so don't want anything precious. I should not have wanted, should not have wanted. I am so tired, so tired and I'll never be the same.

I am sobbing and I'm glad no one can see me, that I am facing only myself, my reflection in the glass. And there, I am walking on water.

When I have pulled myself together, when I am finished with my run, I go to the hotel business center, where I can borrow a computer and send an e-mail. I need to reach out, to communicate with someone; tonight it has hit me how alone and isolated I am here, on the other side of the world from home. I don't feel I can speak on the telephone with this heavy burden of despair weighing on my chest, but connecting to something familiar and known seems like a healthy impulse; I sit down at a terminal and log onto the internet, and find waiting for me a message from Antoinette:

> *Don't forget that nothing is as it appears to be. Time is not linear. Do not allow Alex to torture you. If you must, and no matter how hard it may be, just hand the baby back to her; call her bluff. All will work out, there is soul group activity in action that will assist you along the way.*
>
> *Love and Light,*
> *Antoinette*

She is trying to comfort me, but tonight I cannot be comforted. I am deep inside myself, I can not see my way out. Disappointment and discouragement pushed below the surface in other times are swirling around me, pulling me under, and it seems that the most cherished of my dreams never, ever come true. All the world's teachings seem inadequate in this moment, in the face of these feelings. Do not allow Alex to torture you.....how can she torture me any more than I torture myself? I try to come up with words that do not betray my anguish, for that in itself is a failure on my part, a failure of faith.

*Antoinette,*

*This has been the strangest day of my life. We flew to Guangzhou tonight and during the flight Alex told me once again that she can't take this baby; I was elated, then called my husband and he told me there was no way for us to adopt her due to INS regulations, etc. I am so tired now. Just wanted to fill you in on the latest, I have no idea how this is all going to end. We leave for Hong Kong tomorrow afternoon, will call you from there. Please have words of wisdom ready.....*

I sign off, and go back to our room. Alex fills me in on her conversation with her husband. The lawyer they met with is a family friend, and is very concerned about the INS charging her with fraud. Apparently he has suggested that if Alex goes through with the adoption in China, and brings her back to the United States with the intention of giving her up to us, then the best thing to do would be to relinquish Baby upon arrival.

"Relinquish her, to whom?" I ask.

"He said he could arrange for a Social Services representative to come and get the baby at the airport when we arrive, and have her placed immediately into foster care.

And that's not all; he thinks it would be better to place her in another state altogether, like New York."

"What? Take her to New York? But why? Why not just place her with us as foster parents right off the bat? We already know we want to adopt her," I say.

"He said that if we placed her in another state, the courts would not suspect that this was planned in some way. There might be a better chance for you to adopt her," Alex says, as if this makes perfect sense.

This is insanity. The thought of handing Baby over to a stranger at the airport, having her taken somewhere away from us, made my stomach turn. We cannot do that to her, not after all she has been through.

"No," I say to Alex, "No, we can't do that."

"But it may be the only way for you to adopt her! And I can't leave her here now, in China; we've come too far. So there has to be a plan for when we get back."

So, she has decided not to leave her here; at least we have that. And though I know from comments she has made that she is doing this not for Baby, but to save herself from a life of guilt, I am still grateful and relieved and happy for Baby.

"Well, I'll go to New York with her then, or wherever I have to go. I'll stay with her until I can bring her home," I say.

"You will? You would do that?" Alex asks, incredulous.

Of course I would. I'll do whatever it takes; I have resigned myself to that. I will not leave her to face a strange situation alone again, not if I can help it. "I still believe there's a way, an easier way. I just feel it," I say. Alex looks at me and nods, and we fall silent.

We pick at our room service trays, but don't really eat. Neither one of us has eaten much these last five days, and the stress is starting to show. Alex looks gaunt, her face drawn. She has lost weight though she was already thin to begin with; she hasn't slept. At least I was sleeping, even though it was fitful sleep and full of exhausting dreams.

"I've got to try to sleep," she says, and we get into the big bed. There is a vast unbridgeable distance between us, we cannot comfort each other. Alex rolls to her side, and I to mine, each alone with our private anguish. I try to sleep, but this night, it is I who cannot surrender. I imagine Baby being pulled away from me at the airport, her terror and shock. I try to imagine her being adopted by another family, somewhere in New York.

I want what is best for her, only what is best. I cannot even picture her with someone else, what is best for her is to come home with me! No, I won't allow this craziness! I sit bolt upright in bed, Alex is snoring softly, finally finding refuge in sleep. The baby breathes in her crib, and I look at the clock, it is midnight, I have been tossing for an hour.

I get out of bed and go to the bathroom, there is a telephone there, in a little private room where the toilet is. I go in and close the door, sit on the commode, trying to be as quiet as I can be. I dial my husband's number at work, he should be there now, it is morning where he is.

While I wait for him to come to the phone, I think, how did this happen, how? I feel caught in a dream, one I can't wake up from, a dream that gets more and more bizarre each moment.

He comes on the line, surprised that I have called again so soon. I tell him I can't sleep, I have been turning this over and over in my mind, and that I just cannot accept this, can't accept that there's not another way.

He begins telling me that I need to understand, we cannot adopt this baby.

"No, no! I don't want to hear that, I won't listen to that. I just don't believe it. I know there is some way, we just need to call the right person, the person who can help us," I say, trying to keep my voice low but having trouble doing so, there is too much emotion.

"There is no one to call," he says sadly. "This guy is an immigration attorney, he knows what he's talking about."

"I don't care who he is! I don't believe it, it makes no sense. This is wrong, wrong…all we want to do is bring home a baby that nobody else wanted! Nobody wanted her, not even Alex! And now, because of some ludicrous regulations, some idiot lawyer's opinion, she can't be with us, she can't have a home?"

"It makes no sense, but that's the way it is," he says, trying to keep his own voice low, so others in the office don't overhear.

"I don't accept the way it is! I can't!" I am crying now, loud sobs, I can't hold it back any longer. "Don't you understand? This is life and death, hers and mine. I can't explain this, but if we can't adopt her, I'll never be the same! I've never felt this way before, about anything; I've never wanted anything so much! I don't know why, I just love this baby so much, so much it hurts. I just love her!"

He listens, not offering platitudes or empty words of

comfort, and that is a relief. Finally, he says that he will think about what to do, that he will do what he can. "That's all I ask," I say. "Do what you can."

I hang up, and go to the sink where I splash cold water on my face. I look in the mirror, my eyes are red, my face white. I am scoured out, empty, depleted, weak. Alex is still sleeping when I get back into bed—she hasn't heard a thing.

I am dying, and she hasn't heard a thing. I pull the sheet and blanket up around me, huddling inside, and wrap my arms around my knees, pulling them to my chest. A womb, a cocoon; in this muffled darkness I let go, give in to the tide of feelings breaking free. A roiling, thunderous surf pounds in my ears, my gut is heaving with painful contractions. My cries come from too deep a place to even make a sound.

Why, why, why? Why do I feel this way? A baby I have met only two days ago and my love for her could crack me in two. I would turn the world upside down and heaven inside out if it would bring her to me. Where did these feelings come from? The embers of my heart have been covered with ashes for so long, and now they have become a roaring flame.

I must let it consume me now, I cannot fight this conflagration. May it burn all dross from my being; let the blaze temper my will. My will, yes, my will…what do I will?

> *The human Will, that force unseen,*
> *the offspring of a deathless soul,*
> *Can hew its way to any goal,*
> *Though walls of granite intervene.*

The poem springs to life in my mind…it is one which

I have long admired, but never truly understood until this moment: What if that is true? What if, just what if a decision I make, a steeling of my Will, can hew its way to any goal? What if faith can move mountains? And what if the greatest force is Love?

In the deep lucidity of my pain I see, I have never lived any of these truths, ever. My life has had no real power.

And with this realization, I let it all go rushing out from me, a tidal wave of desire, love, faith, passion, longing; it rolls out into every corner of the universe, to anywhere in any time where God might exist. From this moment of release forward, I am no longer myself alone, but part of that force unseen, which is Life. Someday soon, the cocoon will break open, and I will be free.

> *Be not impatient with delay,*
> *But wait as one who understands;*
> *When spirit rises and commands,*
> *The gods are ready to obey.*

Sleep comes over me like a blessing, to heal my battered soul.

*In the weeks to follow, I spent many nights talking with the Emperor on any number of subjects. He would summon me to his chambers, where an elaborate meal had been prepared, and we would eat together as we talked, sometimes until dawn. He was becoming increasingly alarmed at the continued uprisings in the land—they seemed to be spreading and without any single cause.*

Our talks together comforted him, and he would leave in the morning with a softer countenance, after kissing me chastely upon the cheek each time.

When he left I would return to the courtyard of my chambers, where Chen would be waiting with a bird on each arm. From his waist hung a small leather pouch and I would untie the pouch from his belt, and place into it a jewel which I happened to be wearing, an emerald, diamond or pearl, sometimes sapphire or gold, and I would pull the string tight before affixing the pouch to the fragile leg of the bird.

Chen would then lift his arm and set the birds free to fly outside the palace walls, to a place where Chen had trained them to go, to a place where the jewels might be used to lift those in need, where they might be exchanged for food or shelter or clothing. I watched the birds take wing and each time my mind soared with the birds, to the countryside where the villages lay in quiet humility, where those who suffered did so quietly. And I prayed that the sky open to receive this offering and shelter the birds throughout their journey. Not one bird thus sent failed to return, the empty pouch dangling freely, the offering accepted.

Sometimes I would wrap the jewels inside a thin piece of paper, on which I had written some of the teachings I had received from my Master. If the jewels could relieve suffering, how much more could freeing their minds to see their own power relieve it? For that is what the teachings and the attainment of the White Lotus had done for me, relieved my suffering and given me freedom. My mind was no longer a prisoner of body or walls, for I could release myself from either, merely by focusing my attention, and willing it so. In this way I now moved about the palace, undetected by those who could not see, and knew the intricate workings of the court.

*One evening I was summoned to the Emperor's chamber, and it was clear as I entered the room that he suffered from deep agitation. I felt almost pity for him, so evident was his discomfort. He asked me to sit before him, and I did, the silk of my skirt billowing around me to create a quiet pool in which I floated, listening to his words, absorbing his meaning, letting compassion bathe my awareness. For the Emperor told me he was leaving, that he must travel far into the countryside where there was a ferocious battle being waged, a battle which could determine whether or not his rule would continue in that province, or be overthrown. If the peasants there took control, there was a possibility of other neighboring provinces banding together to do likewise, and the Emperor himself was needed to quell this uprising at any cost, to spur his wearied troops to unqualified victory.*

*The Emperor poured out his heart to me. He told me of his distaste for battle, of his fear of the final outcome. This fear was palpable; it hung in the room and reminded me of the black cloud I had seen the day in the temple, when I had collapsed from its weight. And yet now it did not disturb me, I could feel my strength in relation to it had grown, that its only power was over the weak. I remembered my vow to love the Emperor, and thought that this is what it meant: to seek to encourage and nurture his own strength in relation to this dark cloud of fear, to show him of its powerlessness over one who chooses love.*

*When the Emperor had finished speaking, we sat for some moments in silence. In time a question arose in me, a question whose answer had the power to change that fear into good. "It is possible to be free of fear, to have complete victory over it." I spoke slowly, deliberately. "And yet that victory is never simply given. It must be chosen. Tell me: Do you desire such a victory?"*

The Emperor sat in his abject misery, and when he turned his head from me, I knew that the question had not reached him. "I desire victory over those who seek to overthrow me!" he said with vehemence. "I must defend myself and my lands, those things bequeathed to me through the Imperial lineage. If I lose any part of that which I was given, I have failed!"

Quickly my response came, "On the contrary, it is that which you have simply accepted from others which will burden you utmost! You must choose for yourself, for choice is our only true power."

His anger rose then, "And what of this uprising, shall I just allow it to occur?" His eyes blazed with indignation.

"Sir, it is victory over the self that is the only true victory! You may defeat this uprising, but what of the next? Will you live in fear, will you choose to be a slave to those whom you rule?" I said with a force of conviction which stunned the Emperor into silence.

He put his head into his hands and sat some time without speaking. When he did so it was with pathos and despair, evidence of the destruction which follows in the wake of failed courage. "All I ever wanted was to practice my arts; to learn medicine and science. I did not want this, did not want this…" a lament uttered more to himself than to me.

I sat with him in his agony, his face hidden from my sight. I closed my eyes and prayed silently for his soul, prayed that he make the choice which would release him, prayed that he open his heart to truth. And in my mind I saw the gold-paneled doors, the doors which symbolized the potential within the Emperor's own mind, and they swung slowly to shut, leaving only a slight gap in opening, not yet fully closed against my prayers.

I moved to go, and he reached for my hand. "Wait, for I must know: how do you know these things?" he whispered, without a trace of the arrogance or disdain which was so often a hallmark of his speech.

I answered cautiously, not wanting to reveal that which is sacred. "My father held a great interest in such thought, and he taught me much. But some I know through my own experience, through my own mind."

The Emperor nodded, though he did not understand. "Help me, Empress; help me to see" he said in this unguarded moment, when his fear was greater than his pride.

"How? How can I help you?" I asked gently.

He held my hands more tightly then, and spoke hesitantly, not used to asking, used only to dictating his desires to those who could not refuse. "Write to me while I am away. Tell me of things which you know. I shall be away some months, and when I return, perhaps you and I may…perhaps our duty to the Empire shall be fulfilled at last!"

I promised him that I would do so, and bade him goodbye. That night as I lay in my own bed, my union with the Emperor as yet unconsummated, I felt the stirrings of life within my womb, and I accepted that life, and prayed for its protection. But not for my own.

意願

will

By morning, peace has descended. I wake early, a diffused light glowing through the shuttered windows. I hear the barges passing on the river below, their low rumble hypnotic and soothing. What has passed in the night, what grace has been bestowed, that I could move from agony to acceptance? I still love Baby, still want her; but in that desire there is no longer any fear or need.

Alex and Baby are awake, too, and we get dressed for our last day of official adoption business. The light at the end of the tunnel is visible now; after today, we will know at least one thing for sure: Baby is leaving China. The U.S. Government will issue her visa this morning at the Consulate, and then we are free to go home.

But first, the babies are scheduled for a medical examination. It is routine, a requirement to obtain the visa, and yet there is some anxiety about some serious malady being detected in one of the babies. The group of us walks along a brick-paved promenade in the soft morning air, looking in delight at the pastel stucco buildings which tell of Guangzhou's colonial past. It is beautiful, the buildings are from another time, another place; a little bit of Europe that somehow survived the Cultural Revolution. School children dressed in blue and white uniforms perform synchronized movements on a plaza ringed with colorful flags, attractive couples stroll past arm in arm, and professionals in business suits hurry by with their briefcases tucked under their arms. A Western influence has been allowed to thrive here, and I wonder why. Why were these buildings not smashed and destroyed, along with everything else which reminded the early Communists of the decadence of Capitalism and bourgeois wealth?

We reach the large modern office building which houses the medical clinic. We are ushered inside, and asked to wait on benches outside the examining rooms. I am holding Baby, she cuddles in my arms. Today, she is wearing a bright pink sweater that makes her black eyes look even more exotic and intense than usual. We are comfortable together, she and I. She rests against me as if we've been together forever, and I breathe her in, look into her eyes. She is the most beautiful thing I've ever seen.

The babies names are called one by one, and first Judy and Curtis disappear with their baby behind a glass screen, and then Jimmy and Louise with theirs, Maggie trailing behind. And then a white smocked attendant calls out the name that both Alex and I have been carefully avoiding using all this time, the name chosen for Baby by Alex and her husband, before this trip began. As soon as I hear it spoken, I know it was never meant for Baby, it was never right for her. It is a quintessentially American name, and would have given no hint or nod to her Asian roots. It is a label, an American label that would have been slapped over the Made in China label that was Baby herself, in an attempt to obscure the truth. I am glad that now she will not bear that name, and as I rise to follow the attendant behind the glass, I whisper to Baby, I ask her to tell me her name. I hear an answer, a beautiful name comes, and I tuck it away in my heart, for the time when it can be given back to her.

I hand Baby to Alex and we move into an examining room. A kindly Chinese doctor is there; he speaks to us in stilted English, and indicates that Baby should be put on the table. Alex places her there and he begins gently prodding Baby's abdomen, listens to her heart, measures her head, and manipulates her arms and legs, all the while speaking a sing-song Chinese, which calms Baby. It is obvious that he loves babies; he is smiling at her, maybe telling her she is beautiful, or special. Baby is enthralled; she looks up into his face and is not at all frightened, or anxious. After only a few moments and the briefest of examinations, he says, "This baby, healthy!"

I moved forward, and point to marks we have noticed on her back and shoulders. "What are these?" I ask.

"Bite," he says, pinching his thumb and forefinger together, moving them up and down her back. Ahh, I see; they are bug bites, from the mattress in the orphanage.

I pull Baby up to a sitting position, and indicate my concern that she can't sit up without wobbling and leaning forward. She has no muscle tone at all, no strength with which to steady herself. Her leg muscles have atrophied, too, it is obvious she has not had an opportunity to move very much, if at all. Her records say she is 13 months old, and yet she does not crawl, does not even try to roll over when placed on her back.

"Shouldn't she be able to sit?" I ask the doctor.

"No worry!" he responds, waving my question away with his hand, and leaving the room with a cheery and definitive "Goodbye!" His job is completed, another rubber stamp affixed to a cursory medical exam. But perhaps he has a special sense about this, and does know that Baby is fundamentally healthy, who knows? At least he has found nothing glaring, and there is nothing that will hold up the visa application.

We gather in the waiting room with the others. Anna comes breathlessly into the room; she tells us that we need to go quickly, "Right away!" to the U.S. Consulate. Our appointment is at nine-thirty a.m. sharp, and if we are late, we may not receive the visas at all. They are very strict, she says, and will not grant another appointment should we miss this one. This sets off a panic, and we scurry outside, running down the street, strollers and diaper bags flying this way and that. We reach the heavily guarded entrance to the Consulate out of breath, and with just minutes to spare. We check in with the guard and are ushered inside, past a long line of Chinese people that stretches the full length of the building, waiting to be given a chance to apply for a visa to visit America. They look at us with imploring eyes, envy evident on many of their faces. I feel then the privilege that it is to be an American in this world, to have the freedom to travel wherever, and whenever, we may choose.

Once inside the building, it is America. People rush about efficiently, papers in hand, glancing at watches, keeping to a schedule. Fluorescent lights illuminate tidy office cubicles, where typists click-click at full speed ahead. The hallways and offices are clean and bright, and the workers smile at us as they pass, and speak purposefully to co-workers. It is such a stark difference from the Chinese offices and government agencies we have been dealing with these past eight days—I feel as if I have stepped onto another planet. And on this planet, our appointment time is to be honored, it is not an approximation! Such a small thing, such a big relief; my nervous system locks into the rhythm of this place, this is the pace I have been wired for. I feel a sense of safety here, that we are wanted, that we belong. This feeling of safety is something I take for granted at home, in the United States, and I think of all those who have emigrated there from places like China, how alone and vulnerable they must feel, all the time.

We are shown to a waiting room that is filled with Americans adopting Chinese babies. It is cheerful chaos, books and toys scattered about, the chattering of small children, the happy murmuring of parents about to take home their new children. I play with Baby; she ignores the books and toys and instead climbs on the back of the couch, taking every opportunity to exercise her neglected muscles. Alex goes through the trusty briefcase paperwork for the last time, pulling out thick packets of papers, rifling through in search of this piece, or that. She is nervous; what if there's a problem now? "I don't think I could go through with it if there's a big problem," she says. 'There will be no problem," I say, in a low, calm voice. There can be no problem.

There is no problem. Alex is called to the desk by a young man dressed in khakis and a button down shirt. He has the unthreatening look of a therapist or a teacher in his first job just out of college. We sit opposite him, and he looks through the visa request and asks to see the adoption papers.

Alex slides them across the desk, and he glances through them, and slides them back, no questions raised. Baby is sitting on my lap, playing with the buttons on my sweater, trying to put them in her mouth, oblivious to the importance of the transaction. The man asks for the Chinese passport, and Alex hands over the red covered document, and he stamps it perfunctorily, free to go.

We gather up our belongings, eager to leave the building, the relief is exquisite, we made it through! I want to dance along the sidewalk, to take Baby in my arms and swing her around. You're free, you're free! We're going to put you on a plane and take you home with us, Baby! It is a beautiful day, with warm hazy sunshine, the palm trees sway in the breeze and we decide to take a walk through the park along the river.

We say little as we walk, but it is not an uncomfortable silence. We are each doing the best we can. There is a group of schoolchildren playing in the park, beautiful pre-adolescent girls, running and kicking a ball, laughing, the wind whipping their long black hair. Baby will look like that some day…..I stop to watch, and notice out of the corner of my eye a man standing nearby, looking at me. He might be middle aged but it is hard to tell. His long grey beard is unkempt and wiry hair curls from beneath a floppy brimmed hat. Is he homeless? Why is he just standing there, like he was expecting us? He looks at me and smiles, a broad grin of invitation—'come over, talk to me,' it seems to say; I return his smile and he points to Baby, "Yours?"

I nod, "Yes; mine."

"Ahhhhhh," he says, throwing his head back. "I knew you would be together someday."

Suddenly my vision goes dark; I see bright pricks of stars before my eyes. What? What did he say??

My vision clears and I see he is looking right into my eyes. His are dark, an indeterminate color, and they sparkle with joy. "I knew you'd be together someday," he says, again.

I just stand there, mute, mesmerized, wondering, disoriented. Did he speak those words, or did I hear them in my head? The man shuffles away, torn sandals flapping against his calloused heels, still smiling his smile of secret delight.

I turn to look; Alex and the baby are a few steps away near the edge of the walkway. I want to ask her, did you hear what that man just said? But she is looking away, toward the river and I cannot get her attention, and I know she could not hear.

When I look back, the man has vanished. The park is empty, the mirage of happy girls and wise old man no longer visible, but the echo of laughter lingers in the air.

*The next morning, as I looked out my window, I saw the Emperor's entourage streaming past, on horseback and with carriages, with weapons and supplies. The Emperor himself rode atop his black steed, a formidable horse which carried him high above the mounts of the other men. I could not see his face, but saw the steeliness of his posture and thought he must have come to an acceptance of his fate, or at least a resignation to it. He flew past me on the steed, and then I studied each man in turn; Han was not* among them, he had been left at his post in the palace, left to look after the Emperor's domain. He had not given in.

I had risen very early, before Shiu Lin awoke. I sat at my writing table and thought of my conversation with the Emperor last evening. I wanted to begin writing, to help him understand what I had spoken of and knew to be true. If he could but see....his own agony, as well as the suffering of untold numbers, could be relieved through knowledge that victory over fear was possible, because it was but an illusion, a creation of our minds, joining with many other minds in an agreement that we are separate.

My experience of the White Lotus, the experience of pure love, exposed the illusion to me. So it was this, love, which dispelled fear, totally and irrevocably. But as Madame had said, it was a choice, born of free will, and the choice must be made before the experience could be had. How to convey to the Emperor, that his choices determine his experience, when he was convinced of his powerlessness in the determination of his fate? How to convince anyone who has not yet seen for himself?

It is this fear of death which makes us slaves. And the Emperor was indeed a slave, though he ruled a vast land and millions of people. He could not free his people unless he freed himself. And so, I began:

> To His Highness, the Emperor of China
>
> My thoughts run a course through all time and space. I cannot confine them any more than I can confine the natural love which flows from my heart. I must share with you these thoughts, as you have requested I do so. My hope is that you will accept them as an offering on behalf of the beloved Motherland, China, for my wish is for her to be strong and her people free.
>
> I say to you, there is nothing to fear. Not death, or defeat upon a battlefield. This I know, that what we truly are cannot be destroyed. And I appeal to you, to a mind of intelligence and learning, to open

your heart to the possibility that what you now believe is wrong, and will have disastrous consequences if pursued.

I ask you now to consider the effects of love upon man's spirit. I ask you now: Have you ever truly loved? Only those who have not could fear death. I ask you to consider that what affects one, affects all. If you can but truly understand this, compassion will arise and from compassion the beautiful flower of love springs forth into the sunlight.

My dear Emperor, there is no need to suffer, for you have within your grasp the power to transform the world. Can you not but see? Listen to your heart, and all shall be well.

Yours in Love,
Her Highness, the Empress of China

I sealed the letter, dripping hot wax upon the crease and pressing it with my official seal, and handed it to Shiu Lin, asking her to see it to a courier who would ride day and night overland to where the Emperor fought in a battle for the soul of China, and for his own.

On the morning many weeks later when the Emperor's reply was handed to me, Shiu Lin noticed while helping me to dress that there was a swell at my belly. I had seen her eyes linger there, a quizzical look upon her face, before her eyes came up to mine, and were met with confirmation. "You are with child, Mistress?" she asked.

"Yes, Shiu Lin; I am with child," I replied, and looked past Shiu Lin's happy face to the blossoms on the rose bush which were already fading.

Shiu Lin jumped up, clapping her hands together, "Then we must alert the palace! We must inform the Emperor, and tell the happy news that there will be a continuation of the Imperial lineage," she said in delight.

"No, Shiu Lin. We must not," I answered quietly but firmly.

219

"No one must know."

"No one must know? But...why not? I do not understand...." Shiu Lin said, struggling to make sense of my words.

I sighed deeply, and took her hand. "Shiu Lin, there is something I must tell you..." I began. Drawing her into the garden, we sat for some time as I told her of my chaste meetings with the Emperor, of our talks that went far into the night, of the kiss on the cheek before he would depart, of my return each day without having consummated our union.

Shiu Lin listened, with barely disguised impatience. "But if the marriage has not been consummated, how can you be with child?"

"There was someone else, Shiu Lin," I said. She shot me a look of disbelief, rejecting my statement immediately. "I am with you each moment; Jiang guards our door day and night! There could be no one else!" she said.

"Shiu Lin, do you remember the morning of my wedding, when I slipped away and did not return for some hours? I went to ease my heart, at Black Dragon Pool. And there I found Han, also drawn to this place...."and with that I stopped, as a look of realization had dawned on Shiu Lin's face, and she began to weep.

"Oh Mistress, this cannot be! No, tell me it is not so! For when the Emperor finds out, I cannot think of what will happen, what will happen to us all!" she wailed, sobbing uncontrollably, her head in my lap.

I sat calmly, stroking her hair. "That is why no one must know."

"But how? How can this be kept secret?" she asked through her sobs.

"The Emperor will be away a great while, Shiu Lin. It may be possible, but I will need your help!" I exclaimed, holding her face between my hands, wiping her tears.

"Of course, I will do anything, Mistress, anything at all!" she cried, sitting up and collecting herself at last. "I will tell Madame immediately, she will help us too. Oh Mistress....let us believe we can!"

I smiled at her in gratitude. "I believe we can, Shiu Lin, for we must save this child. But now we must seek to conceal my condition, as you saw today the evidence of it," I said, placing my hand upon the swell at my belly. "My clothing must be made to be loose and unrestrictive. We have some time to prepare our other plans. And now, I must read the Emperor's reply to my letter, as it may guide me in these preparations."

Shiu Lin hugged me tightly, and left me to read my letter. I unfolded the thin paper, and read his words slowly,

> To Her Highness, Empress of China
>
> I received your letter and felt delight at your words, which were beautifully written and wise. And yet, I cannot say that I fully understand your meaning. Are you speaking of religion? For I do not ascribe to a religious view of life, and though in theory the prospect of loving one and all is attractive, in practical terms one cannot be expected to do so. In this life, there are rules that must be followed, or society itself would be jeopardized, not to mention the Imperial rule of China. China can be free only in the context of each man following his duty, as laid down by Imperial decree. There can be no compromise in this. Only one man is ordained by Divine Right to rule this land, and that is the Emperor himself.
>
> As to your question of my having truly loved before...if you are speaking of romantic love between a man and woman, I should say that no, I have never felt a great love for another, but it may ease your heart to know that I should like to do so, should the conditions be favorable. I feel that perhaps it may be possible between us, as I enjoy your company and wish to make our marriage a happy union.
>
> The battle here rages and it angers me to see the faces of these young men who defy me. Any fear I felt on the eve of my departure is now eased, as I am quite protected from harm. Please do not concern

*yourself with my welfare, for I shall return, though when I cannot say.*

*Should you wish to continue to write to me I would be pleased with a response.*

*Loyally,*

*His Highness, The Emperor of China*

I folded the letter slowly and tucked it into the sleeve of my gown. The Emperor had not seen; the void into which his fear had rushed was now filled once more with pride and anger at those who would challenge him. He could have filled it with love, I thought, could have saved himself. In any moment we can save ourselves.

I began to think of ways to tell Shiu Lin that we must think of one who could keep the child safe, once it was born to me. It must be safe outside the palace walls; it could not live within them. And I knew we must begin to pray for its protection, and find a way in our hearts to let it go.

As the life grew inside me, I withdrew more and more into myself. My mind and my heart centered their attention upon it and I dreamed of it each night. It was a girl child, of this I was certain. I could see her, large dark eyes shining, through the mist of my dreams. What fate awaited an orphaned girl child? My heart broke at the thought that she would live without the love of a mother, of the one who loved her beyond time. The one who loved her, I was the one who loved her....even then, before she was born, my love for her haunted me.

Through the next months, I performed the minimal amount of official duties, those from which I could not extract myself gracefully without arousing suspicion. I was attended by many, court ladies and eunuchs, but held only three in confidence as to my condition. Madame knew and only Shiu Lin helped me to dress; and Chen visited me in my inner chambers each day. My voluminous robes and gowns hid my secret well, for no one seemed to notice the impending birth. I had grown little, as if the girl child wished to remain as deeply inside me as she could, assisting in the deception. This only made me love her more, she was my secret life, and she wanted to live.

One evening as I prayed in my garden, Shiu Lin approached quietly, and sat beside me. "Mistress, I wish to tell you there is a visitor here, someone sent to us by Madame herself. She is someone who can help us with…" and she looked down, not finishing the sentence. "Will you see her?"

I put my hand to my belly. "She knows of this?" I asked.

"Yes, that is why she has come," Shiu Lin replied. "We will need help soon, with the birth of the child. The time is approaching and we must prepare."

"And how can the visitor assist us?" I asked.

"She is a midwife, and has delivered countless babies in the Imperial Court. She even attended the birth of the Emperor himself, some years ago," Shiu Lin said.

I was alarmed, and asked, "But Shiu Lin, is it safe? If she is the Emperor's own midwife, will she not divulge the secret and put the child in jeopardy?"

"Mistress," Shiu Lin replied, "she is a friend and confidant of Madame herself. She has been a student of your Master as well, and has achieved a high level of attainment in Buddhist tradition. She understands the situation very well—all is safe! She has agreed to help us, for the sake of the child."

I jumped to my feet, feeling a surge of relief. "Show her in, Shiu Lin, I wish to see her, this woman who knows this child must be saved!" Shiu Lin rushed away, inside my chambers, and I waited *for some moments for her to return, anxious to meet the woman who would assist in the birth of my child. Shiu Lin emerged from within, a strange ashen look upon her face.*

*"Shiu Lin, what is it? What is wrong?" I asked, concerned at her sudden distress.*

*"Mistress, the midwife is here....but..." and she looked over her shoulder in dismay before continuing, "....there is someone else who wishes to see you, and immediately! I...." and before she could finish, an imposing figure emerged from the shadows striding toward me with the air of one who would not be denied. It was Han.*

*"Empress!" he cried, and when he reached me he took both my hands into his own, looking down at me with a mixture of happiness and anxiety. "Empress, we must speak. It has been some time since we have done so, and I...."*

*I reached up, and with my finger to his lips I stopped his words, saying "Not here, Han; it is not safe. Let us walk!" I took his arm, we moved deeply into the garden where all manner of flowers were blooming. When I told Han of my secret, the life which bloomed in me, he collapsed amidst the profusion of blossoms, and cried with heart-wrenching sobs upon the ground.*

*Han lay there for some time, and I stood, my face to the sun, letting its rays warm me, letting its eternal light comfort me. The one inside me stirred, and I took comfort in this also, for she had stirred at the presence of her father. And I thought then that she must see the sun, must run and play in the wind. I could see her thus, hair streaming as she ran and I knew she would be safe, for I willed it so.*

*When Han rose, his face held a look of anguish such as I had never seen. He took my hand again, saying, "Empress, what shall we do? I should remove you today, to a place where you will be safe, where you both will be safe!" he said, his voice strained with emotion.*

I sighed, for I had known he would desire this. "No, Han; I shall not leave this place. For how should we live? The Emperor's power knows no limits, and I should not be safe anywhere in the land. I must stay, and hope to keep the Emperor from knowing of the child. That is the only hope, for all of us."

Han started to resist, but could not, knowing that I spoke truth, there was no other way. His shoulders slumped, his warrior's stance broken, he said "And the child? What will you do with the child? My child...."

I raised my hand to his cheek, resting it there, and sought to reassure him. "I shall have the child; and with help, we shall find a safe place for her to be kept, outside the palace. We must arrange for this before the Emperor returns. Will you help me to do so?" I beseeched him, looking full into his face.

In Han's eyes I saw a fire erupt, roaring up from his depths, and he pulled me to him with primal force. "With every power in me, I shall protect you and the child," he answered. He pulled away, and kissed my hands as he turned to go, tears still in his eyes, unable to contain them there.

When he had gone, only after he had gone, I let my own tears come at last; tears for all that was, and for all that would be lost. And I felt that a presence was with me then, hovering over me, and I saw the lotus which had been at my crown move down until it rested in the womb with my child. My tears became tears of joy, as I knew then that no harm could come to her.

I heard a voice as if from a distance—it was Shiu Lin. "Mistress, will you see the visitor now?" she asked from right beside me where she stood. Beside her stood a woman, one of kindly face and stout physique, dressed in a simple cotton robe, a round charm *pendant dangling from a cord around her neck. When I looked at her she smiled a smile of complete acceptance, of warmth and understanding, and I fell into her arms, and cried out my pain as she stroked my hair and murmured words of comfort. And in time she told me how we should prepare for the birth of the child, the child she called "Lotus," for she had seen... she had seen.*

In the afternoon, Anna takes us on a journey into the heart of the city's shopping district, a huge open-air market surrounded by stores and shops. To reach it, we walk along the same tree-lined boulevards we had traversed this morning, and then cross a high pedestrian overpass spanning a multi-lane highway, which is clogged with traffic. Going from one side to the other is like traveling back in time; on the other side, another culture entirely lives and thrives. The White Swan Hotel, the American Consulate and the international business community are isolated on the beautiful Shamian Island, an enclave of Western architecture and commerce. But surrounding the island is the real China, and as we descend from the walkway, we are immersed in it, surrounded by it, our own little Caucasian island in a sea of Chinese faces.

The contrast is stark. Gone are the clean-swept sidewalks, the pretty stucco villas covered in vines, the spacious plazas. In their places are narrow, broken sidewalks, gritty streets separating rows of grey or brown buildings, with laundry hanging from most of the open windows. Dirt paths, no open space and so many people, all crowded into the confusion of the open air market.

We stand at the entrance, uncertain, overwhelmed. Anna tells us that this is where most people do their grocery shopping, and buy clothes and household goods. Rows of colorful flags wave in the warm breeze. Signs in both English and Chinese indicate stands for vegetables, fish, pig, and rice, among other things. We move slowly forward, and I wonder about the wisdom of coming here, with the babies, when it would be so easy for one of us to get lost from the others, or step from the crumbled sidewalk and fall into the path of a rickety vehicle or into a basket of scorpions.

Anna waves us on from up ahead, "Come on!" She is a little impatient with us in our hesitancy. We try to obey her command, but we quickly fall further behind looking left, looking right, stopping and gawking every few feet. Some merchants sell stacks and stacks of dried lizards, legs splayed out on wooden crosses, a grisly crucifix. Several stands display large shallow bowls or baskets filled with the live scorpions, which crawl frenetically up the sides of the bowl only to slip back down again. Stacked coils of dried snakes are piled high on tables; exotic root vegetables and herbs that look like gnarled human limbs are arranged in baskets and crates.

The produce stands are riotous with color— yellow, orange, red, green; melons and fruits, bursting with life, paragons of freshness, more beautiful than any I've seen in my corner grocery store, or on the prosperous streets of Paris. No shrink wrap, no plastic, just the beauty of the fruits displayed in tiered arrangements of rustic wooden crates. I want to reach out, and so I do; I take a large fuzzy peach into the palm of my hand, and let it rest there, feeling its weight.

A man behind the counter puts up two fingers, and I hand him some coins. When I bite into the fruit a savory burst of flavor fills my mouth and I smile at him, and the old farmer returns my smile.

I move on, coming next to a stand that is dedicated solely to the subtleties of rice. Thirty or forty bags of rice, each with a slight variation in price written on signs planted among the grains. I cannot read the signs as they are printed only in Chinese, but they no doubt tell of what distinguishes one bag of white grains from another almost identical one. I reach into one bag and pinch a few grains between my fingers, and bring them to my nose. A nutty, pleasant aroma wafts to my nostrils. I do the same with grains from the next bag and yes, they do smell different, and I see now that one grain is slightly longer than the other.

In America, rice is rice. It's white, it sits on the plate next to the broiled chicken or fish, and usually it comes from a box. In China, it is a staple, but much more than that. Rice feeds this nation; it is the backbone of the society, served at every meal in every household for thousands of years. It is displayed with the respect it deserves, and shopped for carefully, like the fruit, like the vegetables.

There are live creatures here, too; dogs, cats, floppy-eared rabbits, all waiting in cages to be bought, killed and skinned on the spot. Maggie stops and stares at two skinned rabbits lying on the counter. She looks at the cages filled with live bunnies in line behind them, and she seems to be processing this, brows knit together, putting two and two together. I wonder if the world will be different for her now, now that she knows there are places where they skin and eat bunnies, and kitties, and puppies; but after a few moments she shrugs her shoulders and skips off to the next curiosity, acceptance granted.

We stroll for a long time, in the world full of life and death. Death feeding life, life not possible without death. There is nothing hidden here, no falseness. I think of the grocery store back home, everything shrink-wrapped in plastic, a "sell-by" date stamped on each package. One advantage of seeing your dinner killed in front of you is that you never need wonder at its freshness.

As we wind through the streets of the market I start to feel comfortable, the strangeness wears off. Perhaps not all modernization is improvement after all. I like the human-scale living of this place, the way people shop for just enough food to fulfill that day's needs. I envision myself here, in this life, basket crooked over one arm, picking melons, a small bag of rice, or even a dried lizard or two. Yes, yes, I think; it is not at all impossible to imagine.

We reach the stairs to the overpass which brought us here, and Anna is standing just ahead, waving us on, guiding us once again into the modern world. Just before I reach her, I see a woman crouched down beside a tattered nylon suitcase. In the suitcase is something I can not identify—it looks like bones, there is something sticking out.....I move forward, and crouch down beside her. She is a young woman, and there is a baby sleeping on her back, swaddled in a dirty cloth papoose. The woman wears a chunky stone ring on her left hand, and a large medallion swings from a cord around her neck. She looks up at me with a tired tolerance, "What do you want?"

I look down at the suitcase, and keep looking until my brain can put the pieces of this puzzle together. Yes, they are bones, large femur-like bones, with huge curved black claws attached to it by a tangle of gristle. Bear claws. Beside the bear claws in the suitcase are also horns of different lengths and colors, an exotic collection of hunter's trophies.

I am intrigued, and pull my camera from my backpack. I want to record this scene, but as soon as the woman sees the camera, she begins waving her hands in alarm and saying something that must mean no, no! She turns her head away, shielding her face from the offensive object. Just as she turns her head away I see a small round button pinned to her shirt. It is a picture of a monk, with a shaved head and orange robe.

She must be a Buddhist—could she have come here all the way from Tibet? Perhaps this is an annual trip to the market, to sell the parts collected over the year. And now I have intruded upon her mission, disturbed her peace. I have heard that some people believe that when a photograph is taken, part of your soul is taken, too. How many souls have I stolen? How many times has my own been divided?

I reach into the pocket of my jeans, and pull out the last of my Chinese money, a few bills, and place them beside the torn and dirty suitcase which holds the woman's treasures. She does not turn to look at me, suspicious now, not willing to yield. I feel chastised, contrite; I want to apologize, but there is no way to say it. She is of her world, and I am of mine, and I leave her, in the China we have visited across the bridge of time.

The midwife's name was Huong. All that day, she explained to me the special preparations for bringing a lotus child into the world.

"There can be no doubt that this child will be endowed with a very high level of consciousness, even at birth. And we must ensure that as she passes from your body she is welcomed by those who know of her gifts. Those who do not know will be disturbed by the energy which she will embody, and may seek to harm or even destroy her. This is one reason why children are abandoned by parents. At times, a child such as this embodies, and one or both parents is so disrupted by the energy—their own frequencies and the child's being so discordant—that the child is banished. This happens when the child is at a higher level of consciousness than the parents, and not the reverse; a rejected child is most usually one who will serve to challenge the parents beyond their capacity to grow spiritually," Huong explained.

I felt a wave of relief as I understood her words. "Then one with like frequency may love the child, may even be more compatible with the child than its own natural parent? And there could be one who could love my child, just as I myself would?" I asked.

Huong nodded vigorously, "Indeed, Empress! For the natural parent is a birth channel for the body, but not necessarily the spiritual parent of the child. The spiritual parent of the child is one who has reached the same level of awareness, or higher. And so do not fear, for I know of one who will care for your child in just such a way, and guide her to attainment of all that is good, all that is of love."

As she spoke, the image of beloved Madame flashed in my mind. I saw her smiling, and reaching out her arms.....it was she, it was Madame who was to care for my child! "Oh Huong! I know of whom you speak, I am most pleased, most relieved!" I was overjoyed as I hugged Huong, for I knew of no other who would be suited to be guardian of that which was most precious to me.

Huong patted my shoulders with maternal care, "And now, we must practice the breathing and meditation exercises which will ensure an easy and joyful birth. There is no need to suffer in childbirth...."

At this I raise my eyebrows in surprise, for I had not heard of such a possibility before.

"...yes, it is true! What is thought to be normal suffering of birth is actually a manifestation of fear, of resistance," Huong continued. "It should be, and will be for you, a sublime experience, and one in which you may reach God, as you bring forth this child to earth."

And so we began, and for many weeks we practiced, Shiu Lin assisting me in the meditations, joining me in prayers, helping me to reach that state of mind which would facilitate a sacred birth. Each day, Huong visited through a secret entrance pathway, arranged by Han, so that Jiang would not grow suspicious at the attentions I was receiving from the palace midwife. And as my strength in the practices grew, so also my ability to see the image of the girl child I held within became stronger, so that I knew her, knew who she was, even before birth. I told her each day of my love for her, of my hopes and dreams for her life. I thanked her for coming to me; for the dream of her was all I had now.

One morning when I had grown large, Huong arrived and said, "Today she will arrive!" and with her words came a stirring, a quickening within and a feeling of pressure, and I knew that on this day my child would come forth. Huong took my hand, and Shiu Lin my arm, and we walked together into the room we had *prepared, filled with flowers and candles, the smell of incense and the sound of gentle chimes swaying in the breeze. As my body began its work, I walked or sat, while Huong chanted or rang chimes, calling upon those spirits who might assist us in our task. At times Huong would rub scented oil upon my belly, speaking in soft tones to she who was within, inviting her to come to us, to come to the world. And when pain threatened, she would lead me in prayer or meditation, and it would pass into a feeling of calm such as I had never known. She gave me the medallion which she wore constantly around her neck, and told me to meditate upon the countenance of the great beings which were depicted upon each side.*

*The birds sang at the window, accompanying my labor. Their song transported me, I flew on their wings, tasted the freedom of soaring through the sky. Huong's chanting loosened the strong grip which our ego minds maintain on our thoughts, and I was free—no longer contained in the physical world, no longer limited by time or space.*

*And I saw my child, my own child, and experienced the soul-shaking joy of our reunion which was to be. I saw time unraveling like a ribbon of light, leading from the time of now to the time of then in an unfailing connection, ensuring this destiny. We would be together again, in another time and place, and I saw that it was so.*

*In time my body released her, with a tremendous surge which split the world in two, and I called out to God, who parted the sky to show me Heaven and spoke to me of things beyond knowing. And I knew that whatever I asked in that moment would be granted, but all I desired was to see her, the child that had grown so quietly within and now came into the world without a cry. Huong held her up for me, I saw the dark eyes and perfection of the tiny body, so new and raw, and my heart heaved in agony, for she could not be mine.*

As Huong anointed my child with precious oils and sang out her prayer chants, I fell into a sleep of darkness, where all dreams were extinguished and I knew no light.

My child never cried. For days following her birth I lay with her, she suckling at my breast, content and happy in the warmth of my arms. I sang to her, spoke to her, held her close; she was a world, and I entered that world completely, so that I hardly knew another world outside existed. Time stretched out, so that we lay together for an eternity, and all space contracted to the room in which we existed.

I was dimly aware of people coming and going. Shiu Lin, Huong, and even Chen moved about the room, bringing us food and water, but not disturbing our intense concentration, one upon the other. We looked into each others' eyes, and she spoke to me without words. She reminded me of a baby bird, and that is what I called her....Little Bird, my Little Bird. Though she had been given a name, I never used it; for to me, she was the essence of something so sacred that it must remain nameless.

I memorized her body, her face, her smell; I breathed her in like a fragrance, through every pore of my skin. I whispered to her that though in time we may be parted, nothing would stop me from finding her again, in this life, or in another, and I promised her that I would return again and again to the wheel of life, just to be reunited with her, and that my heart would recognize her, no matter what her form.

One day Huong sat next to me upon the bed. "It has been many weeks, Empress. Should we not prepare the child to be taken to safe keeping? She asked gently, stroking the baby's hand.

I looked down at my child, so small and delicate. "Not yet,

Huong, please not yet. Can we not wait until word arrives of the Emperor's return? For she will be stronger each day, and our bond will grow to be unbreakable," I answered.

Huong sighed, looking at me with eyes filled with deep concern. "Empress, you know that each day brings fresh possibility of discovery. The sooner we take the child to safety, the better for you both." I reached down and pulled my child to me, rocking her and smoothing her hair with my hand. Huong looked suddenly tired, the strain of these past weeks of secrecy showing in her face. "But for now I will agree, and I leave you to each other." Huong departed with a tender touch to the baby's head, and I held her closer than ever before.

Shiu Lin began bringing me garments and I would sew while the baby slept. The tray of Imperial jewels lay upon the bed, and I would pick them, one by one; an emerald, a ruby, diamonds, pearls. I lay them inside an opened seam, and then sewed the pouch tightly shut, hiding my tiny stitches as best I could. Many garments I prepared in such a way, gowns and tunics, overshirts and underthings, so that my child would be arrayed in jewels of value beyond price, a treasure invisible to those who cannot see.

There is a legend in China of the mighty dragon which carries securely under its chin a bright pearl, the most fortunate of gems. It is this pearl that is the source of the dragon's power, for it multiplies anything which it touches. If placed in a bag of coins, more coins will appear; if settled into a sack of wheat, the wheat sack shall bulge with the increase wrought by the pearl.

I chose a large glowing pearl from the tray and held it between my fingers, caressing its smooth spherical surface. If I placed this, a *magic pearl, next to my baby's heart, perhaps more children such as she was would come, would grace earth with their presence. I placed the pearl into a small cloth pouch and began to sew, each stitch binding my hopes in place, my dreams for my baby, my dreams for my people. May a multitude of children spring forth, I prayed; may China be saved by their light. Oh Dragon of China, mythical beast of the land! Protect my child, protect these children, for they have come to save the world.*

When we get back to the hotel, Alex takes Baby upstairs to put her down for a nap. I am glad to be alone, there is nothing to do but wander this giant place and nurse the feelings of sadness which have arisen again during the walk back from the market. This is how it has been for the past seven days; feeling sadness and fear, and then later a transition to acceptance and peace, with an eventual drift back into an even deeper despair which I then have to dig my way out of. I am exhausted by this effort to stay in balance, with the strain of trying to process so much emotional information. It may take the rest of my life to integrate all of this, if I ever do.

Ambiguity is one of the most difficult things to tolerate, and the intolerance leads to poor choices. Not knowing, not knowing how something will turn out, leads to impatience for an outcome. The impatience then results in one of two actions: either a resolution is forced, or there is a move to retreat, to give up. Either way, the result cannot be optimal, for in every situation, a process is working, an intricate, complex process, which has as its goal the highest outcome, the good of the whole, which we cannot easily see or grasp. This ability to allow the process to work can be called faith, and this faith is not a belief, this faith is not passive. The self discipline needed to overcome the anxiety of ambiguity takes enormous effort to sustain.

The truth is that every single moment of every single life is uncertain. We go to great lengths to deny this, so much do we crave the illusion of security. It is as if the knowledge of this ambiguity is too terrible to bear, we must anesthetize ourselves in a myriad of ways or we won't be able to live the false lives we have constructed. True power lies in accepting the fact that everything is uncertain in every moment; it is the truth, and it is where our freedom lies. A small shift in thinking, a slight willingness to admit the possibility, and one can see that if everything is uncertain, then anything is possible.

Anything is possible. I could get Baby, even though in this moment it looks doubtful. It is the certainty of those who are telling me it can't be done which appalls me. The only certainty is the love I feel for her, the only real and solid thing. Everything else is malleable, any regulation is subject to change, any man-made obstacle could crumble unexpectedly. Those who don't understand this fact are always surprised by the turn of events; but I intend to be ready and waiting to scoop up my treasure when all moves aside. The optimal outcome is the only one I will accept.

My only hope is to embrace the uncertainty, rejoice in the ambiguity, let the process proceed. The back-and-forthness of this situation has produced a sort of numbness, a state of suspended animation, which gives me the feeling that I am a witness to my self, as if a part of me were watching from outside. I see myself walking, talking, acting and feeling, and yet there is also a silent part watching, like a stereotypical Freudian therapist, nodding its head, saying, "Very interesting!" but maintaining emotional detachment. I am so grateful for it; the witness allows a buffer between me and the overwhelming emotions, the confusion and fear.

I think about Alex, about the true reasons behind her rejection of Baby, things she has been saying these last few days to explain to me, to explain to herself, how this mess could have happened. It is true that she didn't love her; but any love was blocked from coming forth by her inability to accept that which she did not expect. Baby was smaller than she thought she would be, she was younger, she was dirtier, she was needier. Baby didn't look like she had expected, her nose was too small. And most of all Alex didn't feel the way she had expected to feel, when those feelings were choked off by her own inflexibility. Things must be as she has decided to expect, or she rejects them, they are not real. Instead of deciding to work with and overcome her anxiety, she decides to reject the reality which has caused the anxiety.

If she had worked through it, if she had not let her fear win, what could the outcome have been? For Alex, a profound healing of her heart and a relief from her exhausting need for control; for Baby, a mother that could love her. But the intensity of Alex's fear, the almost total panic she experienced at the thought of raising this baby was too big an obstacle. The struggle between fear and reason has caused what I perceive to be almost a break in her psyche, something like a classic nervous breakdown.

But things are not as they appear, as Antoinette had reminded me so many times. Beyond the psychological terminology was a deeper reality; it was as if a whole new side of Alex's personality had emerged, and was now living side-by-side with the old. It was almost as if two personalities resided there, and control kept flipping back and forth between the two. In any given moment I did not know which side would emerge to be dealt with.

She was at war with herself, and all that had happened here was collateral damage. So I prayed for her, that she find a way to let love win.

In the hotel lobby is a shop selling clothing and gifts, and as I stroll past I notice displayed in the window a pair of tiny Chinese cloth shoes. They are unusual, a blue and white brocade fabric accented with bright red piping. For some reason the sight of them stops me cold; I stand and look at them for a long time before I go inside and ask to see them. A young salesgirl reaches into the window and pulls them out, and places them in my upturned palm. They are as light as a feather, the soles are made of woven straw, they are beautifully made, they are perfect. I stand just looking at them, stroking them, turning them over in my hand, they feel just right.

Baby has been wearing shoes which Alex brought for her, the baby shoes that her son had worn, many years before. Alex has been concerned each day that they will get lost, she is always checking to make sure Baby has not kicked one off or that one is not untied. She wants to keep them for her son, a keepsake. They don't look right on Baby, they are scuffed boys shoes. They are not hers, I am sure that she has never had her own pair of shoes.

I tell the salesgirl that I will take them, and she carefully lifts them from my palm. She takes them behind the counter and tells me, "We will sew button on now." She takes a needle and thread from a sewing basket and begins attaching the little brown button which will fasten the strap across the instep of the tiny foot which will rest inside.

She takes such care as she pulls the thread in and out, making long movements with her arm, aiming for precise placement of the needle. She finishes quickly, and fastens the straps, and holds them up for my approval. Yes, they are perfect, I say, through the lump in my throat. The addition of the simple sturdy button makes them come alive somehow; they are infused with the loving touch of the salesgirl. She wraps each shoe carefully in a fresh piece of tissue paper and then wraps them both together into a tight bundle. She hands it to me, smiling and bowing her head slightly. I feel tears spring to my eyes; I take the bundle and thank her, but silently now because my voice will not come.

Outside the store I take the precious bundle and tuck it deep inside my backpack, on the very bottom, where no one will see it. This is my secret talisman, my act of faith, my leap into the arms of the possible. I have shoes for Baby, waiting for her little feet to fill them. They will be my symbol of hope, and a reminder that sometimes we must walk through pain to get home again.

*I could not release her. Nor could Shiu Lin, Huong or Chen find a way to convince me to let her go one moment too soon, for they too loved the child. And Han, when he finally came one chill day, held her to his breast as a drowning man clings to the one who might save him.*

*"Everything is ready, her safe departure is assured," he said, and yet he held her, and returned day after day to be with us.*

*We were happy for those moments, stolen from some future happiness. It was worth the price, any price, to be together thus, and I cried each time with joy for this gift. And even the day when we were betrayed is counted by me as a happy one, for we were together in love.*

*That day, I was sitting on the bed, while Han held his Little Bird high in the air, for he too called her thus; she gurgled with delight at his attentions, and I was so enthralled with watching them that I almost did not notice a woman standing in the doorway, a look of shocked grimness on her face, which gave way to a satisfied smile of victory.*

*It was Ling Dao, the Emperor's concubine. I turned to see the familiar cold glare which left no question as to her resentment of me and of my place as Empress. I noted her hard beauty which had in the end served to disappoint her; for she had thought it would buy her the Emperor's heart and the key to power over all others, over all women whom she saw as rivals.*

*When I saw her I jumped to my feet with a strangled cry. Han froze with his arms held high above his head, our Little Bird suspended in air for a moment, until he slowly lowered her to his* chest, and turned his back to the one who would be our undoing.

I could not move and stood rooted in place, as the concubine moved slowly toward me, arms crossed, a smirk of cruel delight upon her face.

"And so, Empress," she drawled, "what do we have here? A child? How delightful!" Her hard eyes glittered in the pallor of her cheeks, flushed now with crimson from the excitement of her discovery.

"It has been so long since I, or anyone in the palace, has had occasion to see you, and perhaps this explains why!" The concubine swayed her hips a little as she walked, taking mincing steps to prolong her advance.

"You have been very, very busy, I see...." she went on, "...and my dear Han! Jiang has been so concerned about you these past months. My friend has told me of your many visits here, though he knows that you have tried mightily to keep them secret." She stopped for a moment, splaying out her fingers in front of her and examining her long nails, as if at her leisure.

"I suppose with the Emperor away and so long, that you must have become bored and needed some.....entertainment." Ling Dao laughed a terrible cheerless laugh. "Well. It appears that you have found it! For there is nothing more entertaining than a child, and such a beautiful one at that!" And she moved closer so that I could see the sallow cast of her skin, and smell the sweet heavy perfume with which she had bathed herself.

I stepped forward then, recovering my abilities. I placed myself between this woman and Han, between her and my child. "There is nothing for you to see here," I said, barely keeping my voice controlled. "You must go now, for these are my private chambers." My heart was beating wildly, though I mustered the strength to *appear unfazed at her intrusion.*

*"Oh but I should love to see her!" she exclaimed with feigned delight. "It is a girl child, is it not? My, my, and so it is; what a pity. For a son, now that is something of which to be most proud! I myself should like to bear a son, for only that is important to the Imperial lineage," she said, her voice dripping with condescension.*

*I thought of my beautiful girl child, of the countless women and girls of this land, who for centuries had been enslaved by this philosophy, the idea that male children were of greater value and must be coveted. This idea was the justification for murder, brutality, and cruelty perpetrated by men and women alike, in homage to a freakish concept that had been allowed by all to become ingrained and unassailable in this society. I heard the concubine's words and understood her implication—she would betray her own kind for personal gain, and I feared for my people, feared for the soul of this land.*

*Why, I wondered, desperate in my need to understand such cruelty; why would she do this? I looked straight into her eyes, eyes which were opaque and did not emit light; and as I did so Ling Dao shifted her gaze and sought Han's face. When they found it, the unmistakable longing of unrequited love registered there, and I knew that the jealousy of a woman, that ancient original terror, would be my undoing.*

*It is only from fear and ignorance that such insanity springs, and I worked down my rage, filled myself with the thoughts of the great ones, those who knew, and though I could not feel that balm of compassion for this woman, I felt a sense of peace come over me, that one mind turned to thoughts of love could balance the scales with thousands of hatreds.*

*"I should wish you luck in that, ma'am, and perhaps you could get to that task, and right away. For now, leave us be, for our sake, and*

for your own; for you have no business in these quarters and should have been prevented from entering here," I heard myself speak, and marveled at the voice that seemed to come from another, such calm and strength did it contain. "Shiu Lin will show you out."

And I wondered, where was Shiu Lin? I had not seen her for hours now, where could she be? For if Jiang had failed to stop this woman from intruding, Shiu Lin certainly would not have done so. Her protection of me and the child had been unwavering and seamless.

"Oh, but Shiu Lin is not here!" she laughed. "I had her summoned by Madame this morning for a very important task. It was Jiang who allowed me to enter...such a good friend! For he cares only for the good of the Emperor, and will follow orders given from above at all costs," she said, a self-satisfied smile lighting her face.

Han's eyes met mine, a mixture of anger and deep disappointment evident in his look. His own underling had betrayed him, and had not the honor to confront him with his misgivings. His face quickly changed, it became hard and determined, and I could tell what he was thinking, that there was not a moment to lose.

"It does not matter now, please go," he said forcefully, without looking at the one who had come to poison his well of joy.

Ling Dao hesitated a little, the momentum of the situation no longer resting with her. Before she turned to go, she pulled one last bow from her quiver, held in reserve for the moment of greatest impact. "Oh yes, and Han....it is quite fortunate that I should find you here. For I can tell you both, together! The Emperor is making his return, he rides full out as we speak, and shall reach the palace in the morning, perhaps before the rooster crows. I knew you would both be anxious to know," she said slyly, and turned on her heel, *her cloying scent trailing behind.*

*When I knew that she was gone I rushed to Han's embrace, and he held me there, the three of us pressed together for one last time. And then Han left to complete the preparations that would take my child somewhere far away, to a place where she could not be found.*

*Day moved into evening, the longest evening I would ever know. My baby lay on the bed, unsuspecting of her fate. I moved about the room, looking at her all the while. How could it be that I shall let her go away from me? I gathered the clothing that I had prepared for her, the clothing that was filled with secret jewels, and arranged them on the bed around her. This was all she would take from this place, and I touched each piece lovingly, over and over again, to infuse my essence into the clothing.*

*And then I held her and cooed to her, and when at last Chen arrived to tell me it was time to dress her for her departure, she was quiet and sleepy, her eyes half closed, ready to drop into dreams. I began dressing her slowly, so as not to awaken her, and sang to her softly and she did not awaken as I placed the last of the garments upon her small body. The layers of clothing padded her and when I picked her up I could hardly feel her inside them. Already, I could hardly feel her...I walked with her around the room, singing to her in a voice I prayed she not forget.*

*When Chen entered from the garden he was carrying a basket over his arm. He placed it on the floor in front of me, and removed the lid. Tears glistened in his eyes as he showed me how to place her inside, snuggling her down so that she completely filled the cavity. This is how she had filled my body also, when I had carried her* those months. Fitting so perfectly, the space meant just for her. I would never be filled like that again; this I knew. The empty place inside me gnawed like a hunger and I placed my hand upon my belly as I leaned down to kiss the soft cheek and to say goodbye. Goodbye, Little Bird, goodbye.... In the last glimpse of my child I saw silky lashes resting on creamy skin, the perfect rosebud lips, the sparse hair, and even as Chen placed the lid securely on the basket, I saw her there, sleeping in perfect trust. Something heaved in me as I thought that trust will be broken; now it will be broken, and she will always be afraid.

And then Shiu Lin entered, and through my tears I spoke to her. She was dressed in the concealing robe of the monk at prayer, her head covered in the hood which hid her face from view. Shiu Lin tried to tell me of her pain at the discovery of the concubine's intrusion, that she felt in some way responsible for our betrayal. I shushed her forcefully, for there was none so loyal as she; I told her she was as a sister to me, that I loved her deeply. We embraced and promised to be together again, that we would find happiness, that we would continue the work set to us by Madame and Master. We knew what was to be, and did not dwell upon whether it would be in this lifetime or another, for it did not matter; what mattered was that we willed it so.

Chen and Shiu Lin were to smuggle my child out of the palace by way of a path laid out by Han, who would be waiting outside the gates with horses to carry them off, to a place unknown to me. I was not to be told of her destination, to protect me from myself. Chen lifted the basket and Shiu Lin took hold of the handle and together they carried the precious bundle away, not looking back as they rounded the doorway into the garden.

The sudden emptiness of the room was impossible to bear. Their *departure created a vacuum which collapsed around me, and I imploded in on myself. I fell to the ground under the pressure, not able to resist the power of my grief. I asked my God, how shall I live? Through this night, how shall I live, without my daughter, without my love? A night without dreams of a life, without any tomorrows?*

*And he answered me later, when the darkness almost engulfed me; he answered me only when I could ask no longer. His answer was something I already knew, that the love was inside me and could never be lost.*

That evening we fly to Hong Kong. Standing in a long line in the heat of the airport terminal on a sunny afternoon, with mounds of luggage, baby strollers, bags and boxes, the three families say goodbye to Anna. She shakes the hand of each of the parents, solemnly, bowing a little; she hugs and kisses each of the babies, and tells them good luck. When she holds Baby, Anna has tears in her eyes; they are just barely visible before she wipes them away with the back of her hand.

"Anna," I ask, "What do you think she'll be like?"

She thinks for a moment, peering into Baby's face. "She will be pretty," she declares, "and….naughty!" she laughs with hearty delight at the thought of what "naughty Baby" will be like for her parents to raise.

"Naughty!!" I exclaim. "Why naughty?"

"Well," she explains, "girls from each place have a reputation: girls from Canton sweet, girls from Shanghai smart; girls from Jiangxi have hot temper! But," and she raises her forefinger, lest I think it's all bad news, "Are hard workers!"

I laugh at her comments, thinking how perfect those traits are for living in America. I take her hand then, "Thank you, Anna, for all your help here in China," I say, "you've been a wonderful guide." I have come to like Anna very much, to appreciate her gentle demeanor, her efficient work habits, and her warm heart. It was clear that she cared about these babies, and was happy for them that they were going to have families, and that they were going to America. Anna has no idea that Baby's fate is uncertain, that Alex doesn't want to adopt her, or that she may be with me; I wonder what she would think.

Anna kisses Baby on the cheek, "Goodbye!" she says to her, and hands her hastily to me and turns away, not wanting anyone to see the emotion she is trying to hide. She moves quickly away and does not look back, she is swallowed by the crowd; and then we are alone, and it feels strange. Alex and I stand uncertainly with our belongings, passing the baby back and forth, playing with her, while the line moves slowly toward the checkpoint. Already the little group has started to disintegrate, each family moving away a little from the others, finally to have some space and distance. It is a relief, we are tired of pretending, tired of questions the others ask, tired of having to cover the truth of the situation. Every time someone asks Alex about day care or pre-school or what the baby's room is like, I turn away. Every time someone calls the baby by the name Alex was to give her, I cringe. It is excruciating because I am afraid it will make

Alex change her mind and want to keep Baby. Each time the fear arises I must work it down, work it down, until I can move on and not be paralyzed by it.

Now that we are almost home, in only two days we will be landing in the U.S., the anxiety should be lessening but instead, is building inside me. Walking a tightrope for ten full days; defusing a bomb delicately, one tiny wire at a time, so that it doesn't blow up in my face...my nerves are on edge, frayed and frazzled. And these next two days, we have nothing to do; no adoption proceedings, no travel, no distractions. Just me, Alex and the baby, and plenty of time to think.

And tomorrow is my birthday; I will spend it in Hong Kong. My sister has arranged for us to stay at one of the nicest hotels in the city, the Four Seasons Regent, where she knows the manager and was able to get us reservations. I had been looking forward to this part of the trip particularly, planning on doing some Christmas shopping and having a nice meal to celebrate. Now it seems like just another day to get through, an unfortunate casualty of an unforeseen situation, and I am too tired to care.

Finally we board the flight, over an hour later than scheduled. It is dark outside now, and as we rise above the tarmac the lights of Guangzhou twinkle below. The lights spread out in a giant pool, as far as the eye can see. Barges on the river are strung with festive bulbs, they move slowly and become smaller and smaller as we rise into the night sky.

Baby lay with her head upon my chest, not fussing or squirming, so adaptable, so accepting. What must these last days have been like, for her? The first year of her life she was confined to a crib, or a chair; at most, the world consisted of the one room in the orphanage where she had been placed. I doubt she had been outside much, if at all; the visual and auditory stimulation must be overwhelming. Colors, sounds, movement, music, languages, faces, tactile sensations encountered for the first time. A kaleidoscope of stimuli, a whirling puzzle of information. How was her little brain processing all of that, not to mention her emotions, fears and hopes? I smooth her sparse black hair, kiss her head, she grabs my index finger with her tiny hand and holds on.

My heart thumps against my chest, I love you, Baby! Just then, Alex looks over and sees the tender moment. She reaches out with her finger and strokes the baby's cheek, starts cooing at her to get her attention. The baby lifts her head, Alex reaches for her and lifts her from under the arms, away from me, and begins playing patty-cake, and Baby laughs, delighted. Alex puts her head next to the Baby's, making kissing noises, talking in a sing-song voice.

My stomach churns over, oh, don't watch! Don't respond! I lean over and take a paperback from my bag, open it and stare at the pages, reading one paragraph over and over, and not understanding any of it. The litany of comforting phrases I have been using to assuage my anxiety begins in my head: I do not own her, no one owns her; she belongs to herself, not to me, not to Alex. Feeling this love has to be enough, it doesn't have to turn out any one certain way, not the way you want it to. Only what is best for her, only what is best. Oh, God, I stand aside; only what is best.

I stand aside. I stand in faith that the best outcome will

prevail, even if it doesn't look that way to me. And right now, it doesn't look that way to me. I feel myself slipping into that abyss of doubt, of course, what was I thinking, that it would work out? That I would bring this baby home? I had forgotten so many times, the obstacles. And anyway, a voice says, this is all an exercise for you, a test for you. On the eve of your 37th birthday, have you learned anything? What have you learned? Will you live what you have learned?

The voice shocks me out of my cycle of repetitive thoughts: have I learned anything, will I live what I have learned? Yes, yes; that is the question, in any moment—each situation that arises is an opportunity to live what you have learned. If I let this opportunity pass, I will just have to live this point again, in another time, in another place. I may delay slaying these dragons on this battlefield, but I will meet them again on another, they will be the same dragons. I want to break through it now, while I have the chance, but how? How?

See the lesson, it is the only way. I see her face, she is happy, smiling, laughing. And I hear again the voice, and it tells me, her happiness is yours; all happiness is yours, if you choose it to be.

I reach down and put the book away. And I turn to face the scene which has aroused fear, envy, sadness, anger, all the things which cause pain and limit perception. As I face the scene which has given me a chance to move beyond those things, I say a silent prayer: Thy will, be done.

That night, the night of my greatest loss, was a journey into the heart of darkness, a journey beyond faith. I fought and struggled, pitched battles I had been sure were already won. Hope and love, understanding and compassion, all had to be regained and earned again. In those hours of despair I attacked all that I had pledged allegiance to, had given faith to, and attacked them with a vengeance which comes when one has believed, and been betrayed. I had believed in love, and had loved; I had believed in hope, and had hoped; I had believed there was nothing to fear, and had not feared; and yet none of these things had saved me, for I had never known such pain.

I knew my child would be safe, that she had been saved. And I did not fear for myself, for my death was of no concern to me now. The pain was the primal anguish of a mother when she loses her child, and this pain could not be worked down. There was one way, and one way only; I went into this cauldron of fire, immersed myself and drowned myself and died to myself, and reemerged as one cleansed of a terrible sin, the sin of doubt.

And by some grace I passed that test, and stepped from the ashes of that fire and into a new world. And then a world was shown to me that gave me such new hope that I rejoiced in the certainty of my death, for it is only after death that one may be reborn.

I do not know how many days it was that I waited there. No one disturbed me; I was left to spend the hours in deep meditation, in memories, in prayer for the future. I did not eat, and my sleep was not restful, for my dreams were of an unnatural vibrancy which left me exhausted.

One time I thought that the concubine had come, that she told me she had decided not to tell the Emperor of my transgression, that my child was safe. But I do not know if I was dreaming or awake, wishing it so or experiencing a true encounter. It served only to make me sadder still after my joy died down and I realized again that I was alone in that room.

And Madame came to me, in the emptiness she came to soothe my heart of the pain which sought to destroy me. Her spirit permeated the room. I could see her there, and speak with her of matters which my soul held of highest importance. Could there have been another outcome, I asked her, could I have acted differently, was there another path? And she showed me that all involved had choices and must live the responsibility for those choices.

As her words came to me I saw an image unfold as if behind a veil, and as the veil slowly lifted, I saw Madame, dressed in a tattered robe and tied with thick ropes at the hands and feet to a wet stone wall of a dungeon cell. Madame's face shone with brilliant light, and showed no trace of anxiety as she calmly spoke to someone I could not see, a person in the shadows. I heard Madame say, to the person in the dim, "Do what you will, for you do it to yourself," and then a man stepped forward and slightly turned toward me. It was the Emperor, and he held in his hands a small vial which he carefully brought forward and up, until it was above Madame's head.

"Because you loved me, I shall let you live!" The Emperor said in a thick strained voice. He looked as if he might cry; it was as if he was valiantly struggling to contain an emotion which embarrassed his pride. His demeanor was that of a young boy who in the impotence of disappointment begins to test his powers of revenge.

Madame did not reply at once, but held his fiery gaze with her own tender look. In sadness she said, "I do love you. But it is a love you will never understand."

The Emperor came close to losing his composure at her words; his face crumpled for a moment into a look of deep anguish. "Perhaps you are the only one who has ever loved me," he said in a hoarse whisper.

He struggled to regain his composure, and after a moment he rallied his affronted pride. "You have given me your love and wisdom from an early age," he acknowledged. "And yet you have conspired to take from me that which I hold most precious. Because you have done the one I shall free you; but because of your treachery in the other, I must take something of value from you."

At his words Madame looked up, and as she did so the Emperor tipped the small vial so that a drop of a pearly liquid fell from its rim and into her left eye. As the drops met the soft tender flesh, Madame's face went slack, but she did not cry out. Every ounce of strength was being used by her arms and legs in an instinctual reaction to pull in, to protect, which they were prevented from doing by the thick rope restraints. I could see the corded sinew in her arms as she pulled and thought, she will break out, she will be free! But the arms went slack, Madame's head sagged down; and I could see the flesh around her eye had all but melted, and with it I knew her sight must be forever gone.

Madame still did not cry out, but gave short rasped gasps which burst from her throat in staccato rhythm. As she struggled to triumph over the pain, to not be broken, the Emperor watched with an expression of cruel delight, a twisted smile beneath his hard glittery eyes. He eased backward, slowly, into the shadows, all the while watching Madame's pain rise and crash upon her. Just as Madame could contain herself no longer, she cried out in a pitiable voice an *anguished plea for mercy.*

*The veil descended on the scene and I cried out, "Oh Madame! It is my fault; I am to blame for this horrendous torture inflicted upon you! Oh Madame forgive me, forgive me!!" And I sobbed uncontrollably as I thought of the price she had paid for giving me my freedom, for teaching me of love and beauty. Her words came to me, "This is not your doing," but my grief would not allow me to honor her with accepting them.*

*As I lay sobbing on the bed, I heard the distinctive voice say, "All is well," with such emphasis and strength that I was immediately comforted, and another vision unfolded before my mind's eye: I saw Madame, dressed in a heavy and glorious robe embroidered in gold, her face wreathed by a collar of thick fur, buttoned high up to her chin. Across her left eye was a patch of embroidered silk, which covered the ruined flesh, but did nothing to diminish her extraordinary beauty, and only accentuated the light which shone from the other eye.*

*A papoose of the same fur which rimmed Madame's collar was slung upon her back, and in it slept my baby, in safety and perfect comfort, protected from harm. I saw with delight that next to Madame stood Chen, that he had completed his mission, and I knew that they had come to a place of safety, a high mountainous region beyond the reach of the Emperor's power. Behind the beloved trio rose snow-capped peaks of ethereal beauty, they had reached a heaven on earth. Peace blossomed in my heart, and I rose from the bed to begin a night of prayers filled with gratitude for the jewels mined from amidst the mountain of loss.*

*Finally Chen returned from his sacred mission. The sight of me must have unnerved him, for he did not speak when first he saw me, but came into my chambers and sat upon the bed, put his head into his hands and remained unmoving there.*

*I went to the cage that stood in the corner of my room, the cage which held the bird that Chen had given me those many mornings ago, on the day before I wed. I put my arm inside the opening, and the bird jumped upon it. Drawing it out I turned to Chen, and held the bird out toward him. He shook his head, no; "I will not take it," he said. "I will not leave you."*

*I did not move, but continued to hold out my arm until finally he too brought up his arm, slowly, until the tips of our fingers touched, and as they did so we looked into the depths of each other's eyes. What I saw there locked my attention, for Chen had a story he wished to tell, it was there in his eyes and my own pleaded in response, "Tell me, for I need to know."*

*And without a word the story unfolded. I saw in images the fate that had befallen Chen. There he was, within the Eunuchs chambers, as they prepared for the assault which would rape him of his manhood. And yet, the head Eunuch's face held not cold dedication to duty, but a sad anger, and I felt his reluctance to inflict this pain upon Chen, for he sensed his pure heart and knew of his goodness. The Emperor had sent one too many good men to be castrated against his will, and the head Eunuch, a tall serious man, had tired of performing the cruelties demanded by the Emperor.*

*I saw him come forward, and quietly and deliberately ask Chen, "Are you sure?" And Chen reached out to touch the man's cheek with tenderness and gratitude, and replied, "Yes, I am sure. For it is death, or this…and I must be near her." The old Eunuch nodded, and turned to his assistant who handed him a pipe of opium, to dull the pain and administer some relief from the horrendous shock of the procedure. As Chen put the pipe to his lips to draw in the sweet smoke, the other Eunuchs turned in unison their backs toward Chen; in respect and homage for what was being taken from him they refused to look. This they could give, and this alone, and they gave it with heavy hearts and prayers for deliverance.*

*The image fades and I see in Chen's eyes the perfect love with which he made his choice. This is what has saved him, transformed him and made him whole, and this is what will draw us together, again and again, as we cycle through the earthly existence on the path toward perfection.*

*"All will be well," Chen whispered urgently as he gripped my hands in his. "I shall bring Lo Ming to me now from the village, and she and I will be together; it is arranged! Your daughter shall know us as beloved protectors all the days of her life; do not fear!"*

*Just as I whispered, I have loved you so, the bird took flight across the slight gap between us, and landed safely on his outstretched finger. In the end, we must let go of everything.*

The flight is mercifully short. Hong Kong airport is new and sleek and shiny, and we walk for miles in the immense open space, looking for baggage claim, trying to find customs. All the signs are in English, and it is easy to find our way, but our load of bags and gear is too much for one person to handle alone, as one of us must always be occupied with the baby. We have piled our stuff precariously on a large wheeled cart, and I push carefully; but still a piece slides off here, something gets caught in the wheel there, and we have to stop the whole parade, and re-position the stack.

I do this ten, maybe fifteen times, huffing and sweating, and cursing my tendency to overpack. This episode is perfectly symbolic of the entire trip: there is too much baggage; something falls off, I put if back; we move a few steps forward, and something else hits the ground and I have to stop again to retrieve it. I am Sisyphus, rolling the giant stone up the hill....for ever and ever, into eternity. I am beginning to wonder if this trip will ever end; perhaps we'll just spin off into our own little whirlpool of reality, outside the rushing river of life, moving from airport to hotel to van to bus, city to city, hauling bags and pushing babies, a Hell of our own creation.

And then, after what seems like a lifetime of this, a white-gloved savior appears, in the form of a uniformed driver from the Four Seasons Hotel. He is standing in front of me, holding a sign printed with my last name, he is looking for me. I stop, and point to his sign, too exhausted to speak, and nod gratefully. He says, "Let me take those bags, Madam," and I think, he must be a messenger from God.

Within minutes he is loading our bags and us into a spacious black Mercedes sedan that is polished to a mirror shine. The smell of the leather permeates the car; there is enough room in the plush back seat for both of us to lie down if we wanted to. I am stunned by this feeling of luxury, such a contrast to the transportation we have grown accustomed to these past days in China. Hardly a bump is felt as the car glides down the highway toward the sparkling skyline ahead. It is heaven on wheels.

Baby seems to like it too; she has perked up considerably and is playing on the floor between the seats. I can't move, weakened by our sudden catapult into yet another world, a world of comfort and peace. Sealed inside the car, Alex and I do not disturb the silence, do not intrude upon each others thoughts. I watch out the window on my side of the long back seat, I could ride like this forever, surrounded by the richness of space and silence, a purgatory but at least a pleasant one.

But the ride does end, in no time the car is zipping into a circle drive in front of the glass doors of a tall modern building. The door is opened from the outside as soon as the car comes to a halt. Another uniformed employee helps us out, then scurries around to the trunk to retrieve the stroller, and helps us load Baby into it. He ushers us inside, telling us the bags will be brought up right away, to our rooms. "We have it all arranged for you, no need to check in. We'll take you directly to your room and make you as comfortable as possible," he says, and I wonder if I am hearing correctly. We are being treated like royalty, or at least like some minor celebrity.

My sister must have asked her friend the manager to give us special consideration, and right now, I appreciate it so much I want to cry. Beauty, order, courtesy, softness, quiet; fresh flowers fill the lobby, soothing music wafts through the air. Plush rugs, gleaming marble, the hushed arrival of the elevator that will whisk us to our room. Low lighting in the hallway, nothing glaring or harsh. We enter our room and it is a lovely cocoon of comfort. The bellman goes to the window, and pulling the cord hand over hand, opens the curtain to reveal the most stunning view I have ever seen. The panorama of the Hong Kong skyline spools out before us, the colorful lights on each building celebrating the arrival of the new Millennium, in just three weeks.

I stand transfixed at the window. I had almost forgotten. Christmas is 14 days away, the New Year a week later. My birthday is tomorrow. For the first time since this trip began, I am oriented in time, in space. A huge Chinese dragon made of light spans the length of the skyscraper directly across the harbor from our window. The year 2000 will be the year of the Dragon, a power year, a year when mighty and mythic forces are unleashed in the world. Anna had told us that the dragon is symbolic of the spirit of the Chinese people, and that a dragon year was thought to be particularly lucky, a good year for beginning new undertakings.

Dragon, dragon, spirit of China, beautiful flaming beast; are you real, or imaginary? The Chinese call their land "Middle Kingdom," because legend has it that it floats between Heaven and the underworld. Upon death the Emperor was believed to climb on the back of the dragon and fly to his place in the heavenly realm. I am in my own Middle Kingdom, and I await my dragon, my flight to heaven, my own new beginning.

And so came the morning when a retinue of palace guards appeared at my chamber doorway. Without a word I rose to go with them, walking through the empty rooms of my chambers and across the courtyard which I knew so well. The sky was a piercing blue and against this backdrop I recalled my Master's face, so benevolent and kind. Behind my Master's visage rose a majestic mountain, capped with snow and enveloped in mist. My Master turned to view this glory, and suddenly upon the mountainside appeared a low wooden house perched amongst the crags of rock. A sweeping terrace hugged the hillside, and a woman came from the mist toward the edge of it, toward the sun which was rising between the peaks in the distance. As she drew closer I saw that she wore a robe of heavily embroidered brocade with a collar of finest fur, an ensemble which could be worn only by the very wealthy, only by those with Imperial ties.

The face came into focus as Master and I watched together, and I realized that it was Madame. Her eyes were focused only upon Master, and she slowly reached out her hand, reached with such longing to touch the face of her beloved, from whom now she would be ever parted.

"I will come back to you," she whispered, and I began to sob as I felt the depth of their love, the pain of their separation, and I heard my Master say, "I let you go in all humbleness," as her hand slipped from his face. Just then came the sound of laughter and of feet pattering on the terrace stones. A young girl runs from the interior of the house, barefoot in the cold, and I see it is my daughter, my Little Bird, and she runs into Madame's arms. Madame swings her up high, and she is framed by the rays of the sun, a halo of God's glory above them.

*The image fades and only Master remained in my vision, and from his eye I saw a tear fall. It wounded me so that he should lament our fate, for he, most of all, knew the glory which awaits. Did you know, Master, did you know? I asked. In answer he became a dragon, and flew off into the mist.*

*We know everything. And as I walked between the guards my heart lifted from its depths, and I knew that despite pain and suffering, all was beautiful, and in the end would be well, though we know not when.*

*All would be well. I knew that sleep could become an awakening, and dreams could suffuse reality, that any thought could be a prayer, and that heaven may come to earth. Reality is but a dream within a dream, and all would be well, exceedingly well.*

*We reached the tall red pavilion of the Emperor's domain and we mounted the steps slowly, or it seemed to be slowly, as in a dream all actions are diffuse. I saw the doors, the massive golden doors, and next to them stood the concubine, the one who had betrayed us. And though I knew she felt victorious in our defeat, I felt pity for her, for she had never known a love like I had known. For that is the thing which saves us from ourselves.*

*As we wound through the corridors my perception became clear and crystalline, and I felt as if I was floating or perhaps did not exist at all. My body was weightless and took no effort to move, as if I was lifted slightly by gossamer wings. What are we made of? It is nothing in the end, nothing at all, and yet holds everything we know to be beautiful and true.*

*The door to the Emperor's chamber stood open, awaiting my arrival. I stepped inside as the guards drew back, shutting the door, and ending my reverie. Before me was the massive bed, a bed that was more like a stage where one performs than a place to love and* rest. On the bed lay a gown, a robe of sky blue silk with crimson red at the sleeves, embroidered along the hem with red dragons. It was my gown, my favorite gown; I had worn it that day when I pleaded for the release of the Master's brother. Tradition held that I not wear the gown again, yet here it was, arrayed as if it held a body, but it did not. It was an empty thing, and its magnificence was meaningless without the human spirit inside.

I stood for some time, looking at the gown. I would never wear anything so beautiful again, and I felt released from a burden. When I turned to look about me, I saw that I was not alone as I had believed. The Emperor stood in a far corner of the room, dim at the edges of the shadows, but I could see that he stood next to a table with various items arranged upon it, glass beakers and cups, a tall contraption with tubes, spoons and utensils. Beside him was a tall basket, as high as his waist, the lid tightly in place. As I looked he kicked the basket with his foot, and I thought I saw it move slightly, after he moved his foot away.

The Emperor strode forward and fixed me with a purposeful glare. In his hand he held a pouch which bulged at the sides, and when he reached the bed he held the pouch upside down above it. He loosened the cords and out tumbled all manner of jewels, and folded pieces of paper, which scattered about. I recognized the jewels. They were those which I had sent out to help those in need, when Chen and I released our birds. So they had helped no one, for here they were.

I did not look at him, but kept my eyes upon the jewels. They were so beautiful and I wanted to pick them up and hold them to the light, to feel their weight and look into their depths.

When the Emperor finally spoke it was with a cold, low voice. "You have betrayed me," he said. "You have betrayed the Empire."

I had known he would say these words, for the small mind of such a man can find in all events only reference to himself. A narcissistic will betrays all.

"Look at me!" The Emperor barked when I stood passive and undefended. But I would not, for to look in his eyes would be to give his words legitimacy. The Emperor grabbed at my arm and twisted it behind me, trying with a pathetic show of force what he could not accomplish by command. I winced at the pain but did not yield, did not capitulate to his attempt to disempower me, and this made his rage flare all the more.

"Explain your actions!" he shouted, but it was not an explanation that he wanted. What he demanded was an admission that I had done wrong by him, and that I could not give. When I did not answer he twisted my arm even tighter, but I did not care.

"You have sought to undermine my rule with the trash you have written, and sent out into the countryside. And what did you think might happen, that the ignorant dirty peasants might become 'enlightened' by your words?" At this he gave a snort of disdain. "They shall never understand about law or justice, they must always be led, like lambs to slaughter, or they will wander in confusion on the hillside!" He waved his hand as if to depict those wandering hopeless masses. "You have done them a great disservice in holding out your flimsy hope for freedom; you are a traitor to this land!"

"As I had thought, your Highness, you do not understand my actions," I said evenly; but he ignored me and went on.

"You sought to poison the Imperial lineage with the seed of another," he hissed into my ear. His fury was cold, all emotion distilled to the essence of anger, a single point of reference in a mind convinced of its rightness. He threw down my arm, and massaged his tight fingers.

"I care not for your bastard girl child, that is of no importance," he continued. "A girl can be sold on the corner for a tarnished coin, and I suspect that will be her fate." I made no reaction to his cruel remarks, but held the thought of the lotus which was with my daughter always.

"But you are a dangerous element, and have corrupted one of my best and most trusted men," he went on. "He, too, will have to be destroyed, did you not know this?"

My heart froze, and in that fleeting moment the Emperor saw my panic. Destroy Han...I had not thought, had not realized the Emperor would so completely succumb to his terrible pride.

"But you gain nothing by killing Han; he has done nothing of harm!" I cried, not able to disguise my fear.

"Kill him? Oh...." And he gave a little laugh, a cruel sound. "I shall not kill him. For now he is harmless, he has been ruined by you! His integrity and honor is in tatters, he has taken what does not belong to him. But there are ways that he shall suffer for his deeds, for his betrayal of my trust. This beautiful gown...," and he waved his arm, indicating my robe upon the bed, "....this beautiful gown shall be his, but alas! When he receives it, it shall not contain the Empress!" This last he said with mock despair, as if playing to me, his audience, for effect.

His behavior sickened me, and I felt my anger rise at the thought of Han. "He has taken nothing, for no one can own another, except through love," I retorted.

The Emperor threw his head back and gave a hearty, false laugh. "Love? You speak of love? Another of your dangerous notions, and one for which you shall pay dearly. You spoke of love in your letter, and I was willing to indulge you this quaint idea for a time. But speaking of love as the answer to all questions is of such

265

stupidity, such ignorance, that indeed it makes me question your sanity."

I thought of his reply to my letter, wherein he acknowledged a desire to love, and knew that it was anger and pride which spoke, and not truth. "In your own letter, your Highness, you spoke of the possibility of love between us; have you forgotten your words?" I asked in an attempt to bring him back from the edge of the abyss on which he now stood. For I did not wish to see him, or anyone, fall into such a pit of hatred and despair as to denounce love's true power.

"No, I have not forgotten. On the contrary, I think of it constantly. It causes great pain when I remember what a fool I was, if even for a brief moment. There can be no love between us; our marriage was based upon tradition only, a desire to bring forth heirs to the Imperial lineage," the Emperor asserted, and by the mechanical way he spoke I knew it was a rehearsed response, and that even he himself did not believe it.

And then I took action without thinking. In an instinctual desire to reach him I grabbed his forearms and pulled him to me. I placed my lips upon his, my lips which kissed the sweet flesh of my daughter, which spoke words of love to Han. The Emperor stiffened in surprise but did not pull away, and I held my face next to his, and saw his eyes grow wide with astonishment. I looked directly into them, and saw the eyes of a little boy, hurt and confused, and sent thoughts of reassurance to him, as a mother would her child.

At first I thought he would break through his pain. He did not pull away, and did not strike out at me. But as I looked into those eyes I saw another facet of his spirit emerge—an unrelenting, angry, and vicious beast, and I pulled away in horror. This beast he had nurtured and grown in his heart, and it stood between him and any type of love that might threaten to enter there. He was now the beast's domain, he was lost.

The Emperor pushed me backwards onto the bed, and I did not resist, for I knew it was futile. I lay next to the gown and amidst the jewels scattered there, while the Emperor strode back and forth, muttering to himself in words I could not hear. An epic internal struggle, the nexus of all choice, was upon him. Ego or spirit? Love or fear? Humanity or brutality? Hope or despair? Life or death? In every life there comes a time when the final choice between opposites must be made.

That time was upon him, and I watched as he struggled. There was nothing I could do, as this choice represented the ultimate use of free will. This is the choice we all must make, all and every one.

Finally, the pacing ceased. The Emperor stood for a moment, and I saw his face ease into a slack expression, the relief of having made a decision, no matter what the decision might be. He was no longer in turmoil, and had thrown himself behind a course of action from which there would be no return.

The Emperor turned briskly on his heel, and strode to the table arranged in the shadows. He came to the tall basket, and without hesitation he raised the lid, and reached his arm into the bottom. He looked intently into the basket, and his arm moved in strange motions, as if mirroring a partner in a dance. He made a quick gesture with his arm then, and when he pulled the arm from the depths of the basket, in his fist he held a thick black snake, which writhed and tried to evade his grasp.

He held the snake with both hands, obviously practiced at handling the beast. With one hand he held near the end, and with the other he made a pincer with his thumb and middle finger at its jaws, forcing its mouth to open wide. He stood holding it aloft, with an expression of something like pride upon his face, a look of boyish delight at having control over a wild thing.

He turned sideways so that my vision of the scene was not blocked, and moved to the table that held the glass beakers and strange devices. He pushed the head of the snake forward, placing the protruding fangs over the lip of one of the beakers. He held it there, his own face pulled into a grimace of concentrated effort, while drops of liquid fell from the fangs into the glass. When there was no more liquid dropping from the fangs, he turned and pushed the snake into the bottom of the basket in one motion, and quickly slammed the lid down upon the venomous beast.

With the detachment of an alchemist, or a doctor preparing his medicine, he held the glass beaker aloft, and peered into the milky substance. He put it down upon the table and chose another beaker, filled with liquid that was a strange smoky shade of blue. He mixed the two together, pouring them carefully back and forth between the beakers. When he was satisfied, he turned toward me, and came forward across the room, the liquid sloshing at the rim of the glass.

The Emperor knelt before me on the floor, as if genuflecting, as if in homage. It was a final act of sadistic sarcasm, the twisting of pure intent. When he raised his head, his look held something I had never seen, it was not human, but devoid of all that makes us so.

His lips moved as if to speak but no sound emerged, until finally I heard the words, spoken barely above a whisper, "You have poisoned me." And putting the glass to his lips he drank the liquid, which caused one last hope to rise in me. He held it in his mouth, not swallowing yet, and came forward toward me.

It was then I saw into him, saw beyond him, saw that his choice had already led him into hell, and there was no need for me to wish him there. My little bird of hope died as he put his lips to mine.

For a moment, he held them there, and our eyes locked in a final dance of wills. When he saw that I still did not fear, that I lived free and whole within myself, he used the force of his tongue to open my mouth and I felt the foul liquid spew forth, the poison of hatred and fear filling my mouth and throat, the same mouth which Han had kissed, the same throat from which came songs to my child.

I denied the instinct to swallow my death, and willed my throat closed to that which would extinguish my light upon the earth. But suddenly a sharp pain seared my consciousness, and I realized the Emperor had bitten my lip, had created a pathway for the fatal poison to surge through my blood and into my heart, the same heart which loved and longed for those I had lost.

I lay down upon the bed. My fingers touched the gown which would be sent to Han after my death, and I willed my energy to flow into its fibers, so that when he knelt and took it in his arms in despair, some measure of comfort would reach him. I felt a warmth and tingling at my fingertips, and the last of my energy left me as I had bid it do.

The room swirled about me in a kaleidoscope of images, faces of those I loved, scenes of beauty and tranquility, the reflecting pool with its lotus that serenely floated upon its surface. When now it was certain I would begin my journey to another time and place, I turned my thoughts to that which is eternal, and what I saw was beyond any dream of heaven.

I felt myself evaporating into nothingness, losing that thread which keeps us rooted upon the earth. And just before the darkness fell I saw a light so bright that I was blinded with the brilliance, and felt a joy of letting go as I went to it, to the place where all is one.

*Where is she?*

I sit bolt upright, and throw the heavy covers back. Where am I? My heart is pounding; I cannot get a grasp of my surroundings. An almost dark room, a curtained window, a bed, a crib......a crib. Yes, yes, the crib, for Baby. I take a deep breath and remember, I am in Hong Kong, this is our last day in China, we are going home. I throw my legs over the side of the bed and walk to the crib, I need to see her and make sure Baby is alright.

She sleeps peacefully on her back, I can hear the steady breathing and I feel a sense of relief, from what I do not know. As I am peering through the bars of the crib, the startling ring of the telephone makes me jump, but Baby goes on sleeping, as does Alex, snuggled beneath a mound of covers on the other bed.

I reach the phone and pick up the receiver, say a quiet "Hello?" so as not to awaken them; my husband's voice comes over the line, and the first thing he says is, "Happy Birthday!!"

I tell him I'm not sure how happy it will be; I am exhausted, and focused only on getting us home tomorrow. "Well," he says with a mischievous tone, "maybe this will help: we can adopt the baby, I have it all figured out!"

I sit in stunned silence, afraid to believe, how could it be that simple? Just yesterday he had said that there was no way this could work. What had happened, how had he gone from "no way" to "it's done" in less than 24 hours? Here is the miracle I have been expecting.

"I called Antoinette….," he says. This is surprising, they had never spoken before. He knew very little of the conversations I had with Antoinette these past months. I had kept our work together mostly to myself, for fear he might not understand. But somehow, he had been moved to call her because, he says, "I did not know what else to do."

"What did she say?" I ask.

He tells me that she had said that the important thing now, while the outcome was not yet clear, was for him to make a stand, to declare his intentions. "Do you want this child?" she kept asking him, over and over again, until all his qualified answers of "buts" and "ifs" were exhausted, and he finally said a clear and definitive "Yes."

He tells me that when he said it, he felt a literal lifting of his spirit, as if something that had been weighing him down was now removed, and he was free.

He had then called a friend, someone who had adopted two children and knew of an agency that could help us; and after speaking with a lawyer at the agency, it was clear that there was a process for this type of adoption, and he had laid out the steps.

I listen to the details, but keep thinking over and over, I knew this would be the outcome, I knew there was a way. How did I know? It's as if all along someone has been whispering in my ear that this was meant to be.

My husband is elated. He is giddy with happiness, and the last thing he says is, "Bring our daughter home."

I hang up and Alex pushes back the covers, "What's going on?" she asks in a sleepy voice. I tell her what he has said, how it can work, and she jumps from the bed and grabs me in a hug. "Oh, thank God! This is an answer to my prayers!" she says, and she is crying. It is genuine emotion, and I feel a strength and calmness spread over me, that no obstacle remains, and all will be well.

I tell Alex I want some time to myself; Baby is still sleeping, it is just barely dawn. I leave the room and find the rooftop terrace that juts out over Hong Kong harbor. The misty morning air creates an ethereal scene, it is as if the terrace is floating in the clouds.

I sit on a little wooden bench, and think, how will I explain all of this to others, and to myself? I think of a time two years ago when I was having dinner with an old friend from college. She brought up the fact that, though I had professed for years that I wanted children, I remained childless to that day, even after more than ten years of marriage. "What are your plans?" she asked, "I'm just so concerned! I think you would be a great mother, and you know, we don't have forever, time is moving on!"

I thoughtfully considered what she was saying, and then told her that I knew what she was saying was true, but I was just not worried about it, and I didn't know why. "If it's meant to be, it will happen," I had said. And she reminded me that for something to happen, I would have to take action of some kind. I told her not to worry, that I knew it would work out. We had dropped the subject then for the rest of the dinner, but later, after sharing a bottle of wine and lots more conversation, we stood waiting for the car outside the restaurant. Suddenly I turned to her and said, out of the blue, "I know I will have one child, it will be a girl, and I will have her when I'm 37 years old!"

She looked at me blankly, stunned at my declaration. "Well!!" she said, after she recovered. "That was definitive!! Where did that come from?" I looked back at her, shocked myself at what I had just blurted out. "I have no idea!" I said. And I did not.

Now, two years later, it is the morning of my 37th birthday, and my husband has just told me that we will adopt a child. A strange, unexplainable coincidence, just one more in a long list in relation to this situation. I have no explanations. And for now that is just fine, none are necessary.

I sit for awhile and watch the boats in the harbor. When I return home tomorrow, my life will have been completely altered; I will not be going back to the life I left. I will not even be the same person as I was before, and that is an answer to a prayer. For what does not change must die, and I want to live.

We go out into the city. There is a place called Stanley Market, where there are good things to buy, children's clothing and linens, souvenirs, silk robes, everything made in China, and sold there for a pittance. We hail a cab in front of the hotel, and begin the long ride, through the city and along the curving highway that hugs the harbor. The view is breathtaking, the high hills surrounding the water, the buildings built precariously into their sides. I watch out the window, noticing how different Hong Kong is from mainland China. It is the West, the British influence is so obvious; and yet, the faces are Chinese. It is the nexus of two worlds.

I should be elated. This is my birthday; I have just found out that we can adopt Baby. I am in an exciting city and we are to spend the day exploring. And yet, an anxious nausea set in when I returned to the hotel room this morning, and has been increasing during the ride. Once again, Alex's behavior has changed markedly. She is now so interested in Baby, wants to hold her and care for her—she got her dressed for our outing, and even now is playing patty-cake with her as she sits on her lap in the car.

I pretend as if I don't notice, I play along. But by the time we reach Stanley Market, I feel as if I'm going to cry. For not only is Alex displaying such maternal behavior, but Baby has begun to clearly favor her over me. When I try to hold her, she reaches for Alex, squirming to get back into her arms.

I try to reason myself out of despair. For one thing, I pulled away from Baby, just when she had bonded with me and felt secure. She had trusted me, and then I distanced myself. And though I knew the reasons for my actions, she could not; how could she understand what I had to do? I don't blame her, don't blame her at all. She is looking for what she needs, her survival is at stake.

But what of Alex's actions? What to make of them? I keep thinking, she has to know how this would make me feel, she has to know. Only a dunce could not see that this sort of back-and-forth would play havoc with my emotions, and she is anything but stupid. But this morning she had seemed so sincerely happy that we could adopt the baby; was this just innocent affection? Relief that now Baby would have a good home? But her behavior makes me feel so uncertain, what if she decides, after all this, that she wants her?

I don't want to ask Alex about her intentions, to even introduce the possibility into our conversation. And though I keep repeating the thought that she is mine, it does not matter what I tell myself; I feel sicker and sicker as we stroll through the market, my energy draining from me as the moments pass. I have to get out of here, I just want to go home; and by the time we finally hail a cab to return to the hotel, I feel it is the worst birthday I have ever had. All during the ride, Alex's heretofore unexpressed affection for Baby is in full bloom. She laughs with her, tickles her, plays fun games; and I think, I just can't do it; can't pull myself out of this one. I will just stay here in despair—you won, you won!

I do not know what to make of this. Of course I have to remember that until an adoption is legally finalized, Alex could change her mind at any time, and take Baby back. She would have every right; there would be nothing I could do to prevent it. Am I willing to live with that possibility? It could be months of such worry, can I handle it?

Outside the taxi window, the chaos of Hong Kong swirls in dizzying confusion, and for a moment my mind, exhausted and overwhelmed, slips into a groove that has been worn by the dreams of these past days, and I see the face from my nightmare of last night, the beautiful hard face of the concubine. It is there before me, so vivid for one moment that I am frightened and unsure if I am dreaming, or awake. And then the image is gone, but a shiver runs through me and on a warm day in a tropical city my body goes cold as ice.

And then I look into Baby's laughing face, and decide not to let our future slip away.

When we let ourselves into our hotel room, the phone is ringing, and I run to catch it. It is Antoinette. While Alex gets Baby settled, I go into the other room so I can speak to her in private. "How did you know to call, on the worst day of my life?" I ask her.

"Worst day of your life? It's your birthday!" she exclaims. I tell her of today's events, how the morning started with such bright promise, and how the day has degenerated into a tangle of fear and doubts. A thicket of despair, I can't find my way out…I tell her I have a bad feeling and I just want it all to be over. I want it all to be over, the pain, the ups and downs, the anxiety, and even the hope; the higher my hopes reach, the deeper my despair later; the higher the cost. "We anesthetize ourselves, don't we?" I say to her. I realize that I always have; that I've always chosen to do without heart-stopping joy if I could avoid the other end, the blind despair that comes with the inevitable loss of that joy.

Antoinette tells me I need to find some time to be alone, to pray. "Have you been praying?" she asks. "Non-stop," I answer. "It just comes spontaneously now, I am always praying, always praying…..." I, who until now had had a hard time even saying the word God; who until now had only prayed the stale memorized scripts of the Catholic mass. I was praying for my very life. I had never understood about prayer, what it was, or what it was supposed to do, so I had rejected it, never practiced it at all, until Antoinette taught me that prayer was using your will to align the mind with the highest principles, to open a channel through which peace could come.

And then I tell her about the dreams; how this morning I woke up in a panic from a dream I can only half remember. The dream still won't let me go, snatches of it have been coming to me all day. It was a dream of loss, of death, of endings and searching for salvation. I cannot organize the images into a pattern but the emotional tone is of a piece, and has woven itself into my waking life so that I don't know if my sadness and loss of heart is its residual, or caused by events of the day.

We talk for a long time, she giving me encouragement, and I wanting to believe. She tells me that I must write down the dreams, that I must discover what they mean, that freedom lies in understanding.

"And one last thing," she says, before we hang up. "When you are on the plane tomorrow, when you leave China, hold the baby against your heart." I don't ask why, knowing that everything Antoinette says has meaning beyond the obvious. She can see things that others can't; though she has told me over and over that she is not psychic. Her gift allows a glimpse into the world beyond this one, where our actions have consequences beyond our understanding.

So I just tell her that I will; it sounds so beautiful that I don't need reasons. In the other room, Baby is asleep. I tell Alex I'm going out for awhile. I take the elevator once again to the rooftop terrace, and find it deserted and quiet and eerily still.

I sit on a bench overlooking the steely waters of the harbor below. Boats glide by in uncanny silence and all seems in its proper place. It is a projection of my own inner calm thrown onto the screen of the world. My love has found a channel, it has somewhere to go.

I had often wondered, would it be possible for me to love an adopted child as much as one to whom I had given birth? Wouldn't there be a difference in intensity, or less of an identification, less of a bond? But what I know now is that love is a mysterious force, powerful beyond all measure. That I could love, so intensely, a child that some other woman had given birth to, defied my own conceptions of what love was. Life longs for life, and that longing is the force which draws all living things together.

After a time of reflection, I take out my notebook, and looking out over Hong Kong harbor, the grey waters shadowed by the tall buildings in the distance. I feel something rise in me; an agitation, a release from this lethargy. Joy unmasks itself in my heart, and I begin to write.

The first dream seems so long ago now, on the plane ride here. But I start remembering, the memory is stored there though I had not been aware of its existence. The details come effortlessly, it is as if I am watching a movie unfold in my mind...I write as fast as I can, to keep up with the images. And when I finish with that dream I begin on the next, and continue on, until I realize I can barely see it is now so dark. I move into the hotel hallway where there is a bench and continue writing, continue recording my dream of a life.

I write while tears stream down my face, tears of realization, tears of discovery. I begin to see, I see......all my life operating as if that was all there was of it; as if it had a discrete beginning and end, as if my choices in this life were determined only by the events of this life, when in reality this life had been an echo of something begun long ago.

Those I have loved and needed and lost, cycling with me in desire to meet again, to try again to perfect our experience in this earthly domain. Friends, family, lovers and enemies, all playing their part through time, all seeking to balance the scales so that they may go home again.

Hours later when the pages are no longer empty and my tears have faded in the joy of knowing of a greater existence, I return to the room and begin to pack. We are going home, and all would be well.

*When I wake I don't know where I am. It takes several minutes before I remember I am in the Emperor's chamber, he has poisoned me, I have lost everything. I have lost everything...but how can this be? I feel my body, I am in my body, when a moment ago I was in the place where all is one, the indescribable domain.*

*My eyes will not focus for they are still blinded by the light I saw there, the light of love and peace which engulfed me. I want to go back! A grief assails my heart as I realize I am no longer beyond the pain of the physical realm. The words "you must go back" echo in my ears, again and again, and I shake my head no, no. I cannot, cannot endure that which is required on earth. I cannot...cannot.....*

*"Empress! Open your eyes. Empress! We have not much time, we must hurry. Empress!"*

*The voice is a raspy whisper, an echo of a voice I once knew. Am I dreaming? I must return to sleep, to the arms of the all-loving presence which had surrounded me. Pain breaks into my awareness; I vaguely hear the sharp slap of a hand against my cheek. No! Leave me be!*

*"Empress! Now! Wake up!" The voice calls again, louder this time, louder and more insistent; it will not let me rest, the voice requires my attention. I struggle to comply, to flutter my eyes open a little, to find the source of my torment and make it go away.*

*A figure swims before me, it is the Emperor!! Oh, it is he...I struggle and writhe to get away, what nightmare is this? I pull hard away from his grasp, only to feel his grip tighten around me, pulling me even closer toward him on the bed.*

*"Empress!!! Wake up!!! We have no time to lose!!" The voice insists; and again I feel the sharp crack of a hand upon my flesh, the stinging slap pulls my consciousness up and out of the fog of confusion.*

*Before my startled eyes is the face of Han, he is so near to me that I can feel his breath on my cheek. This is the wishful thought of a dying lover, to see the face of the beloved once again. It is a torture and a blessing, and I curse the power of my mind to bring* forth that which I most desire.

I close my eyes against this unreal image, and it is then I feel myself being lifted from the bed by the arms of this apparition. The strain of trying to discern what is real from what is unreal overwhelms me, and I lose again the thread of consciousness, and fall into darkness.

The earth is shaking and rocking and loosening me from sleep. Where am I? How long have I been sleeping? I feel a swaying motion, and realize that I am moving. I feel a nausea rise and must work down the impulse to vomit. I open my eyes and look around the interior of a carriage, window curtains pulled to block the light. A figure sits on the bench opposite, and when it sees I am awake, it jumps forward toward me, to come to my aid. It is Jiang, but how can this be? I do not understand, do not understand what has happened, cannot fathom a turn of events which would produce this outcome. I try weakly to speak, but my voice will not come. There is a burning in my throat and my heart beats feebly in my chest. I cannot muster the energy to do more than raise my head.

"Empress.....you are with us!" Jiang says softly, and strokes my hair as he looks into my eyes. They plead with him, tell me! But first he brings a beaker to my lips and says, "Drink," and the liquid trickles down my throat and soothes the raw flesh and makes me feel stronger and more attached to life.

"Empress....do you understand? You are saved...all are saved!" Jiang says, and when he sees the anxious look cross my face, he knows what I am thinking, and goes on.

"Your child is safe! She is safely hidden and with Chen and Madame awaiting us. All is arranged, all will be well... for Han's devotion knew no bounds. He took great risks to subvert the Emperor's plans and has succeeded in a grand strategy. We will shortly be far from the Emperor's reach, and live the life we had dreamed!"

I struggle to bring forth sound. "How...Han?" I venture, and Jiang nods his head. I can speak no more, and Jiang begins to tell me of the details of the plan which released us from bondage.

"Han possessed intimate knowledge of the Emperor's true self. As you must be aware, Empress...the Emperor had much difficulty with the act which would plant his seeds and produce an heir. If known, this inability to perpetuate the lineage would threaten the Empire, and Han convinced the Emperor to let us go, in return for keeping his dangerous secret. Chen secured the ships and supplies necessary to spirit us away."

The slow realization of this truth begins to take over my mind. I am alive...my daughter is alive...Han has rescued us....we are safe. And all the grief and pain I had endured in thinking all was lost comes like a tidal wave upon me, and I sink into the bench and sob with uncontrollable fury, for I would no longer be the person I once was. I had died to innocence, and must now rise, a phoenix, from the ashes of loss.

In the morning my unnatural buoyancy seems to unnerve Alex. She is quiet, withdrawn, while I happily get us all moved about, from the hotel to the airport, to our gate, onto the plane. We are settling in, the airplane is packed, a popular Hong Kong to San Francisco flight, filled to capacity.

I am standing with Baby, arranging our things, when a

middle-aged woman approaches, looking quizzically at me and up toward the seat number.

"9-D?" she asks. "Are you in 9-D?"

"Yes," I tell her, "this is my seat."

"I have the same one, look!" and she hands me her ticket stub, and it says 9-D. I pull out my own, it too says 9-D; we have both been assigned the same seat. Irritation arises; can't this last part of the trip go smoothly? But the woman moves away, she goes to find a flight attendant who might solve the problem, and I settle into my seat, thinking squatter's rights; they won't make me move.

In moments the woman is back, flight attendant in tow. It turns out that the seat next to me is empty, the only one available on the flight. It seems we are destined to sit together, this woman and I, and she settles her belongings and immediately reclines in the seat, closes her eyes and goes to sleep.

How can someone sleep when there is so much commotion going on, people boarding the plane, stuffing packages overhead and bags under the seat, flight crews making announcements over the intercom? But she is, my neighbor is snoring soundly. I look at her, she is around middle age, slightly overweight, a little disheveled. She is an Asian woman, but she spoke perfect, unaccented English.

The plane finally taxis for takeoff, and Alex, sitting on my other side, also snuggles down to sleep. I hold Baby, and as we race down the tarmac, gathering speed for our ascent, I pull her to me, pull her to my heart. I feel hers beating next to mine, in perfect rhythm, and when at last we leave China, she looks up at me, and smiles.

The dinner cart has reached us, and my neighbor finally stirs. She has been asleep since we boarded, and so has Alex. Baby fell asleep shortly after take-off and I was left to stare into space, keeping vigil; I have slept enough. I have slept a lifetime, and from now on sleep will serve only to awaken me.

We start to make conversation, the woman and I. Almost immediately she asks me about Baby.....have you adopted her? Where is she from? What was the process like? She is very interested.

I tell her my friend Alex has adopted her, I stick to the story. We have just left China, nothing is certain. The woman listens well; she nods and absorbs the story. I begin to see that she is a kindly and thoughtful person, that she asks good questions and makes astute comments. I tell her about visiting the orphanage, about the terrible problem of abandoned babies, mostly girl babies, and of my grief at having seen those who must be left behind.

"I left China long ago, when I was just a child," she tells me. "I have heard of this but have never traveled there to see." She tells me that she has lived in California for over 20 years now, and is an American citizen. I see a sadness when she speaks of China, and she gently steers the subject away, toward the life she has now, the one she has built in America.

"I am coming from India, I have spent two months there studying with a guru," she tells me. A Buddhist, she has devoted most of her adult life to studying and teaching. It is then I notice her jewelry, prayer beads around her neck, a medallion with a picture of a monk, a bead bracelet used for meditation. I ask her many questions about her practice, about going to India. And after a time she points to my wrist and asks, "And are you a Buddhist?" I am wearing a bracelet purchased from a street vendor in Guangzhou, the day we went to the market. It is a string of jade beads, very simple; it looks almost exactly like the one the woman has on her own wrist.

I had almost forgotten I had it on. I take it between my fingers, seeing it, really seeing it, for the first time. Am I a Buddhist? How to answer this question? I do not practice any religion, but believe in universal truths. I am a Buddhist in that I believe that the Buddha spoke truth. But I am a Christian too, I believe that Jesus attained the ultimate in human potential, Christ consciousness, and that to follow his teachings, his authentic teachings, will save us.

"I am not a practicing Buddhist," I answer. "But I have studied the teachings, and accept them as truth."

The woman nods, and begins telling me that she recently saw the Dalai Llama, that she heard him speak at a conference, a gathering of Buddhists at a small college town in the Midwest.

A small college town in the Midwest......my mind slowly reels back, to a day just 3 months before, when I was running through the streets of my alma mater, having just arrived in town to deposit my step-daughter at college. I saw a poster, in the window of the hotel lobby; apparently, there was a major event taking place there, just that weekend: the

Dalai Llama, the spiritual leader, was to address an audience of thousands of Buddhists, and perform a rare ceremony which had something to do with enlightenment. He was there in this little town because his brother was administrator of a large Buddhist center there, and had invited him to come.

When I saw the poster I was overwhelmed with a desire to go, to find the gathering, to see the Dalai Llama. But we were to be in town only a few hours, we had to get back home. How could this be, to be in the same place at the same time as the eminent figure of the Dalai Llama? It was strange to think, that our paths had come so close to intersecting, and in such an unlikely place as this.

I did not get to see the Dalai Llama. But now this woman, a native of China, a traveler from India by way of Hong Kong, a resident of San Francisco, who by some fluke happened to be assigned my seat on the flight, was telling me that she was there too. Our paths had crossed twice, in three months time.

The shocked look on my face makes her ask, "What's wrong?" And when I tell her, "I was there, too; I was in the same little town that same weekend that the Dalai Llama was there," she laughs a delightful tinkling laugh, and she almost seems like she is not surprised.

And suddenly, we both know that our meeting is no accident, no accident at all, and we begin urgently talking, putting our heads near each other to catch every word. Just then, Alex gets up and leaves her seat, and I say to her, "I have something to tell you!" And I tell her the story.

Her name is Grace. She tells me this as she pulls the jade amulet from the bag under her seat. Grace, yes…this has been a Grace, to have this woman next to me during this long flight to a new life. I unburden myself, for the first time since the ordeal began; I tell her of my hopes and fears and of the tremendous love that has blossomed in my heart. She listens with deep understanding, she nods and affirms.

She asks softly, "And why do you think your friend could not take her?" I tell her that I think, deep down, she was frightened of Baby…frightened of what it would take from within herself to raise this particular child. "She couldn't do it," I say, and she asks, "Can you?" And I get the feeling that her question is more than casual interest, as if she is a proxy and is receiving my answer on behalf of something much larger than herself. Her eyes hold intense expectation, and bore into mine. After a moment of reflection I answer, with no hesitation or restraint, "Yes," just simply, yes. And she smiles in relief and says, "That's right!" and begins to take things from her bag, as if by my answer she was free to bestow gifts upon Baby, in celebration of this event.

Grace brings forth a string of prayer beads, and says they were blessed by the Dalai Llama. "Hold these for her, so that she may use them later," she says, and I take them in my palm with reverence. Baby touches them; she is very gentle and acts as if she knows that they are holy.

Next she pulls out a medallion which dangles from a thin red cord. On the medallion is a tiny painting of the

Goddess Kwan Yin on one side, and a photograph of a monk on the other. "See what she does when she sees this," she says, and holds it in front of Baby. Baby reaches for it, and looks for a long time. She flips it over and looks at the monk, and looks up at Grace; she looks down again. I look over to see Grace nodding, obviously pleased, but she does not tell me the significance of the medallion, or who is pictured on it. "Keep that for her," she says, and I put it carefully away with the prayer beads.

And then she takes the bracelet of beads from her wrist, the one that looks so similar to my own, and places it in my palm. "This is for you, from me," she says, and there are tears in her eyes as she holds my hand there. "You have both been blessed."

I feel a chill run the length of my body as she says these words, and I cannot speak. Alex returns to her seat and we spend the remainder of the flight in silence. When the plane lands and we rise to gather our belongings, I bend to pick up Baby, and when I turn back to speak to Grace, she is gone.

At the end of the ramp I stop to put Baby into her stroller. "You push her when we go out," Alex says to me, her voice tired and strained. I am relieved as I have been wondering, worrying about this moment. Would Alex want to be in charge of Baby upon our arrival, would it be an awkward moment? Both of our husbands were to be there waiting at the gate, and I wanted, so badly, to have her in my arms when my husband first saw Baby. But she seems in a hurry to move ahead, and she walks quickly away, not stopping to help get Baby situated in the stroller.

I push her slowly up the ramp, my legs weak and shakey. I can't walk faster, it is as if I am in the slow motion world of a dream. I look down at the top of Baby's head, she is sitting forward a little, expectantly.

I don't have a chance to take her from the stroller before I see him. He is standing just inside the doorway, at the back of a crowd of people knotted at the end of the ramp. He is standing on tip toe, straining to look for us over the top of the heads in front of him. His face holds a look of anxious expectation and hope; of joy denied, of dreams about to come true. Our eyes do not meet, he is looking for her, his daughter. And when he sees her his face crumples in such a way that I know we have achieved an incredible victory of the heart, it is a divine reunion.

We reach him and he hugs me tightly to him. He stoops down and says hello to our baby. I kneel down too and everything in the world disappears, everything but the three of us.

We are laughing and crying; the pain of years, of lifetimes, burns away, leaving only our joy. There has been no time since we were last together, for time does not exist, and we go out into the world to begin again where once we left off, redeemed in love, our spirits whole, our souls renewed, this journey complete.

重生

epilogue

How do we know where our journeys may ultimately take us? One year ago, I went on a trip, and returned with an understanding that life is not as we suppose. I returned with a baby, with a piece of myself, with the ability to see a pattern in what before had looked like chaos. Our lives, part of a tapestry, woven through time by threads of our choosing. This is our story, Lily.

You play with your father a few feet away, at the edge of the ocean, at the edge of the water that touches each part of the world, a sea which connects us all. The sun shines upon us, the same sun which shone above me in China last year, and in any lifetime which has ever existed on this earth. How could I not have known that what affects a tiny orphaned girl in China affects me too?

And yet I had not known, not really known. This past year has been spent uncovering truths long buried, mining the rich earth of dreams and clues given but not noticed before. Praying for guidance and receiving it, in abundance; refining my will so that my life can be a force for good.

And loving you. For six weeks after we returned, you could have been taken from us at any moment. Legally you were not our child, and I bathed you, fed you, rocked you to sleep, and held you close with the thought always hovering: this could be all the time we have together; we have only now. The sheer joy of being near you protected me from despair, and those first intense days of uncertainty were a crucible in which the final shreds of my old life were burned away.

The Empress was with us in those weeks, watching, a

quiet but unmistakable presence, enjoying the happiness of our reunion. I could see her now, I no longer had to dream in order to reach her. It was as if our release from China had released her, too. I would become aware of her presence as I watched you play, or as I went into meditation. Very often when I was running, visions of her life came to me, and I experienced her most intense emotions, the pain of loss, the agony over her decision to return to life. The feelings were overwhelming, and at times I could no longer discern what was her reality and what was mine. It seemed we had fused through this process, a journey of recapitulation. I no longer asked myself why she had come, or what it meant. The truth of her was beyond question.

One day as I felt her presence, the urge to write overcame me and I sat down and let her voice flow through me and onto the page.

*What if this is real, what if I'm not dreaming? I see the sparkling blue-grey water long before we reach it. As we descend the cliffs which rise up like a wall against the sea, I can make out in the distance the white sails of two ships billowing against the sky. These are the best of the Chinese Empire's trading vessels, and Jiang has explained to me that Chen has procured them for our departure to safer lands. I had not been aware of the extent of Chen's influence among the entrepreneurial eunuchs, so absorbed in my own dilemma that his growing power had escaped my notice.*

*As we descend, the Emperor comes to my mind. I see him weeping, unable to muster the strength to go on. I send out a silent prayer of forgiveness, forgiveness that will release us all from his cruelty. I pray for the concubines left behind, for those women who must continue in that confinement. I pray prayers of thanksgiving, for the miracle that will allow my daughter to live free.*

*As we draw nearer and nearer, my excitement begins to grow, for I shall see my child, I shall see her again, and hold her and look into her eyes. She shall know I have not abandoned her, she can grow again in trust. I begin to make out a knot of people on the beach, moving to and fro, carrying boxes and bags, readying for our departure.*

*At long last we reach the sands. I have grown in strength in the many days since we have traveled from the Imperial City, and I feel a surge of energy propel me from the carriage and onto the beach. I begin running, and the knot of people moves apart and I see Madame, and Chen, standing with a bundle in his arms. Next to him, lying on a pallet on the sand, I see Lo Ming, his love from the village, she is here, he has made good promise.*

*I run for what seems an eternity and then I am there, and with tears in his eyes Chen hands the bundle to me. I unwrap the cloth and I see her, my child. Her eyes are huge and dark and luminous, and they hold no recrimination for me. She is at peace, and in that peace I see my own salvation. My daughter looks at me and smiles. My heart rises up, a winged joy takes hold and propels my prayer thought to heaven: thank God, thank God.*

*I turn then and see Han standing a distance away, a retinue of armored men on horseback arrayed behind him in protection. His men, who did not forsake their true leader, have risked their lives to bring us safely here. In the cliffs above the beach, I make out more men on horseback, and there is the unmistakable figure of my Master among them, descending to join us for our journey to another world.*

*My eyes lock onto the face of Han, who waits in expectation.*

*The look on his face speaks of the pain he has endured, and the hope which remains. I begin running, holding our daughter tight, running with the wind. She begins to laugh, a burbling of joy rises from the bundle in my arms, it is the music of angels, the echo of my own heart. I run to reach my love, my spirit reborn.*

Her joy is my joy, and I weep at the triumph of love transcendent which is her life.

One cold grey day two weeks after we returned from China, the day before Christmas Eve, Alex called and said she needed to come and see me, she needed to talk. As I hung up the phone I knew that this is what I had been dreading, that somehow the time had come when I would have to make a stand.

When Alex arrived she was visibly nervous, and she sat down at my kitchen table with hardly a glance at you, playing on the floor, happy and content. "I think I may have made a mistake," she said, and I thought, here it comes: the denouement, the crisis point, the Waterloo of this lifetime epic. "Maybe I should take her home for a day or so, just so I can be sure?" Her tone was firm but her words, the "maybe," the "So-I-can-be-sure," told me everything I needed to know about her true intent. Her tentativeness fanned my anger and gave me courage. I took a deep breath and rose to my full height in the chair, and something like righteous certainty permeated my mind.

"You can't do that," I said, loud and strong. "You will not take her from this house." You will never take her from me again. The Empress and I speak together, her energy coursing through me in that moment.

Alex slumped in her chair, the nervous bravado gone. She had instantly become like a shell of herself in the face of my declaration, and she said, "I know" with such sheepishness that I almost felt sorry for her. It surprised me how easily she let it go, and as she began trying to explain herself and save face, I knew it was done. The final act of our drama had been played out and the curtain fell, releasing us from our roles in each others' lives.

I walked her to the door and as I stood in the cold and watched her go, I felt a cloak of such calm descend upon me; my worst fear had been faced. I knew with certainty that nothing would ever separate me from you again, and that certainty allowed me to release all blame. I said a silent prayer of thanks to her that in the end, she had done the right thing; and from the deepest part of me came forgiveness, and I let her go.

And now I think of how I had been seeing you with me for so long, in dreams or visualizations, that it is almost as if my longing brought you into being. For years during visits here I had seen myself holding the hand of a little girl, and walking on this beach. She is with me now, that girl I dreamed of; and I watch as you laugh and play in delight at the water's edge, and I can hardly believe this dream is real. Through the grace of you my life has blossomed.

Last year when I had returned from China, when my family met you, my sister asked me if I remembered the time I had spoken Chinese.

"What? I have no idea what you are talking about!" I had said.

She was stunned that I would not remember. We had taken a family trip to San Francisco, the summer I was 15. I remembered walking around that fog-shrouded city; it had seemed like a dream. We had been to Chinatown one day, and apparently that night in the hotel room, I sat up in bed and began speaking. My sister told me that I was quite upset about something, and kept waving my arms around, saying something about a baby. I was crying, and then I lay back down and went to sleep. She said she was quite scared, and that she was sure I was speaking Chinese.

"How do you know?" I asked her.

She said it sounded exactly like what we had been hearing all day in Chinatown.

"That's why I wasn't surprised," she said.

"Weren't surprised about what?" I asked.

"About you bringing home the baby. I always knew you were Chinese."

A chill of recognition rippled over me as she spoke those words, and I thought, yes; I am Chinese. Perhaps I have been every race, color, creed and nationality in some lifetime which I do not recall, but which influences me still. Since bringing you home, whenever I see a Chinese or Asian face a feeling of kinship, of connection and knowing, rises in me, to meet that person with the same eyes, the same hair, the same skin as my Lily. How could I not be one with them, when I love you so? I forget at times that when they look at me, they see someone different, someone separate; and when

I remember that, it feels like a betrayal.

I want to say to them, do you not see? We are the same, underneath these superficial characteristics that make us look different to one another. I want to share with them what I know: that it is there for us to discover, the offspring of our deathless souls, in our dreams and desires, in the places that beckon us, in the people we long for, in the loves and fears with which we dance.

But I do not say it, I never do. I just hold you close, and hope that they see in our love a hopeful beacon calling them to life. And now you call to me from the water's edge, your father waves, and I go to you and am reborn.

# About the Author

Beth Nonte Russell was born in Jasper, Indiana. She received a B.A. in History from Indiana University and an M.A. in Psychology from Marymount University. She lives near Washington, D.C., with her husband and daughter. This is her first book.